I0693763

Copyright ©2025 by A.E. Faulkner
AuthorAEFaulkner.com

All rights reserved.

No part of this publication may be reproduced, distributed, or transmitted in any form or by any means, including photocopying, recording, or other electronic or mechanical methods, without the prior written permission of the publisher, except as permitted by U.S. copyright law.

The story, all names, characters, and incidents portrayed in this production are fictitious. No identification with actual persons (living or deceased), places, buildings, and products is intended or should be inferred.

Cover Design by S.E. MacCready

Divided States Logo Illustration by Riley Haring

# Uprising

by AE Faulkner

Book 2 of the Divided States Series

Seek wisdom, not knowledge.
Knowledge is of the past, wisdom is of the future.
- Native American Proverb

# Contents

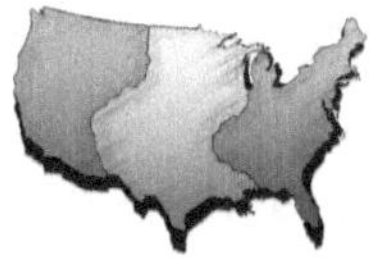

# CHAPTER 1 ~ KIERA

## UPPER DIVISION, CENTRESTATES

"Leader Imperant, I've brought something for your consideration." I slide a ten-page proposal across the desk's smooth surface. Every thought is complete, meticulously outlined with recommended actions and rationale. His eyebrows twitch slightly but he barely glances at it, clearly disinterested.

"Give me a summary. In one minute or less." He slumps in his chair, letting his neck and shoulders relax into the pillowed headrest. I refrain from pursing my lips together, instead forcing a compliant smile across my cheeks.

"Of course. Basically, I believe it's time to officially end the delegation. We've gotten what we needed, and more, from them. There's really nothing else to be gained."

"You've run all your tests? Or whatever you're calling them – theories or experiments." His mouth twists in disbelief.

"Yes." It's a slight untruth, but a necessary one. "We were right. The Eastates delegates have no compliance chips. Everyone else does."

"How many days are left? Why not just let it run its course?"

"We're actually ahead of schedule. They've completed everything we needed. Having them here ties up resources needed to analyze all the data we've gathered."

Before I know it, he raises a fist in the air and slams it down on the desk. My pulse surges as I nearly jump out of my seat.

"What aren't you telling me?" He turns a pointer finger at me.

"Sir, a few of them have . . . discovered some information they illegally accessed on our servers. If they would share that information, it could be quite . . . incriminating against us. If it were to get in the wrong hands, Eastates and Westates could unite against us. We have to eliminate them. It's not ideal, but it's the only way to ensure that they keep quiet."

His lips press together into a tight line. Fury radiates off him as his cheeks flush red. He crosses his arms and spits out another round of questions.

"Kiera, what you're proposing incriminates us too. How is that a better alternative? And how did a bunch of kids break into our systems? Are monkeys running our digital security efforts?"

Smoothing out my hair, I regain my mental footing. I can make him understand.

"Sir, this is an opportunity. We can use this to start the war. We blame the delegates for an act of defiance against Centrestates. We make it look like they attacked the power grid and we were merely trying to save it for everyone. Then we roll out the alternative source we've been testing. It paints us as heroes and positions us in an authoritative role. This is as good a time as ever."

Leader Imperant's eyes latch onto me. I hold my posture and meet his gaze. I won't wilt under his scrutiny. And if he's going to buy into all of this, I have to show him that I believe it will work. It has to. Everything's on the line. We've been preparing for this for years. It's just all happening sooner than we anticipated.

Once we go through with this, there's no turning back. Regardless of how risky he perceives it to be. He's already the leader of one Territory, so we're a third of the way there. You don't overtake a whole country without taking risks.

I stand and saunter over to the window to admire my Territory. In the distance, lush rolling hills fade into the horizon. As my gaze travels closer, clusters of buildings rise and drop in varying heights. Their smooth glass framed by sharp silver panes glint whenever they catch the sun's rays. Manicured flower beds dot the city streets below. I want it all. And more. Every last inch of the Divided States.

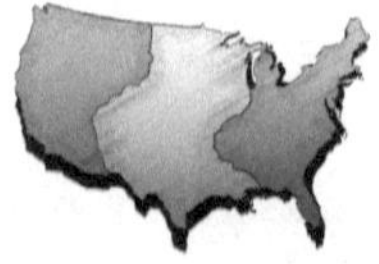

# CHAPTER 2 ~ EVERLY

## UPPER DIVISION, CENTRESTATES

"Everly, you feeling okay?" Saya asks as I push scrambled eggs around on my plate. Considering I yawned no less than four times on the walk over here, she must know I'm tired. Hopefully she doesn't suspect anything else. "You just don't seem like . . . yourself."

The sleep-deprived, irritable part of me that tossed and turned most of last night wants to lash out with something like, "You don't even know me. How could you possibly know if I'm not acting like myself?" Thankfully the rational part of my brain manages to make an appearance.

"Just tired. It's been a long week, you know?" My smile falters, but I try. I'm not sure she believes me, but she nods and changes the subject. *That's the kind of thing Josli would do.* The difference is that

Josli would know exactly what was wrong because I would have told her every last detail about our big escape last night. That is, if she wasn't right there beside me for it.

Either way, I want to put this whole experience behind me. Of course, that's impossible. My temples pound, probably from the level of overanalyzing my brain has done over the past twelve hours.

Everything Beckett told me plays through my mind on repeat. Someone, part of the Uprising, made sure he was chosen to be a delegate. My mother, who is a leader of the Uprising, asked him to find me. The whole time he was here, it was to gather information about Centrestates and try to connect with me.

There's no reason for Beckett to lie about all of this. He may just be trying to recruit me for this Uprising, but what do I have to offer? In less than a week, I go back home. We'll never speak to or see each other again. And in Eastates, I have no power, no ability to do anything that would help their movement. *So what would the point be unless he was telling the truth?*

If what he told me is true, it would explain why he started conversations with me when he didn't seem interested in talking to anyone. And all those times I caught him staring at my birthmark . . . he knew exactly what to look for. That raised reddish-brown spot just below my left ear forms a near-perfect heart. It was an easy way to verify my identity. In early school, kids loved pointing it out, but as we all grew older and my hair grew longer, mostly hiding the mark, they forgot about it.

Up until last night, my plan was to serve the delegation and basically count down the days until I could go home. But now, that would mean being even farther away from the family member lost to me for years. Although, it's not like I have special privileges to go to Westates when this is over anyway. *Would Dad even believe me if*

*I told him that Mom's alive? If we joined the Uprising in Eastates, could we send messages back and forth with her?*

I prop an elbow on the table and rest my head against a clenched fist. *How am I going to think about anything but this today?*

"Hey, are you sick again?" Saya nudges me, her eyes trained on me in concern.

"No, no." I force a smile. The last thing I want is for Kiera to notice that I'm more distracted than usual today. If I can't keep it together at breakfast, I'll never survive the inevitable scrutiny upstairs. Curiosity draws my attention around the table. *Are the others at all bothered by what happened last night?* Between sneaking out, getting separated, and stopping Beckett and Callan from trying to pound each other into the pavement, I can't be the only one out of sorts.

Apparently, my fellow delinquents have lapsed back into our mutual barely-acknowledge-each-other relationship. Ryland and Kinsley act as if this is just another day, enjoying their breakfast and socializing as usual. Even Chander and Callan act like nothing out of the ordinary happened last night. The only difference I notice is the crack in Callan's bottom lip and his slightly swollen jawline. Every time he takes a sip of juice, he cringes. *Serves him right.* I've decided to not solely blame Beckett for the mess last night turned into. I blame all of them.

Just the passing thought of Beckett awakens my curiosity. *Did he sleep last night? Does he feel guilty about sneaking out? Is he planning to reintroduce his fist to Callan's face again today?*

I fight against the instincts urging me to seek him out. My emotions alternate between anger and want. I never should have gone, but it was too easy to agree when he asked me. I clearly don't fit in with them, and it's a miracle we weren't caught. Beckett certainly made sure there were enough chances. As if stopping to talk to the old man wasn't enough, he practically attacked Callan. The guy's a jerk, but that kind of violence would never be tolerated in Eastates.

*Eastates!* I didn't even notice if Hayes came to breakfast. I twist in my seat, looking left and right. Of course, Hayes has planted himself at the head of the table. He and his brainiac twin, Vanen, are caught up in a deep discussion. I can tell it's serious by the way Hayes motions with his hands and examines the ceiling as if in thought.

Maybe they've learned more about whatever this delegation truly is. I've been so caught up in Beckett's stories and knack for leading me into reckless situations that I forgot about everything Hayes and Vanen have been doing. Besides, catching up with Hayes may help take my mind off the Uprising.

***

When we reach the Unity Room, I plant myself beside Hayes. He and Vanen rush to hand out everyone's computing devices. When they finish and return to their seats, he slides his glasses up the bridge of his nose, watching me. There's no time to chat now, but he must know I want to talk, considering I rarely make a point to sit beside him.

Muffled conversations fill the time and space as we wait for another day of useless discussions to begin. Within minutes, two voices rise above the others. Their vicious tones spread a hostile charge through the air. Every head turns to the back of the room – toward Callan and Beckett. Their eyes are locked, their faces twisted in anger.

"I guess you didn't learn your lesson last night, huh, *Beckey*?"

With that taunt, Beckett launches a fist toward Callan, connecting with his jaw. After raising a hand to his face protectively, Callan hurls himself toward Beckett. Before any of us can react, they collide with a table, knocking it onto its side as it crashes to the floor.

Frenzied footsteps echo from the hallway. Whoever's coming is in a hurry. As the guys stand and face each other, Kiera rushes into the room with her assistants, Lisum and Wynter, just a few steps behind. Their jaws drop for just a moment before they storm into the scuffle.

"Stop that right now!" Kiera commands through gritted teeth. She inserts herself between the two guys. "That type of behavior is unacceptable and will not be tolerated." Rage reflects in her narrowed eyes. It sends a shiver down my spine. *I'm just glad I'm not on the receiving end of whatever she plans to do.*

The guys stand and brush away the remnants of their struggle – running fingers through their mussed hair and straightening their clothes.

"You two have officially earned yourselves a trip to our security and defense departments. It seems you both lack the ability to maintain peace even if you don't like each other. And that is a critical skill when we are working toward a renewed peace treaty. Lisum, Wynter, please escort these gentlemen, and they *will* behave as gentlemen, to my office."

Her assistants jump at her command, rushing to collect Beckett and Callan. Before the door closes behind them, Kiera takes a deep breath and smooths her hair. She bends down to pick up the red notebook she dropped during the scuffle. As she presses her fingertips together, a smile curves her cheeks. With the two offenders gone, her demeanor softens. Slightly. Disapproval precedes her words as she strides to the podium and takes her usual place behind it.

"This was supposed to be a very special day, and for most of you, it still will be." She leans forward, resting her palms on the podium's smooth surface. "You are halfway through your delegation duties and you have made wonderful progress."

*Really? Does she know something I don't?* It feels like we just sit around and argue most of the time. I throw Hayes a sideways glance, but he's too focused on Kiera to even notice. Unwilling to seek out another potential conspirator, I turn my attention back to her.

"In celebration of your success thus far, and in acknowledgment of the incredible sacrifices you've all made to be here with us, your hosting Territory, Centrestates, is granting you a brief afternoon visitation with a loved one. Today."

Audible gasps chase her words. Some delegates stare straight ahead, unblinking. Others share a wide-eyed glance with the person next to them. My heart hammers in my chest as I process Kiera's announcement.

*I get to see Dad or Easton today!*

# CHAPTER 3 ~ EVERLY

## UPPER DIVISION, CENTRESTATES

Reckless anticipation surges through me like lightning. Inner giddiness threatens to crack the unemotional wall I want to maintain.

"Lisum and Wynter have coordinated all the arrangements." Kiera purses her lips. "They will meet your visitors at the train station and escort them here."

*My visitor must be Dad. There's no way he would let my little brother travel alone on a train, to an unfamiliar Territory. The only other person I'd want to see right now is Josli, but I can't imagine they would send her before a relative.*

"I had planned to spend the morning with the entire delegation so we could start drafting a new Alliance Agreement. But instead I need to address the bad behavior we all witnessed just moments ago." She releases a deep sigh. "So that leaves you without anyone to guide the conversation."

Hayes raises his hand. She turns her head toward him, raising her eyebrows expectantly. "Yes, Mr. Crimshaw?"

"We've been working together long enough to know what to do. You can trust us to do this without any supervision. Vanen and I can take notes and write a report so you can see what we come up with."

Kiera licks her lips and glances around the room. *Honestly, without Callan and Beckett, the group is pretty easygoing.* Ryland and Kinsley can be a little annoying but for the most part, they're harmless. The hostility searing the air evaporated as soon as the guys left. And once Kiera announced that we were getting visitors, the mood quickly shifted to excitement.

"I think that's a good plan, Mr. Crimshaw." She nods and flashes him a brief smile. "I'm going to display an outline on the screen. If you follow that, it will lead you through each section of the agreement. Work through them in order. Each section is complete only when you can all agree on the terms. Work through as much as you can, but don't rush it. You'll get a little break from this after lunch, when your visitors arrive."

We actually spend the morning in productive discussions. It's the most engaged I've ever felt with the group. The promise of seeing my father serves as a powerful motivation. The others must feel the same way – everyone seems genuinely interested in creating a new Alliance Agreement.

With a renewed perspective, I look around the room, seeing my peers for what feels like the first time. We're here to create a plan that the Societal Order Leaders could enact in each Territory. Even if they make changes to what we give them, these are our words and our ideas.

Just as quickly as a sense of pride flashes through me, it's gone. I can't ignore the warning signs that this delegation isn't what it's supposed to be. Hayes and Vanen finding the IND, or indicator, list of people we know from back home. The old man saying that war is coming. Beckett trying to convince me that I should be part of the Uprising. The reminders deflate my spirit.

***

By lunchtime, my stomach churns with eagerness more than hunger. As the clock ticks closer to noon, Hayes suggests that we finish up any last thoughts so he can add them to his notes.

Just as he closes the file and sets the computing device aside, the door swings open. Callan and Beckett trudge inside the conference room, followed by Kiera. The guys avoid eye contact and drop into seats while she stops mid-step to announce that all the delegates will be eating lunch together. As soon as we are done, we should report back to the Unity Room. From there, we'll be taken to spend some time with our visitors. Fueled by the lingering promise, the group rushes out the door and down the steps.

"I can't believe they're doing this for us." Saya elbows me as we keep pace down the stairs.

"I know . . . I mean I guess for you it's not that big of a deal, right?" She is staying at Centrel Quarters like the rest of us, but she lives in this division.

"Even though I'm close to home, I still miss my family," she admits. "The time here is going by fast, but I wouldn't mind seeing my mom or dad."

"Yeah, I can't wait to see my visitor too. It's got to be my dad." He's never talked about leaving Eastates, even just to visit a new place. I wonder what he thinks of Centrestates, not that he'll get to see much of it. I'm sure he'll go back home later this afternoon. He can't miss work, not more than he already will.

Even as Saya and I join the lunch line and grab food, my gaze wanders to Beckett. I wonder how much trouble he really got in. I want to ask if he's okay, but both he and Callan wear unapproachable, emotionless masks. Neither appears the least bit interested in talking or even making eye contact with anyone.

Talk at the table is light as everyone seems focused on gulping down their lunch and cleaning up. As they finish eating, delegates wander back to the stairs in small groups of two and three. Beckett lags behind at the table as Saya links her arm through mine and tugs me away.

"Maybe our visits will start early if we're all back in the room!" she says, playfully jabbing my side with her elbow. The prospect prompts me to move a little faster. In no time, ten of us are perfectly perched in our seats, awaiting Kiera's return. Callan and Beckett slink into the room just moments before she arrives.

The random chatter quiets as soon as the rhythmic clacking of her heels echoes in the hallway. Kiera prances into the room with Lisum and Wynter a few steps behind. Just seeing them twists my stomach in knots. If they're here too, that means they're done retrieving all our visitors. *Did one of them greet my dad at the train station? Did they just see him minutes ago?*

Our host flashes a broad smile, clearly pleased with the power she holds over us right now. It feels like she commands every heartbeat and breath, but I don't think anyone cares. Other than Beckett and Callan, the rest of us generate a buzz of excitement that swirls in the air.

"Now," Kiera tilts her head and scans the room, seeking us out individually as she speaks. "Your visitors have arrived and they are waiting for you in private rooms. You will have two hours before we return to our duties."

*Two hours? That's it?* They brought all these people here for such little time. It feels like a waste, but I guess I should just be happy that it's happening at all.

"As part of the delegation, there is information you are not permitted to share with anyone at this time. For instance, you may not reveal any parts of the Alliance Agreement we've been working on. Everything we've discussed is considered confidential." She twirls a wrist in the air, adding the last part as if it's an amusing afterthought. "Think of it as trade secrets that stay within this room."

I scan the others. Most of them allow their excitement to shine on their faces – eyes bright, smiles hopeful, posture relaxed. Kiera could probably tell us to walk through fire to see our visitors and everyone would readily agree.

"Also, and these are such small requests that I'm certain you won't have any trouble adhering to them . . . after the visits are over, you may not discuss your visitation with any of the other delegates. This is for your privacy as well as your loved one's privacy."

She smiles broadly, as if she's just awarded us all a throne to rule the whole Divided States.

***

Kiera, Lisum and Wynter divide up their babysitting. They each usher one Territory's delegates to conference rooms throughout the upper floors. Of course Kiera takes the Eastates delegates, so Hayes and I are stuck with her.

On the other side of each door awaits whoever each delegate's visitor is. As it nears closer to my turn, my nerves tingle with anticipation. When Kiera leads me to what must be my room, she encroaches my personal space, gently brushes a stray lock of hair behind my ear. I suck in a sharp breath as my back stiffens and goosebumps erupt along my arms. The intimate gesture is inappropriate and unwelcome, but it happens so quickly, I'm too stunned to respond. She cocks her head in amusement. I vow to pay closer attention the next time she's near me. *I won't let her catch me off guard again.*

"Enjoy your visit, Everly. And remember, not a word about the delegation's treaty." She presses a slender finger to her lips, in a shushing gesture.

*Yeah, I get it.* She turns on her heel and marches away as my fingers reach for the handle in nervous anticipation. Besides putting a physical barrier between me and Kiera, I crave the comfort awaiting me on the other side. This is exactly what I need right now. Just a few hours with my dad to remember the life waiting for me back home. Six days from now, I can pack my bags, bid superficial farewells to the other delegates and watch Centrestates grow smaller in the distance as the speed train transports me back home.

I gulp. *How could I forget?* No one seems to know for sure that we have a ride home. I make a mental note to ask about it.

Twisting the door handle, I tug a smile across my cheeks and release a deep breath. My eyes immediately land on the only other occupant of the room as the door slowly swings open. But it's not my father, or my brother.

My heart seizes and my jaw drops as I come face-to-face with a ghost.

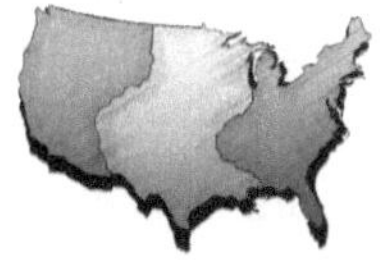

# CHAPTER 4 ~ EVERLY

## UPPER DIVISION, CENTRESTATES

Memories flicker through my mind as it struggles to comprehend the person before me. She rises, slowly but steadily, pushing up from the small square table her chair was tucked beneath. Her deep brown eyes mirror my own.

That's where the similarities end. While my long brown locks are streaked with honey-gold highlights from the sun's rays, hers are crowned with silvery strands of gray and white. Wrinkles sprout from the corners of her eyes. A smile bursts across her cheeks, pulling them taut. Her outstretched arms reach for me. I shake my head, slowly at first, but the motion grows erratic as she steps toward me.

"Everly, honey, I've missed you." *It can't be her. She was sick. She died. Years ago.*

"It can't . . . can't be," I stutter, still shaking my head. A gray jumpsuit hangs loosely from her thin limbs. It's cinched at the waist, a single belt looped twice around her wiry frame. Even with only a moment to assess her, the word *weak* springs to mind. But Beckett said my mother was strong. And he said she was in Westates. *Why is she wearing gray?* No Territory wears gray.

"But it is. I'm right here." She stops abruptly, eyeing me like I'm about to sprint back through the door I just came through.

My face scrunches in confusion and her image blurs as tears build. "This isn't possible. Dad said you . . . died."

She reaches for my face, but I angle my chin away. My instincts hesitate to welcome this person's touch. At the same time, my posture slackens as I suddenly feel too weak to stand.

"I know, this is hard to understand. I know, honey." She inches closer and rests a hand on my shoulder. When tears roll down my cheeks, she wraps a lithe arm around me. With a strength she doesn't look capable of, she blankets me in a tight embrace.

"And part of what you said is true. I was sick. They took me away to help me, to heal me," she whispers in my ear. "But I'm here now. I'm real."

My heart rockets as my throat swells. I focus on verbalizing the cluster of words swirling in my brain. Squirming out of the hug, I step back to examine every wrinkle and scar, evidence of the time that's passed between us, of a life she led that I wasn't allowed to be part of. Time presses on me like a massive weight, just waiting to steal my mother from me. Again.

*We're supposed to have two hours together, but how can I trust anything that anyone says when she was sent away for so long?*

"But where have you been? Why would they let me see you now?" I have so many questions but a wrenching feeling in my gut promises that this moment will pass in what feels like seconds. There's no way I can glean years' worth of answers in the meager time we have together.

She squeezes my hand and leads me to the table, motioning for me to sit. When I slide a chair out and lower myself into it, she does the same. Leaning across the table, she slides her hands toward me. I hesitantly reach for her open palms, somehow craving and fearing the physical connection. We stare intently at each other as she pours explanations into a rush of breathless sentences.

"Everly, I did things . . . some things that I shouldn't have. I questioned the Societal Order, the laws and rules, and I tried to turn others against them too." She shakes her head slowly, as if disappointed with her actions from so long ago.

"They provide for all our needs, and all they ask in return is that we contribute to our communities. But I couldn't appreciate that." She presses a clenched fist to her mouth. I can't tell if she's trying to stem emotion or if she's forcing words out that she doesn't believe. I observe every facial tic and expression as she continues.

"After my sickness was cured, I was asked to demonstrate my loyalty to the Societal Order by serving time in Westates. I'm just grateful that the Societal Order trusted me to contribute again. I couldn't come back home but at least I get to see you now." She laces bony fingers together and drops them in her lap, her solemn gaze following their trajectory.

"Mom, I don't care what you did. You've been gone for . . . six years. You've missed so many things, and most of Easton's life." My tone grows indignant. "You've been punished long enough. Our whole family has been!"

Panic flashes in her eyes. She scrambles around the table and wraps me in another embrace.

"Everly." Her breath tickles my ear. If she weren't that close, I'd never hear her words. "It was all my fault. The Societal Order did what they had to do to maintain peace." I tense, flinching, but she pulls me closer and continues. It's almost like her side of the conversation is on a continuous loop meant to detract from anything I say. It's not worth wasting time arguing, so I clamp my mouth shut. When she realizes I've calmed down, she scurries back to her seat. Instead of pushing for more answers, I sit back and listen.

She describes the time she spent away from us, helping to assemble furniture and other hard goods for all the Territories. She doesn't mention anything about Beckett's family. Digging into the recesses of my memory, I search for hints of recognition the entire time she talks. She's blinking a lot. *Did she used to do that?* I can't remember. I never had a reason to scrutinize every move she made. Her hands are almost always in motion, either fidgeting or clasping and unclasping together. *Is she nervous?* It's not exactly suspicious to be nervous about seeing the daughter you left behind six years ago.

When I ask why she's wearing gray, she explains that it's because of her past infractions. It's meant to serve as a constant reminder that she no longer fits into any Territory. It seems cruel, but I sense she's evaluating my reaction, so I keep that thought to myself.

After a moment, she stretches her arms across the table and takes my hands in hers. "I've talked enough. I want to hear about you. Now tell me, you haven't done anything that could get you in trouble, right?" She pauses, catching her breath. Her grip tightens, as if in anticipation of my answer.

"No, of course not." Eastates Everly never did anything that would be against the rules, but I'm not about to admit that Delegate Everly has been a different story.

"It's okay, you can tell me." She watches me intently, but I can't bring myself to admit any recent wrongdoing. My mind is still in shock that we're even sitting here. And a small part of my brain wonders just how different she is compared to the mother I knew six years ago. My silence invites her to continue.

"I don't want what happened to me to happen to you or Dad."

Her absence left a raw, irreparable hole in my existence for the years I thought she was dead. But in this moment, as brief as it may be, I look to her for answers, for guidance. The instinct floods through me, a deep yearning for a parent to reassure me that everything will be okay, an empty promise I'd gladly accept without hesitation.

"I haven't done anything. None of us have. We all follow all the rules." My rushed words sound defensive, but that's exactly how I feel. Disbelief flickers in her gaze for a moment before she shifts to a different topic.

"I've missed all of you. How are your father and your brother?"

That question is easy enough. I spend the next several minutes telling her about Easton's schoolwork and how we both help Dad with the chores. It reminds me of those last days at home before coming to Centrestates, and everything that waits for me there.

"Mom, remember that perfume you had? In the red glass bottle? I still have it. I found it when I was packing to come here." Maybe this will trigger her memory and draw out the person I used to know.

"Of course I do, honey. I'm glad you kept it safe." She runs a hand through my hair. Now I lean into her touch, relaxing in the moment. Is the shock wearing off, or do I so badly want this to be real that I'm willing to blindly shift into belief?

"Sometimes I open the lid and just take a quick whiff of it," I admit, releasing something between a sniff and a giggle. "It's almost all dried up."

"Maybe we can get more of that perfume," she whispers. "And maybe we'll get to see more of each other, Everly." She squeezes my hands a little tighter. "I am certainly going to ask if there is any chance for that."

My jaw drops. I hadn't even thought about what's to come after our time is up. I eagerly devour her words. They aren't exactly promises, but they're more than I would have ever hoped for. A sob bursts from my throat. I raise a trembling hand to cover my face. Squeezing my eyes shut, I hear the scrape of her chair drag along the floor. Within seconds, her warmth envelops me. I stand to meet her hug.

"Don't worry, my sweet Evy," she mutters softly, rubbing my back.

My eyes fly open wide. A lump forms in my throat as my stomach drops. *Evy? She never called me that. She was the only one in the world who called me Lyly.*

I'm thankful we aren't facing each other, or she'd see my reaction. Forcing my trembling lips to move, I form the only question I can think of to test the warning signals my brain is sending.

"The perfume, Mom, do you remember how it smelled?"

"Of course I do. Roses." She turns my chin to face her as a smile lights her whole face.

I force a smile back. The red hourglass-shaped bottle holds the last drops of my mother's lilac perfume. *Did she forget?*

Three swift knocks strike the door, nearly making me jump out of my skin. It's the official end, or at the very least an interruption, to our privacy. Before either of us can respond, the door swings open.

Wynter clasps her hands together and bounces toward us. "I hope you enjoyed catching up, but it's time to conclude your visit."

The initial awkwardness returns, snaking its way between us. My mother nods to Wynter before turning to me.

"This is just goodbye for right now, not forever. I really believe that." She cradles my cheek in her palm. "I love you, Everly. Please tell your father and brother that too."

"I will." I nod. My throat seems to constrict with each breath. Every inhalation is an effort. "I love you too, Mom. Bye."

I stumble out of the room in a daze. *Did that really just happen?* Even if it did, I have no way to communicate with my father. I'm trapped between confusion and disbelief. Heavy tears threaten to spill as an utter sense of loneliness slams into me. No one can understand how I feel right now. My temples pound as confusion swirls in my mind.

The delegates meander, one by one, back to the Unity Room. Like me, it appears that their feet carry them on muscle memory alone. No one speaks. Some of them wear a forlorn look, as though they've seen their own ghosts while others appear relaxed, perfectly content with however they spent the last two hours. I'm too consumed with my own thoughts to wonder who any of their visitors were.

# Chapter 5 ~ Caro

## Uprising Headquarters, Westates

"You're not going to believe this," she states. Her words are slightly muffled. Her mouth must be pressed to the receiver. "Today we brought in visitors for the delegates. It was some high-priority task Kiera came up with two days ago."

"That doesn't sound concerning. Are the kids homesick maybe?" I can't help but ask, even though it feels like I'm disregarding her assessment.

"Nothing here is harmless," she insists. I don't need to see her to know she's clenching her teeth, barely restraining herself. "Let me put it this way. Some of the visitors weren't real."

"Weren't real? I'm not following you." There isn't time for idle chitchat. We've got a secure line but who knows for how long. Clearly her emotions are hampering her ability to get to the point.

"Caro, one of them was supposed to be you!" Her explanation hits me like a cannon to the gut. My mouth goes dry. There's only one delegate who would have met with "me" as their visitor. The thought of it twists my nerves into an angry knot. We have to end whatever sick game Imperant is playing.

"Are the delegates okay?" I have to keep my questions general. I can't afford to allow my emotions to spiral out of control.

"Physically they're fine, but emotionally . . . they're tired and confused, I think." She pauses before lowering her voice. "And some of them figured out they aren't on the transport list to go home when the delegation ends. I've been checking every file I have access to and can't find any record of return travel itineraries . . . for any of them."

"Could it just be an oversight?" I chew my bottom lip in thought. *Does that really mean anything?* The arrangements could have been made but she just didn't find the details.

"There aren't any oversights here," she mutters. "Kiera makes sure of that. Everything runs exactly as she wants it to. She's got Leader Imperant in the palm of her hand. She even—" She stops mid-sentence, sending my heart into a racing gallop.

"Are you still there?"

"I can't talk much longer. But there's something else . . . " Her voice drops, replaced by the sound of papers shuffling in the background. I wait, hoping no one interrupts this conversation. *We just need a little longer.* Her next words spill out in a rush. I don't dare interrupt. If she gets caught sharing information with me, especially at this level of government, I don't want to imagine what would happen to her.

"I've been snooping around and I found some projections about the power grid," she says. "Without major upgrades, it will be out of transmission capacity by the end of next year. The population is increasing in all three Territories, and the trajectory of demand is far beyond the current system's ability to keep up. A research team here has developed a system of regional power grids that they're testing . . . some sort of fuel cells that convert natural gas into low-emissions electricity. I don't understand it all, but I wonder how much of it the other Territories know."

"If the Societal Order leaders know, they certainly aren't sharing any information with citizens," I mutter.

"And that's not even all of it. I think things are much worse than what we thought." Her words run together as she pushes them out in one breath.

"What have you learned?" Aside from how limited our contact is, our plan is working brilliantly. Plant a member of the Uprising in Central Hall. Directly under their noses. Of course we have multiple contacts there, but she is our highest ranking, meaning she's the closest to the top. And right now, that information is critical. I just wish it was reaching us faster.

"In between watching over the delegates, I've been researching what we talked about and I . . . I believe I found proof of the . . . compliance chip."

She can't see, but my mouth drops open. Rumors and theories have swirled through whispered gossip for years. I never wanted to believe that the Territories implant us with a small device to limit our ability to make decisions for ourselves. But this doesn't sound like just another story that she's heard. Whatever she's found has her rattled. She's not one to struggle for words, especially since our conversations have to be kept brief.

"Keep going," I encourage her.

"I found . . . production reports . . . showing where the chips are made and how they get distributed to medical centers . . . throughout each Territory."

"So Centrestates supplies chips for the other Territories too?" If that's the case, then leaders Huntsman and Ault are just as guilty as Imperant. A small part of me had hoped that he was the only Societal Order Leader at fault for the Divided States' oppression, but of course that couldn't be true. If it were, I never would have been ripped from Eastates and thrown into Westates. That requires coordination that crosses boundaries and borders.

"They do." She pauses, likely expecting my next question.

"Can you get me that paperwork? Whatever it is you found?"

"It's too risky right now." She hesitates for a moment. "But when you're ready to strike, I could lead you to all the information you need."

"That's fair." There's no point in smuggling out one small piece of evidence when we might be able to gather a treasure trove of it in just a few more days. *Besides, what if she's misinterpreting what she found?* My thoughts drift to the one counterclaim that always made me dismiss the compliance chip theory as an overimaginative premise. I can't help but say it.

"If everyone had this chip, then the Uprising would never exist. We'd all be happily playing by their rules, never questioning anything."

"According to their data, some chips are defective," she explains. "One hundred percent perfection isn't possible. That could have led to some people – who ended up with defective chips – slowly sabotaging the system. If a baby is born and implanted with a defective chip, and that child grows up and becomes a medic, they might feel an ethical tug-of-war with certain rules and, perhaps, act on it. Who knows if there are people out there who secretly refuse to implant the chips but somehow stay under the radar?"

"That is believable and over a span of decades, it's entirely possible." Maybe everyone would be a part of the Uprising if they didn't have the chip. "Anything else?"

"I found some summaries of studies they conducted on citizens who have the chip, testing their loyalty to the Societal Order through verbal and written questioning. All the subjects were from Centrestates."

Fiery anger surges through my core. So the Territories have resorted to experimenting on their citizens. *What's next? Creating generations of mindless puppets they can program to work, serving their leaders with no other purpose? That's not living.* I shake my head, banishing the wandering thoughts. I can contemplate this later. Right now there's something she needs to know.

"Good work. I've called the other leaders for a meeting. They'll all be here by tomorrow." *And they won't be willing to risk exposing the Uprising without strong evidence that we can succeed in our mission.* I soften that message slightly. "They will expect proof of the Societal Order's indiscretions before committing to a mission strategy. I trust you'll keep gathering information?"

"I'm confident that there's an abundance of incriminating evidence against the Societal Order, and I am committed to finding every last detail of it."

Just as I open my mouth to reply, her tone drops, fast and low. "Someone's coming, I've got to go!"

The line goes dead. I stare at the phone for a few minutes, processing all that she's told me.

Today's update only confirms what I already knew. The Uprising has waited long enough, and it can't wait any longer.

# CHAPTER 6 ~ EVERLY

# UPPER DIVISION, CENTRESTATES

"I trust you all enjoyed your visits." Kiera raises her eyebrows expectantly but waits no more than a breath for anyone to respond. "Well, most of you anyway. Callan and Beckett forfeited their visitation privilege. Instead, they spent those two hours right here," she plunks a finger down on the podium, "with me. Working together, poring through all your notes, calmly discussing any opposing viewpoints and drafting a new Alliance Agreement. I'd like you to spend the rest of the afternoon reviewing what they've come up with."

When I glance toward Beckett, a shimmer of light catches my eye. He's actually wearing the lapel pin Kiera presented each of us on our first day here. I still marvel at the detail of the raised eagle figure emblazoned across the golden surface, its talons stretched out to the round edges. Until now, that was the only time I ever saw it on him. *I wonder if Kiera finally said to him, "Wear this or else."*

Hayes' hand shoots into the air. "Will everyone need their computing devices?"

"Thank you for asking, Mr. Crimshaw." She pauses for a moment, considering his unspoken offer. "Yes, you can hand them out. I'd like everyone to focus on the screen up here, but if something we talk about gives you an idea, take notes on your devices. We'll go through each section of the drafted agreement and I will capture any changes the group agrees on. Lisum and Wynter won't be joining us. They're busy ensuring that all of today's guests make it back home safely."

When her eyes flicker toward me, I instinctively drop my gaze and attempt to shrink into my seat. I hate that she knows anything about me personally. She knows who my visitor was, and she obviously knows my mother wasn't brought here from Eastates. It's unheard of for relatives to live in different Territories, so Kiera must know at least some history of her whereabouts.

"Unless there's anything else, I'll pull up the first section, we'll pause for a moment so everyone can read it and then we'll dive right into any suggestions the group has."

After those brief announcements, we're thrust into debate and discussions. My mind struggles to concentrate as thoughts war with each other. Honestly, everyone seems quieter than usual, probably lost in their own thoughts. If Dad had been my visitor, I'd probably be swimming in homesickness right now. Some of the others are probably wrestling that emotion.

The rest of the afternoon fades into a blur. My temples throb the more Kiera attempts to force the Alliance Agreement on us. Is

she purposely trying to distract us? And what was the distraction –
having visitors or scrutinizing the stupid agreement?

As I struggle to bury the conversations that replay in my mind,
realization dawns. Beckett! I need to tell him that I saw my mother.
Of course Kiera said we aren't supposed to talk about our visits.
But what does it matter? Beckett certainly would never tell her,
or anyone. *How can I be expected to keep this inside?* It's already
consuming me and I still have another week here.

After a few hours, Kiera dismisses us, acknowledging that we've
had a busy day. Of course she would never admit that she's pushed
us past our mental and emotional limits.

"I hope you all have a restful evening. And remember," she pauses
long enough to ensure every set of eyes in the room has landed on
her. "Your visitations are private and confidential. You are not to
discuss them with each other." She raises her eyebrows as if daring
someone to question or challenge that statement. No one does.
Instead, they tidy up the tables and chairs before making their way
to the door.

Although my body is prepared to spring toward Beckett, I restrain
my muscles and instead slowly meander near him. Positioning
myself beside him as the delegation flows down the stairs like a river,
I act uninterested. He doesn't even glance over at me, but I lean
toward him and whisper, "We need to talk."

As if he fully expected the request, he whispers back, "Garden.
Thirty minutes."

I nod as a faint smile passes over my lips. Relief momentarily
numbs the flood of emotions my mind has processed over the past
week. *Who would have ever thought I'd seek comfort in confiding in
Beckett?*

***

The slight breeze carries his crisp, woodsy scent to me before I see him. Even surrounded by plants and flowers, I know it's him and not the foliage. As soon as he reaches me, my eyes drift to his collar. The pin is gone. *It must have been for show. To appease Kiera.*

"What's going on?"

"I needed to tell you about my visitor." I chew my lower lip, wondering if he'll believe me. I barely know him, and his whole demeanor suddenly feels distant, detached. It's like the connection I thought we had is evaporating right before my eyes. And I can't stop it. Before I can change my mind, I blurt it out.

"Beckett, I talked to my mother today. That's who my visitor was. Well, she said she was my mother but something about her seemed . . . off."

His gaze latches onto me as if he's finally noticed I'm standing before him. He lunges toward me, clutching my arms in his hands.

"What exactly did she say? What about it felt wrong? It couldn't have been her!"

His intensity makes me wilt, once again questioning everything I thought I knew.

"I . . . I mean, she told me that she said things that . . . got her in trouble. Things about the Societal Order. And she wanted to make sure no one else in the family was doing anything like that."

He rubs his chin, giving me time to turn the questioning on him.

"How can you be so sure it wasn't really her? You weren't even there." I have my doubts, but I'm the one who saw her and talked to her while he was trapped in a conference room with Callan.

His narrowed eyes pierce me. "She'd never willingly come here. And besides, I guarantee they wouldn't go to the trouble of bringing visitors here for us. It was just for show."

His words sting. They imply that the person he knows would never come here even if it meant seeing the daughter she left behind so many years ago. As if he knows my own mother better than I do. What hurts the most is that he probably does. *If he's even telling me the truth.*

"What do you mean it was just for show? For us? For the visitors?" His accusations are making my head spin. There's too much to process right now. I thought he could help me work through this, but he's just making it worse.

"For anyone who'll listen. 'Look at how wonderful we're treating the delegates. They're being interviewed, they're getting the best food, they're deciding our future, they're so important.' Everly, you can't believe any of it. There's a reason for everything they do here, and it isn't good."

I'm not sure what else to say. He squeezes his eyes shut and pinches the bridge of his nose in concentration. After a minute, he slowly relaxes his features and faces me. I can see the intensity of thoughts spinning in his head. He quickly closes the small gap between us and leans close to my ear.

"I just thought of something," he whispers. "Everly, up until a few days ago, you had no idea your mother was alive. And now, all of a sudden, they bring her here."

"It can't be a coincidence, right?" I ask. That's an awfully big one.

His eyes dart left and right. "What if they've been listening to us and all this was intentional?" he whispers. Without another word, he grabs my hand and we hurry back to Centrel Quarters. My brain stretches to remember everywhere we've talked about my mother. It was never around the other delegates, so I don't think any of them would have told Kiera anything.

Without stopping, Beckett leads us straight to Hayes' room. Sure enough, Vanen's there too.

"You two interested in testing a theory?"

Hayes slides his glasses up the bridge of his nose and nods. "Always."

***

The guys listen intently as we explain that we think Kiera's listening to us and using those conversations against us, to test us. She's already said we're test subjects. Maybe this experiment is unfolding with each day.

Vanen convinces us that the only way to test the theory in the time we have is to bring everyone in on it. We all know about the INDs, or indicators, as we believe it stands for. We found a list with one IND for each delegate – people we know from back home. As if that wasn't weird enough, each delegate also had three letters next to their own name – either CON or SUB. We haven't figured out what any of it means yet.

Maybe it's time to chat about our visitors today. We can find out if they were all INDs and see if there are any repercussions. If we all talk about it, no one can be singled out. At least, that's what we hope.

Dinner becomes a message chain, where one delegate passes a note along to the next, beneath the table. It simply says, "Meet in room 412 as soon as we finish eating. Say NOTHING out loud about it until we're in Hayes' room."

I shovel the food into my mouth so quickly that the flavors blend together in a savory rhapsody. Even mushed together, it tastes amazing. Everyone's quiet during the meal, likely contemplating what's to come next.

As soon as we funnel into Hayes' room and click the door closed, Beckett abruptly announces why we've gathered here.

"We need to know who everyone's visitors were today." His jaw tightens and he clenches his teeth. Hayes and Vanen shoot him an annoyed look. *This isn't the way they would handle this.*

"What? Why?" Ryland asks. "What do you care? You didn't even have a visitor!"

"It's none of your—" Arjun adds before Saya jumps in.

"You know we're not suppos—" Saya starts, looking around the room for support.

"I don't care! We're also not supposed to be an experiment, but here we are!" Beckett waves a hand around, fury rolling off him in waves.

"An experiment? What?" Kinsley plants her hands on her hips, waiting for an answer.

"Too much, man." Vanen raises a hand toward Beckett. "You're just making everyone defensive."

"We need to talk about this," Beckett insists. "Okay, I'll go first. I didn't get a visit, but Kiera made sure to tell me who it was going to be." He slides a palm across his chin. "My visitor was supposed to be my brother, who is also my IND."

"Why would she tell you that?" Kinsley asks quietly. In the charged silence her question is crystal clear.

"We were told he was locked away, serving a life sentence. That we'd never see or hear from him again. But somehow they could have just delivered him here, along with someone to taunt every other delegate, pretty easily."

I scrunch my face. *Taunt?* I wouldn't have described it that way. Unshed tears sting my eyes as I bite my lower lip. Now that he suggests it, I wonder if he's right. That's kind of how it felt when Kiera took me to the room for my visit.

The others solemnly admit who their visitors were. Exactly half of us met – or were withheld a visit – with our INDs. Vanen fires up his computing device. He and Hayes pound the keys, reviewing the previous information they found.

"We've got something here!" Vanen announces. "When we cross-check the visitors with the list of CONs and SUBs."

"The SUBs met with family members. The CONs met with their INDs," Hayes adds. "Now we have to figure out what it means."

# CHAPTER 7 ~ EVERLY

## UPPER DIVISION, CENTRESTATES

Thoughts churn, spilling into sidebar conversations.

"So what does it really matter?" Kinsley asks. "I mean, we got a break from the same old meetings every day and spent some time with people from home. How is that bad?"

My eyes dart to Beckett but I keep quiet. The room descends into discussion on its own. I share a knowing glance with Hayes. This get-together was just a test to see if we're being listened to. The others don't have to know everything that's going on.

I slip past the others, casually meandering to Beckett's side. He seems to understand that this isn't the place for us to talk, but it is a chance to listen to the others. Besides that, my heart pounds as my gaze gravitates toward the door, just waiting for Kiera to burst through it and scold us for doing the very thing she told us not to. *Does she know we're all in here together?*

Hayes and Vanen descend into their own world, trading whispers, quieting every few minutes to tune in to the conversations floating around the room. After about twenty minutes, one voice rises above the others to announce that he's had enough.

"Why are you all so obsessed with overanalyzing everything?" Callan huffs. "So we had visitors. Did you ever stop to think that maybe the Societal Order was just doing something nice for us? No, because you're all too busy looking for some crazy plot that doesn't exist. I'm done wasting my time on this." He throws his hands in the air and stomps to the door. A wave of doubt rolls through the room in his wake.

"I'm kinda tired of thinking," Ryland says. She rolls her neck from side to side before arching her back in a stretch.

"Me too." Kinsley nods and the two of them make their way to the door. "See you in the morning."

They both throw a wave to the rest of us before slinking into the hallway. Soon after that, the conversation fades to awkward small talk until the remaining delegates either claim to be tired or suggest that we're probably making this a bigger deal than it really is. One by one, they filter out the door.

"You want to walk back together, Everly?" Saya asks.

"I'm gonna stick around for just a little longer," I say.

She raises her eyebrows and motions toward Beckett as a sly smile slides across her lips. "Gotcha. I'll see you in the morning."

***

After the last of the others leave, Hayes faces our small group. All that's left is him, Beckett, Vanen and me.

"So we know the pattern of who met with their Indicators." Vanen scratches his head. "Aaaaaaaand we think we have a theory as to what's happening here." He motions toward Hayes, as if we don't know who the "we" is that he's referencing.

Hayes tilts his chin to the bathroom and we all scramble inside the small room. The four of us huddle together, uncomfortably close as the sink, shower and toilet occupy most of the space. Hayes speaks first, his voice just above a whisper. It's almost laughable. Just moments ago we purposely wanted to see if Kiera could hear our conversation. Now we've switched into top secret mode, as if the bathroom is an impenetrable chamber where conversations remain private.

"We think the hypothesis here is that certain citizens are *predisposed* to break the rules, more likely to question the Societal Order, or give them trouble. If they can predict that, they can prevent problems before they happen."

Goosebumps erupt along my arms. That makes perfect sense. It's like his words sharpened my focus, allowing a picture to come into view. And it's crystal clear. Kiera and Leader Imperant never cared about our opinions, not for a real peace treaty, they just wanted to invade our thoughts. The supposed peace treaty was just to get us talking. *Are the other Territories in on this?*

"That has to be it," Vanen adds. "That would explain why this whole thing is happening. They thought they could study us for two weeks and walk away with answers to some formula." As if tag-teaming, Hayes explains again.

"Some of us are part of a control group, not really considered a future threat. But then some of us have Indicators that are more closely watched. It's like they're the real test subjects."

My breathing grows shallow as I consider this theory. Beckett and I are real test subjects and Hayes is here as a control subject. It's entirely possible he's right, no matter how bitter a taste it leaves.

"So now what?" Beckett asks. Has he really processed all this already? Because I'm just lucky I can still blink and breathe without being reminded to do those things.

"Well," Vanen starts, "we'll find out tomorrow if we're being listened to. But we need to plan our next move either way."

"Even if they don't know we talked about our visits, we have to be ready for anything," Beckett insists.

"What can we really do? Most of us are far from home," I wrap my arms around my middle, as if that could protect me from whatever is to come. "I mean, whatever they say, we have to do."

"What I'm saying is, do you really think they'd just let us all go back home and pretend like nothing happened here?" Beckett raises his hands in the air.

"You're right," Hayes mutters, his gaze dropping to the floor. "We know too much. And if we truly are just an experiment to them, what happens when the experiment's over?"

His words grip my heart in a vise. Of course the Societal Order wouldn't trust us to return home. Even if I tried to bury the knowledge that my mother is alive, reality would barrage my mind the moment I saw my father. And brother. There's no way I could keep it from them.

"So what do we do?" Vanen asks, knowing none of us has an answer.

"We play along until we can figure it out." Hayes declares, sliding his glasses up the bridge of his nose. "We're on our own. There's no one we can trust here and our visits are done, so it's not like anyone from home can help us."

"All of this is happening because they wanted it to happen," Beckett says. "The Societal Order controls everything. It doesn't matter where you live or what you do, they control every one of us." He throws me a side glance. *I know where this is headed. He's going to tell them.*

"There are people who can help us," he continues. "They're everywhere – in all three Territories. People who want to live their own lives, not how the Societal Order tells them to live. And they're willing to fight for it."

***

I leave Hayes' room feeling numb. *Could we really be right about all this?*

"I can't believe you told them," I whisper as Beckett walks me back to my door. He withheld some key details, like my mother's role in the Uprising, but he did show them the symbol behind his knee and explained that this resistance network spans all three Territories.

"As I see it, we're marked now. The Uprising may be our only hope at making it out of this." He stops and faces me, his intensity searing into my soul. "At this point, we're a liability . . . alive. But dead, all their secrets are safe."

"So you need to find that old man again, right?" My eyes flash wide, anticipating his answer.

"Him or someone else." He scratches his chin. "If we could even find someone else, but it's risky."

"I'd say everything is risky for us right now. There's no secret handshake or password or something? Like no way to know unless you hike up your pants and show off some skin?"

He smiles shyly. It's such a rare look for Beckett. All too quickly, it fades. His eyes turn serious again. "I know what we have to do."

I gulp, already knowing that whatever it is can't be good.

"We have to break into Kiera's office. Hayes and Vanen found the list of our Indicators, right? So maybe she has notes or a list of suspected members of the Uprising. If we could get a few names, we could try to find one of them."

My hand flies to my mouth, covering the gaping hole left when my jaw dropped. "You think Kiera knows about the Uprising? Or Leader Imperant, do you think he knows?"

"They have to," Beckett reasons. "It's not like they'd ever admit it publicly though. That could stir up fear, or maybe even interest." He smirks. "If more people knew about our cause, I bet they'd join us."

He might be right. I had never heard of the Uprising. And if my dad knows about them, he certainly never mentioned it.

"So even if there was a list of names here, how could we possibly find anyone on that list? Neither of us knows anyone here. Maybe we should ask Hayes and Vanen to search the files? If they found the first list, they may be able to find another one."

"Would they really know what to look for? The less they know about the Uprising, the better. We only tell them what we need to." He huffs out a frustrated breath. "It's just the two of us, Everly. The more people who know, the more likely we are to get caught."

I shake my head. What he says makes sense, but he also has a record of getting us in trouble. *How are we supposed to do this?* "Do you remember the last time we tried this?"

"Of course I do. Look, just give me tonight to think of a plan. We need more answers, and the only place we can get them is in Kiera's office. I bet something's in that red notebook she carries around."

He's not going to drop this. Somehow, I've become entwined in his plans. It would be really exciting, if it weren't so dangerous. But, considering we're in this situation and there's no way I can figure to get out of it, I'll leave it to him.

"Okay. Just think of something good."

***

Breakfast is quiet. I try to catch Beckett's attention a few times, but when our eyes meet, he subtly shakes his head. *He doesn't have a plan to get us into Kiera's files yet.* Part of me hopes he'll change his mind and forget about trying to find a list of Uprising members. I think I'd rather try to find that old man again. Maybe he'll come around now that he knows at least one delegate is his ally.

As if the prospect of breaking into her office doesn't rattle my nerves enough, I wonder if we're already in trouble for talking about our visits last night. *Does Kiera know? Is she plotting our punishment right now?* Hayes, Vanen and a few other delegates exude guilt. They focus a little too intently on their plates, for the most part avoiding eye contact and conversation.

Suspicion hangs over us like thick clouds threatening to unload their burden at any moment. I can easily imagine the emotions flowing through the other delegates right now – confusion, disbelief, uncertainty. Most of us saw our Indicators yesterday. While some of those reunions were happy, others – like mine – were beyond unexpected.

Talking about it last night left the group divided. Like Hayes and Vanen, I expected everyone would suspect Kiera was somehow plotting against us, but when we parted ways, most of the other delegates weren't convinced. Some didn't even see the visits with our Indicators as anything of concern. So much for coming together in unity.

# CHAPTER 8 ~ EVERLY

## UPPER DIVISION, CENTRESTATES

As we climb the steps to the conference room, Saya scoots close to me and whispers, "You don't believe all that stuff last night about us being some sort of experiment . . . do you?" Her wide eyes look hopeful that I'll dismiss it all as a stupid overreaction, but I'm not willing to admit how I feel. Or everything I know.

"I'm not sure what to believe." It's not a complete lie, but I am inclined to trust the combined brainpower of Hayes and Vanen – and they both seem pretty certain about what's going on here. I also heard a firsthand account of Kiera and Leader Imperant referencing a control group and subjects. Not that I could ever tell Saya that.

"You know, the other girls don't think you and Beckett act like a couple." Her eyebrows jump as she chews her bottom lip. It makes me wonder if she's the one who doesn't think we act like a couple. Although it's totally believable that she told everyone about us. And of course, our little lunchtime escape to a private table would have fueled any gossip.

I gulp before reacting to the topic I didn't expect. "Well, um, we don't know if Kiera and the others would be angry if they found out. I mean, they might think we aren't taking our time here seriously, that we're just here to have fun together." *Okay, that wasn't a great answer since nothing here has been fun. Well, other than Saya's slumber party.*

"Yeah, I get it." She nudges my shoulder and lets the conversation drop as we reach the Unity Room.

"Good morning," Lisum calls as we take our seats. "We'll just pull up what you were working on yesterday afternoon and pick up from there." As she and Wynter retrieve yesterday's notes and project them onto the screen, Beckett stands and approaches them. *What is he doing?*

"We'll hand out computing devices," Hayes announces as he and Vanen jump out of their seats and rush to the cart. I strain to catch any hint of Beckett's conversation but the guys ensure that doesn't happen as they unlock devices from their docking stations and dash from delegate to delegate, delivering each one.

After a hushed exchange, Lisum and Beckett head to the door while Wynter draws our attention to her. It's time to start our work on the Alliance Agreement. I'm powerless to stop my gaze from tracking Beckett. *Where is he going?* As if he senses my curiosity, he turns his head. When our eyes meet for just a few seconds, he lifts his chin and flashes me a crooked smile. I can't help but smile back, even as I wonder what he's up to.

When Hayes hands me my device, he gives me a subtle thumbs-up. I narrow my eyes, wondering why everyone seems so odd today. He leans down and mutters under his breath, "No one's acting like they heard us talking last night."

*How could I have forgotten about that?* I guess the real test is when Kiera prances in here, whenever that might be. I listen and pretend to type random notes as Wynter leads the discussion. My foot taps a steady beat on the floor as I imagine what Beckett could be doing. If he was going to the bathroom, Lisum wouldn't have left with him. Maybe he's sick? He looked fine at breakfast though.

A few minutes later, Lisum slips back into the room and joins Wynter as if nothing happened. There's no sign of Beckett. *Where did she take him?*

About thirty long minutes later, he finally returns. I watch his every step from the moment he crosses through the doorway until he touches down in his seat. He raises his eyebrows when he catches me looking but obviously can't tell me anything right now. *I know who I'm sitting beside at lunch today.*

***

When Lisum and Wynter dismiss us to eat, I follow Beckett like a shadow. For every step he takes, I take two. I nearly bump into him before he acknowledges me.

"Missed me, huh?" he smirks, clearly enjoying the attention.

"Where were you?" I can't help demanding the obvious question.

"Let's get through the line and meet at our table. Then I'll tell you." So that secluded spot in the corner is now *our* table. I actually like the sound of that.

While he carefully chooses a salad with deep purple lettuce and yellow tomatoes, I rush to grab anything within reach. A bowl of green beans – perfect. A flatbread smothered in sauce and cheese – sure. Time slows as my impatience soars. After what feels like hours, he plunks a roll on his tray, grabs a cup of water and leads us to *our* table.

"So where did you go this morning?"

"Let's just say I was on a recon mission." He tears off a piece of the buttery roll and plops it in his mouth.

"What?" I plunk my elbows down on the table, a little too hard. I want answers, not some riddle to figure out. He takes the hint and finally spills what I've been waiting for.

"Okay," he says, raising his hands in the air. "I went to talk to Kiera today. I said I was sorry for how I've acted and that it may have influenced some of the other delegates. I said that our time here has shown me that I shouldn't have done it and that I'm the only one at fault. Everyone else should be excused from any blame."

I cross my arms and eye him suspiciously before realizing I should be looking at him as if he's the love of my life. If we want the others to think we're interested in each other, I can't exactly let my annoyance with him be on full display. Recovering quickly, I relax my posture. "Really? Why?" *Why would he even bother? Kiera would never listen.*

"I did. Everly, you got in trouble because of me. You didn't deserve that and I wanted Kiera to know." He pauses, those endless blue eyes imploring me to understand. "But while I was there, I also used that time to scan her office. You know, trying to see if she had anything that looked important just sitting around. Something that might help us find someone who's part of the Uprising."

Heat flushes my cheeks. I know I should focus on the last part of what he said, but my stomach flutters with tendrils of wonder. He actually tried to fix things for me, even though we both know it isn't possible. I try to push a nonchalant response past my lips.

"You really thought she'd just keep something so important out in the open?"

"It was worth a try, and besides, she did put that red notebook she carries around in the top right drawer of her desk." He clears his throat before continuing. "It seems pretty important to her. And now we know where she keeps it."

"So?" I have a feeling I won't like where this is headed.

"So that's got to have something important in it. We have no idea what they have planned for us, but I'd bet my life that it isn't anything good. We're in danger just being here. Our only hope is the Uprising. If Hayes and Vanen didn't find anything about the Uprising on the servers, then I bet it's on paper. And I bet it's in Kiera's office. She probably keeps it close to her so she can scribble down any evil thoughts that pop into her head."

"Please tell me you don't want to steal the notebook so we can read it." My stomach drops and any remnants of an appetite disappear.

"No, of course not." He shakes his head as his gaze drops to his tray.

"Good," I sigh. "Because that would probably be the worst idea I've heard yet."

"I'm not stupid enough to steal it, Everly." He raises his eyebrows and crosses his arms. "I just want to read it. And I think you should be the lookout when I do."

I squeeze my eyes shut and blow out a deep breath. Time is ticking away and I haven't even told him about Saya's earlier comment.

"Before you try to convince me to help you and I refuse, Saya said no one believes we're a couple." Heat flares within my cheeks as my words rush out. At least the frustration I'm feeling from what he's proposing is put to good use.

"Then we make them believe." He leans forward and stretches a hand across the table. When my eyes follow his movement, he wiggles his fingers. "Holding hands is a good start."

Slowly, I slip my hand into his. A jolt of electricity pulses through me as we touch.

"Now, I've got an idea for how we can sneak into Kiera's office."

A war erupts between my brain and my body. Practical thoughts command me to shut this conversation down before it truly starts, but the simple physical connection we share softens the harsh objection I should have.

"Haven't we gotten into enough trouble? I've been thinking about it and we should try to find that old man again." He cringes but doesn't release his grip on my hand. I seize the silence to boost my argument. "The old man wants to help us. We already know that. He tried to warn me that first day."

"We could try, but that could take days." He releases his grip and slides back in his seat. "But that notebook is right there. And we could have our hands on it in just a few hours."

After a few minutes of silence, he says, "How about this – we try both of our ideas? We're stuck here anyway all afternoon. So we'll try to read Kiera's notebook and if that doesn't work or nothing's in it, we try to find the old man?"

With no fight left in me, and no other ideas, I nod slowly. It doesn't seem like there's much of a point in arguing with him. And besides, I bet we won't even make it into Kiera's office. That thing must be locked down. At least that's what I hope.

# Chapter 9 ~ Caro

## Uprising Headquarters, Westates

"You've got to come soon!" My contact is on the line again and this time her voice is shrill with panic. She's never been this forceful yet unhinged at the same time. It worries me. She's working right under the Societal Order's nose in Centrestates and if they find out . . .

"What's changed? Do they suspect anything?" My tone is smooth but my pulse races. *Did someone blow our cover?* That's all it would take – one traitor willing to spill our secrets to one of Imperant's lackeys. Anyone who sides with Societal Order Leader Imperant craves that rush of importance. Trust is dangerous anywhere, but in Centrestates it's deadly.

"I don't think anyone suspects anything, but . . . tomorrow night . . . something big is happening." Her words fade to a near-whisper. "I can't talk much longer. Kiera could be back at any time."

"Wait!" My command comes out harsher than I intend. I've got to tiptoe through this conversation. A compromised mental state can cause even the strongest personality to wilt in the face of demands. Softening my tone, I lower my voice. It might make her feel more comfortable if we're both whispering. "What's going on? I'm not sure we can deploy that quickly. We planned on having another three days."

"All I know is that they're taking a trip to the power grid—"

"So?" I cringe, even though she can't see me. She could disconnect at any minute, and interrupting her isn't going to reveal the information I need any sooner. She takes a deep breath before speaking again.

"Kiera's been meeting with Leader Imperant every day . . . and every time, she seems so frustrated after. I don't know . . . I just have a bad feeling about what's to come." I practice patience and stay silent in case she wants to add anything.

"Caro, I know it doesn't sound like anything unusual, but I just sense a growing . . . agitation . . . here. This whole delegation was Kiera's idea. It's her pet project and, for whatever reason, I think it's not turning out the way it was supposed to." She drags in a ragged breath. "And the other thing is, I was able to get a hold of the projected transport lists for the next week. None of the delegates are on it. I can't imagine there would be a separate list because the trains run no matter what. There's a list for every week."

I gulp. Centrestates leadership doesn't seem like last-minute planners. Based on what I know, at least about the delegation, every detail has been laid out and scrutinized before any plans were put into motion. They wouldn't overlook a detail such as sending the delegates home. And the only way that was intentional is if they never planned to send them home.

"So tomorrow evening, you think the delegates will be . . . in danger?" I can't bring myself to say that their lives will be threatened. I can't bear to hear it, even from my own mouth. The intel she's provided hasn't been wrong so far, and this Uprising member is our closest connection to the top. Although the timing isn't ideal, I can't ignore her concerns.

"I would bet my life on it." The sincerity in her tone leaves me momentarily speechless. But leaders have no choice but to find the right words.

"We'll be there. Whatever it takes, I'll make it happen." I disconnect the phone. That was the easy part. Now I just need to convince the others that our current timeline isn't going to cut it. Our next move has to happen now.

***

"Thank you for gathering on short notice," I start, folding my hands as I gaze around the rickety wooden table, meeting each of my colleagues in the eye. The other four Uprising leaders graciously agreed to join me for an unexpected, expedited meeting. Well, all but one of them is gracious.

"Try *no* notice," Zai mutters, planting an elbow on the table and dropping his chin into his palm. His scruffy black beard swallows his knuckles, which I'm sure are white from the pressure of his clenched fist.

"You're right, but it was necessary." I face him, matching his intense gaze, daring him to challenge me. He puffs his chest but it doesn't make a difference. We're all equal leaders here – five of us. I shift my focus to the others and continue.

"I've heard from my key contact in Centrestates. The delegates will be taken to the power grid tomorrow evening, and she has strong reason to believe that their lives will be in danger." I pause, ensuring that the others are listening, hanging on my every word. "We've got to make our move then."

"Absolutely not!" Zai booms, raising his dark bushy eyebrows. "We're not ready. We agreed, we *all* agreed, we move in three days. The delegates will still be there."

The others chime in, agreeing with him.

"There's no reason to rush," Daxton says, leaning back in his chair as he runs a hand through his tousled, sandy hair. Welch sits beside him with his muscular arms crossed. He doesn't respond, but he's clearly evaluating the conversation.

"What proof does she have? We can't blow our whole operation because someone has a hunch," Orla adds. I feel a definite kinship with the only other female in the group, and I was hoping she'd support me on this.

"Are you compromised by your daughter's presence there, Caro?" Zai asks, narrowing his dark eyes. "Maybe you should excuse yourself from this discussion."

"I will do no such thing!" I slam a hand down on the table. It shudders. "My contact has reason to believe the delegates are in danger. Imminent danger. All the delegates, not just my daughter. If I was interested in being reckless and just getting her, she'd already be here by now. This is a mission and if we can't complete it as planned because Imperant changes course, then it's all wasted."

The others glance to each other, caught between disbelief of my intentions and the reality of our truth.

"This delegation is the perfect distraction, and if it ends before the fourteen days, then we have to start all over. War is inevitable, whether we like it or not. This is our one chance to prevent it. So what do you want to do?" I look around to each of them. "Do you want to stick to the original plan as if nothing has changed, or do you want to act upon the most recent information we were given? You all know it's a risk every single time we communicate with someone on the inside. We can't afford to lose any of our contacts there. And we can't afford to wait for the perfect time, because it will never come."

I cross my arms and lean back in my chair. My dissertation is over. There are five of us so that there's never a tie. The majority wins, simple as that.

"Then let's vote," Zai says, planting his palms on the table, leaning forward. We're on the same side, but that guy has always managed to test my last nerve. "I'll go first and I say no. We'd be foolish to move now. It would put the whole mission at risk."

We debate for nearly half an hour. As the discussions wind down, Daxton agrees with Zai while Welch sides with me. Ten minutes later, Orla casts her vote to end the standoff. She chooses action over caution. I allow a satisfied smile to spread across my cheeks.

It's official. We're sending in a team to evacuate the delegates and capture Centrestates' leaders.

***

"So it's decided then." I steeple my fingers, elbows resting on the worn, notched surface of our tattered table. It serves multiple purposes – whether we're sharing a meal or debating a strategy – the Uprising shuns the Territories' frivolous ways. Or at least the Societal Order leaders' frivolous ways.

"We'll split up. It's the only way we can neutralize all three leaders at the same time. One of us targets Leader Huntsman here in Westates, two of us capture Leader Ault in Eastates and the last two capture Imperant in Centrestates. The pair going to Centrestates will also intercept the delegates and return them to their families. Of course five of us can't do all this, so we'll activate our allies in each Territory."

"Yes, that's what we agreed to," Orla interjects. She's always been straight to the point. I like that about her. "Now, who's going where?"

"I'll take Centrestates," I announce. It's the most dangerous of the three missions, but it's the most direct route to Everly. I've been patient long enough. The time has finally come to see the daughter I lost too long ago.

"Of course you will," Zai mutters. He raises a finger in the air. "Sign me up too."

I cringe inwardly. Respected leaders don't roll their eyes at the prospect of teaming with their least favorite person.

"I'll take two of our top soldiers and focus on Huntsman," Orla offers. "That is, if you two are comfortable taking down Ault." She nods toward Welch and Daxton. They concur.

"Not a problem." Daxton meets my gaze, silently confirming that he believes in this mission even if he didn't vote for it.

"Look forward to it." Welch cracks his knuckles on a stretch as if we're planning a picnic.

"We leave in one hour." Before I can continue, Zai huffs out an exasperated breath. *We already know he doesn't agree with the accelerated timeline, but he can't let a chance to remind us pass by.* I throw him an impatient side-eye before continuing. "Each group takes a two-way radio. We check in only when we have news."

"And by way of distance, my team should be the first to report back," Orla says. "Welch and Daxton should be last."

"Our mission should be extermination," Zai spouts, for probably the tenth time today. "This whole *neutralize* crap is just wasting time."

"As we agreed, we can't go in guns blazing. This has to be quiet and, ideally, a peaceful transfer of power. Or at least consideration of our proposition." I temper my words, even though I feel like grinding them out through my teeth.

"And tell me again why any of the leaders would willingly give up their throne so we can all live together in harmony and sunshine?" Zai asks.

A dull throb pulses behind my temples. This man has been part of the Uprising his whole life. I have to remember that. He has everyone's best interests in mind, but diplomacy isn't one of his strong points.

"We have evidence of how the Societal Order has controlled citizens," Welch states, "and we have the technological capability to share it to every home through the information broadcast. The best case is if they listen to reason and agree to work with us."

"And then it's back to my plan when they don't," Zai sneers. It's enough to make me pound a fist on the table, which I do but instantly regret. When I respond, I force an even tone in my voice, even though impatience flares within me like a burning coal.

"If we are to gain people's trust, we can't come in heavy-handed. That just sets it up for an '*us versus them*' mentality. And while we are initiating this takeover, there are more of 'them' than 'us.' We can't afford to make everyone hate us."

"I don't care if anyone hates me." Zai crosses his meaty arms and leans back in his wobbly chair. *Of course you don't.* The words burn on my lips but I bite them back.

"She's right, Zai," Orla concedes, flipping her long auburn braid over her shoulder. "They won't listen if we slaughter the only leader they've ever known."

"I didn't join the Uprising to lead people by fear," Daxton adds. "And I don't intend to start now."

"Fine, fine." Zai raises his hands. "We'll *neutralize* the leaders, try to talk some sense into them." He pauses, clearly believing our plan won't work. "And eliminate them as a last resort."

"Last resort." We all agree. It's not the best option, but we all know it might become the only one.

***

Our headquarters is a simple space – Zai's home. His wife graciously started preparing a mishmash of their leftover rations for us as soon as she heard we were leaving on a mission. The food is ready by the time we finish gathering minimal necessities for the trip: weapons, provisions, appropriately colored Territory clothing and long-range radios.

The five of us sit for one last meal together before we part ways, some of us at least. I'm stuck with Zai but I'll definitely need help in Centrestates. And, despite his expertise in fraying my last nerve, he's an ideal mission partner. He'll debate every angle of a strategy, but when the time comes to put it into motion, he sticks to the plan. It's our best chance at succeeding and, ultimately, saving lives. If the Societal Order knew how many Uprising members are secretly working right under their noses, they'd squash us like bugs.

A core team will remain on standby in our Westates headquarters in the lower division. If any one of us reports back through the radio with the code word "united," then our technical experts will release a recorded message through the information broadcast that outlines inequities across the Territories: Centrestates' lack of resource conservation, and Eastates' and Westates' manipulation of food ration additives.

Would citizens actually believe us? Certainly not all of them. And that is where Zai stands – convinced that it's too soon to act. We need more time to infiltrate more areas and build our numbers until there are more citizens who know the truth. While I know he's right, I can't ignore that my daughter is among those in Centrestates right now, blindly walking into what could be a plot to erase her existence. And I'm the one who put her there.

We tested our technological capabilities by breaking into the delegate files. When candidates were being considered, our experts manipulated the Centrestates' program to recommend the most suitable prospects. At my request, they added Everly Scott to the Eastates selection.

I've waited for six years, transforming from a timid stranger dropped in a strange Territory to a commander in an anti-government movement. We won't stop until we've abolished this divided way of life. It's not living.

The time has finally come for the Uprising to strike.

# CHAPTER 10 ~ EVERLY

## UPPER DIVISION, CENTRESTATES

Another day starts just like all the others. We all meet for breakfast and then head up the stairs for our daily meeting. Soon after we assemble in the Unity Room, Kiera charges through the doorway, followed by Lisum and Wynter.

"Good morning, delegates." She wears a bright smile. "I continue to be impressed with your progress. And, as a reward for your dedication and hard work, I am pleased to share that we have a very special treat for you this evening."

A few audible gasps sound around the room. Saya's eyes widen and her eyebrows jump as she shoots me an excited glance. After yesterday's surprise announcement – our visitors – the thought of something else sends a wave of queasiness through my gut.

"We will spend today discussing our proposed Alliance Agreement, but . . . ," she pauses for effect. "After dinner this evening, you will be treated to an exclusive tour of the energy grid." She presses her palms together, nearly bursting with giddiness. "It's the most powerful, most useful resource in the entire Divided States, and it's imperative that you all gain an understanding of and appreciation for Centrestates' main contribution to all Territories."

Hayes' hand shoots into the air. She nods toward him, granting him permission to ask the question burning in his mind.

"Will we get to see how it runs, behind the scenes?"

"I appreciate your enthusiasm, Hayes. As delegates, you will see parts of the power plant that no one other than the workers see. Now, I've got to work out some final arrangements, so Lisum and Wynter will stay here and facilitate your discussions. After you finish the agreement, they will review details about how the power grid functions and its layout."

She waves a hand through the air. "Of course this will all be reinforced tonight during your tour, but let's just say it will give you a head start. Something I'd like you to consider tonight as you learn about the grid's inner workings is if there is room for improvement or efficiency. We'll discuss it tomorrow, but pay close attention to everything you see and hear on the tour."

Kiera straightens a few papers on the podium and charges out of the room with a smile still plastered on her face. She seems genuinely happy. Which makes our theory that she's been listening to our conversations seem completely wrong. If she knew we all talked about yesterday's visits, she would have flown in here ready to punish us. I'd say by now, Hayes was right and we don't have to worry.

Just as the group prepares for the day's discussion, I catch Beckett's eye. He jerks his head to the hallway before raising a hand

and asking to use the restroom. About a minute later, I do the same. Lisum and Wynter don't seem at all interested or concerned that we both asked at the same time. I scurry toward the bathrooms, practically running into him.

"I've got a plan for how we can check out Kiera's office." When I cross my arms and scrunch my face with doubt, he continues. "We'll stay here when everyone goes back to their rooms. It's our only time to snoop around. We have to do it before dinner."

"But workers will still be here." Not to mention, I'd need an excuse to tell Saya when she asks to walk back to Centrel Quarters together.

"That's why it's perfect," he says. "We're supposed to be here. They won't know exactly what time we're done. It's not always the same each day."

"Okay, but what about the other delegates? They'll notice if we don't leave with them all."

"I thought of that too. Leave something in the room. We'll both forget something and turn around to go back for it." As I contemplate his idea, he huffs out a frustrated breath. *We don't have a lot of time to debate this.* "We have exactly zero other options."

"Fine."

***

Although I pretend to be interested in the discussion, my mind drifts to possible ways to accomplish our secret mission. As much as I try to avoid it, my thoughts and eyes keep wandering back to Beckett. *What does he really expect to find in Kiera's office? Would she just leave her evil plans to take over the world sitting out on her desk for anyone to see?*

If we're going to have a shot at finding anything, I need to figure out what to leave in the room that's so important I can't just get it in the morning. Other than my clothes, it's not like I have much of anything. I can't leave something so obvious as a shoe. Sweeping my gaze across the room, I search for an idea.

After a few minutes, my mind settles on an obvious choice – my delegate pin. It's easy enough to remove and Kiera's ingrained in us that we're supposed to cherish this gift from Centrestates. It makes perfect sense that I'd be distraught if I lost it. Settling back into my chair, I relax into the seat and try to hide the satisfied grin tugging at my cheeks.

***

The day wears on and a few hours after lunch, Lisum and Wynter dismiss us with a reminder that they'll meet us at dinner and escort us to our exclusive tour when we're finished eating. As everyone powers off their computing devices, I scratch my neck, allowing my fingers to brush against the golden pin. It's not enough. The stupid thing's fastened in place.

Beckett glances over at me, our eyes meeting. His widen as if to say, hurry up. I pick up the papers and pencils at the table, organizing them into a small pile. Knocking one of the pencils on the floor, I bend down, nearly crawling under the table. With a quick glance to make sure no one's watching, I rip the pin from my collar. The backing slides down my front, safely tucked within my shirt. The ornate face tumbles to the floor.

Satisfied, I stand and drop the pencil on the table before sliding my chair beneath it. Saya rushes to my side.

"Ready to go?"

I nod, finding it hard to meet her eyes. Our peers shuffle into the hallway. We follow a few yards behind them. Just as we reach the first step leading downstairs, I feign disappointment.

"My pin, it's gone. It must have fallen off."

Saya stops. "Let's go back and look for it. It must be in the room."

"No, you go ahead. No need for us both to go. It's probably rolling around on my chair right now."

"Okay . . . stop by my room and we can walk to dinner together, okay?"

"Sure!" I'm getting too good at ditching her when I need to. Turning away from her, I rush back toward the conference room. I pass Hayes and Vanen on my way. They both raise their eyebrows expectantly.

"Just forgot something," I mumble as I brush past them. They watch me suspiciously. Of all people, they would understand that something's up. But now isn't the time to explain it. Besides, Beckett doesn't want to tell them just yet.

I return to the conference room to find Lisum and Wynter buzzing around the space, straightening tables and pushing in chairs.

"Everly, what are you doing back here?" Lisum's eyes track me as I rush toward the chair I was sitting in. Flicking my gaze across the room, I realize Beckett's not here.

"I think I lost my pin. I'm hoping it's here." I bend down to the exact place I dropped it, raising it in the air as if it's a prize I just won. "Found it. Thank goodness." Turning on my heel, I bolt for the door. Fury chases each step as I wonder if Beckett is planning to show up. *Did he go to Kiera's office without me? Is he on his way back to his room and didn't bother to tell me that plans changed?*

As I round a corner toward the steps, a hand grasps my arm. I nearly jump out of my skin.

"I had to find a place where we could hide until Wynter and Lisum leave," Beckett whispers against my ear, pressing his nose into my hair. "They can't see us hanging around." Inhaling a deep breath, I try to calm my rattled nerves.

"Where can we go that no one will find us?" I whisper as my eyes dart up and down the hallway. My senses ignite, hyperaware of any approaching presence as if I've instantly shifted into some invisibility mode.

"How about that supply closet they showed us on the first day? I bet no one ever touches it. And it's close."

I nod as my pulse quickens. *It's not a big space.* Just the thought of cramming in there with him makes my cheeks flush and my stomach twist. He steps away and motions for me to follow him. We both walk confidently. If anyone sees us, they have to believe we're supposed to be here.

No one's around when we reach the half-closed door. Notebooks, tape and other supplies line the shelves in neat stacks. A thin layer of dust assures me the items aren't of much interest to those who work here. Beckett and I step inside, and he pulls the door closed. The space seems to evaporate around us. My arm brushes his and there's not enough room to pull away. The temperature skyrockets and my limbs feel shaky. The only way to avoid pressing up against him is to hold an awkward position. *I won't be able to do this for very long.*

The silence hangs like thick humidity in the air. If we just stand here without saying anything, the seconds are going to feel like hours. Beads of sweat pool along on my forehead. I blurt out the first thing that pops into my head. "So, what do you think of the food here?" I whisper.

He cocks an eyebrow at me, crinkling his nose as if it's the dumbest thing he's ever heard. When he doesn't immediately respond, I rush to fill in the awkward silence.

"Like, I noticed that the food tastes different here. Like, a lot different." He just watches me, probably enjoying how I squirm under his scrutinizing gaze. "We basically eat mush back home. It has hardly any flavor and none of it is fresh."

"Same." His shoulders relax a little. "We don't have food like what they've been giving us. Not even close."

I release a breath. Somehow the harmless conversation helps take my mind off what we're doing. *What would Josli talk about?* She would love to be in this situation right now – hiding in a closet with a cute guy. *She wouldn't have any trouble talking about something . . . anything.*

"So, do you believe that they put things in our food to help us physically, like things to help you stay awake at night?" I peek at him, hoping the question isn't offensive. The whole night dweller thing might make him feel uncomfortable. Callan certainly acts like night dwellers are inferior. Although he acts like everyone is inferior to him.

"It's just a rumor," he says, brushing a hand across his chin. "But I wouldn't be surprised if it turned out to be true."

There's so much more to say, about my mother and about whatever this delegation actually is, but I can't risk bringing up anything that might hijack my emotions right now. If we're actually going to sneak into Kiera's office and find something useful, we both need to stay focused. We share a contemplative quiet for a few more minutes before he nods toward the door.

"We should probably go now. We don't have much time before dinner."

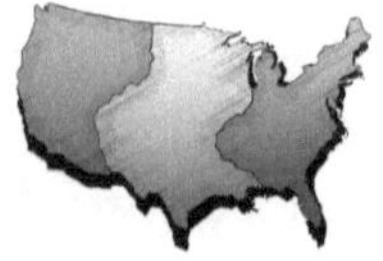

# CHAPTER 11 ~ EVERLY

## UPPER DIVISION, CENTRESTATES

We slink through the door and down the hallway. The Unity Room is empty and dark. While the overhead lights cast a bright glow up and down the hallway, the offices running along each side appear vacant. *That's a good sign.* We scurry toward Kiera's lair, constantly checking behind and in front of us. *So much for looking like we belong here.*

When we reach our destination, we cautiously peer inside. Sunlight spills in through the windows, stretching across the wall and settling in a corner. A small cluster of seats faces the prominent desk with a high-back chair neatly tucked beneath it. Confirming that no one's here, at least at this moment, Beckett grips the handle and twists it, squeezing his eyes shut as if bracing for the worst. The door could be locked or on the verge of triggering a screaming alarm to announce unwelcome visitors.

By some miracle, or maybe what is about to become our latest bout of misfortune, the handle turns in Beckett's palm, giving way to the motion. His eyebrows jump in surprise as he swings the door open and barges inside.

"What are you doing? Just walking right in?" My head swivels back and forth, certain someone is about to catch us. Still, I quickly shuffle inside behind him, feeling too exposed in the hallway.

"It's like diving into cold water. We just have to do it." He points to a bookshelf near the window. "You start over there and I'll check her desk. Try to stay low, and be quiet!"

Without a thought as to what I'm doing and how much trouble this could land us in, I dash to the bookcase. Neat rows of multicolored spines and notepads line each shelf. I'll need to make sure anything I touch is returned to exactly where I found it. I have a feeling Kiera would detect anything out of place in about half a second.

Beckett doesn't share my thought. He drops into Kiera's lush chair and shuffles through drawers carelessly, shoving papers back inside before sliding them closed. Rolling my eyes, annoyed by his carelessness, I run my fingers across each shelf, seeking anything that could be of interest. Nothing stands out though. I choose random books to flip through between briefly admiring the geometrical decor on each shelf – golden stars, about double the size of my fist, stand proudly between groupings of books.

Just as I blow out a sigh of frustration, Beckett mutters a few choice words under his breath and jumps to his feet. "Only one drawer's locked! It must be in there."

"A lot of good that does us." I slide the yellow notebook I've been flipping through back onto the shelf and rush to his side.

"I know how to pick a lock." He flashes me a smirk before plucking a paperclip off Kiera's desk. "One of the few benefits of being the child of an Upriser." In a few breaths, he unwinds the metal and jams the tiny rigid rod into the lock. After fishing it around for a few minutes, a faint click announces his success. He proudly slides the drawer open.

"Well lookie what we found!" He flashes the cover toward me in victory before thumbing through the pages, his eyes scanning from top to bottom and side to side. After a few page turns, his face pales and his gaze slides to me.

"Everly, look at this." The handwritten letters are rigid, forming words I know but don't want to comprehend. Each one leaves an impression in the paper, as if Kiera's pen stroke was firm, making her word choices definite, deliberate. My stomach twists and my throat dries. Everything she wrote promises violence and destruction. It's like an outline of plans for the delegation.

*Phase 1: Convene meetings, generate baseline data, build rapport, observe subgroups that form naturally*

*Phase 2: Mix subgroups, minimal exposure to trigger (Indicators), verify compliance (confidentiality test, chip scan)*

*Phase 3: Plant evidence of deviant behavior, eliminate nonconforming subjects through an act of war*

*Phase 4: Present evidence of delegate plotting, declare necessity to defend Centrestates, launch military attacks*

*Phase 5: Power restrictions, food supply disruption, Xone wall destruction, unification under one leader*

I raise a trembling hand to cover my mouth as my throat goes dry. The walls seem to close in on us as the pieces of this puzzle slide into place in my mind. It's true. We're on the horizon of war. And this whole delegation was the first step in launching it. That's all we ever were to them – a stepping-stone to take over the Divided States. Beckett's doubts were right the whole time.

We might as well be a million miles from home, with no hope of returning. I can't even warn my dad or Josli. And if my mom really is still alive, out there somewhere, then fate delivered one last cruel blow – my entire family is about to slip away before we were able to reclaim what we once were.

Beckett turns toward me, dark clouds of anguish and anger brewing in his eyes. My ragged breaths clip the air. He snaps the notebook closed with too much force. "I know we said we wouldn't take it, but the Uprising needs to see this notebook!"

Unfocused, I nod. We need all the help we can get, but if anyone's going to believe us, we need proof. The crazy old man was right. War is coming. And it feels like I'm standing right in the middle of the battlefield. Beckett and I face each other, realization weighing our features with worry. We share a panicked gasp when a melodic whistling drifts through the hallway. He grabs my hand and pulls me under Kiera's behemoth desk. We tuck ourselves into every available square inch just before our unexpected company arrives. Our limbs tangle before Beckett's knee jams into my ribs. While it hurts, I don't have time to contemplate anything other than the jolt of electricity running through me as we squeeze together in the cramped space.

The door swings open as I chew my bottom lip and pray that whoever it is picked the wrong office and abruptly leaves. I know that isn't happening when a rhythmic squeaking draws closer, like wheels rolling across the tiled floor. When it suddenly stops, a voice begins to hum an upbeat tune as a shuffling sound reaches my ears.

Beckett and I share a wide-eyed look, rising anxiety passing between us. He presses his fingers to his forehead and silently inhales a deep breath. We will be caught – it's just a matter of how soon.

After what feels like an hour, but is merely minutes, Beckett drops his eyes to the floor and slowly shakes his head in defeat. He pushes off the floor and stands, lowering his hand as if telling me to stay down. In that moment, I know that it's not his fault we're here. I'm strong enough to decide for myself and I chose to come here just like he did.

I rise to my feet, joining Beckett, much to the alarm of our visitor – a middle-aged bald man wearing traditional Centrestates tan clothing. He's no one we've seen before. The broom in his hand tells me he's here to clean Kiera's office. Daring to release the slightest breath, I watch him with wide eyes. *At least it isn't Kiera, but is he going to tell her?*

"You're delegates, aren't you?" He rests a hand on the broom handle and eyes us intently. We both nod. "What are you doing in here?"

"We had some extra work to do and Kiera asked us to drop it off at her desk," Beckett smoothly lies. *How does he come up with this stuff?*

"Hmmm, then why would you be hiding under a desk? Sure doesn't look like you were just dropping off a few papers," he smirks. I gulp as bile burns the back of my throat. *This is it.* We're caught and this guy's amused by our stupidity. Beckett shoots me a wilting glance that promises he's sorry.

When the man notices our reactions, he waves a hand in the air, as if to take back what he said. "I was just messing with you." He leans closer and drops his voice to just above a whisper when he asks, "Is there anything you want to show me?" The smile he wore moments ago fades and his features turn serious.

Beckett tilts his chin in the air, holding the man's gaze, fully focused on processing the question. He reaches down and starts to tug his pant leg up, pausing for a momentary glance at the stranger. The man nods once. After Beckett shows him the U symbol tattoo, the official mark of the Uprising, the man drops a hand on Beckett's shoulder.

"That's what I thought," he mumbles under his breath. "Now, what are you really doing in here?"

"We were hoping to find a list of . . . members of the Uprising." I can read the conflict playing across Beckett's features. He knows we can trust this guy, but it still feels wrong to admit, especially out loud.

"And what were you planning to do with that?" The man crosses his arms as if there's no possible answer we could give that would justify us wanting that information.

"Look, we need help! This whole delegation is an act." Thoughts rush past Beckett's lips so fast that the words blend together. "It was created to set us up. To make it look like we tried to sabotage Centrestates somehow and we were—"

The man raises a hand, stopping the seemingly endless rant. "How did you figure that out?" His eyebrows arch as he awaits an answer.

"We found something in Kiera's notebook . . . about phases of the delegation." Beckett sidesteps toward the stranger and thrusts the red notebook toward him. I didn't even notice Beckett was holding it behind his back until now. He opens it to the page we found earlier and the man's eyes slide over it before focusing on us again.

"I've been keeping an eye on that notebook for quite a while. She keeps it locked in that top right drawer in the rare moments it's not in her clutches," he mutters, eyeing the notebook like it's a precious commodity. He walks around the desk and places it back inside its home.

"What are you doing?" Beckett asks, his tone laced with a dark edge.

"This stays here. We can't raise any red flags." When Beckett fixes him with a death glare, the man explains, "Look, I've been monitoring it and the information is working its way through our channels. Those who need to know will know, but we can't tip off anyone here."

As much as I don't like it, what he says makes sense. And part of me is relieved that people are actually looking out for us, even if we don't know who or where they are. *I just hope they plan to do something soon. Very soon. Like, before Kiera does.*

I place a palm on Beckett's arm, willing him to back down. When our eyes meet, his posture visibly relaxes, slightly.

"Fine," he agrees, answering me before glaring at our new ally. The man runs a palm over his bald scalp.

"Look, it's important that you act like you don't know anything. Trust me, people are watching, both ours and theirs." He glances toward the door. "You two should go. A bunch of them are in a meeting, but it'll probably end soon. And that means someone could walk past here at any moment."

"Okay," I answer, tugging Beckett's hand. This is our "out," and we need to take it before we're caught by someone who really will get us in trouble.

***

It feels like the prize we earned was snatched out of our hands almost as soon as we got it. Neither one of us talks as we hurry to Centrel Quarters. Too many thoughts and questions ricochet through my brain to settle on just one. Although he followed me out of Kiera's office, Beckett's sour mood is palpable. I don't blame him. He had proof of everything he ever doubted in his hand, and he had to give it up.

We part ways in the elevator. By the time I reach my room, my mind is in overdrive. I crawl into the bed and bury my face in the pillow. Scrunching my eyes closed, I concentrate on pushing each thought from my mind, pretending they evaporate into faint wisps of air that flutter away. My breathing slows and my muscles relax. My body completely melds into the mattress as exhaustion overtakes me.

# CHAPTER 12 ~ EVERLY

# UPPER DIVISION, CENTRESTATES

While my body rests, my brain takes me back to a recent place. One that will likely replay in my memory many more times.

*Kiera leads me to a conference room. My vision is hazy, but goosebumps spring up across my arms. I know what's coming. As we stand just outside it, the door swings open. Just like yesterday, I come face-to-face with my Indicator, my mother. She wraps me in a tight hug, but it feels wrong. Forced. An invasion. I slowly start shaking my head no but she ignores it and whispers in my ear, "It's much easier if you cooperate, Everly."*

*A sharp knocking jolts me out of the embrace. Is this really my mother? I turn toward the door, which rests on its hinges, partway open. All that's beyond it is a dark, empty hallway. No one is on the other side. But the knocking grows faster. It finally yanks me from the room, and the swirling memories of my mother.*

I swipe beads of sweat from my forehead and inhale a deep breath. It was just a dream. I think my brain subconsciously knew that the whole time, yet it still wraps me in anxiety. I push myself up in bed to sit and rub my eyes, yawning. I nearly launch into the ceiling when a round of angry thuds pounds on my door. Someone's here, and they're quite impatient.

Dragging the clock within my range of hazy vision, another yawn rattles my whole body. It's 5:37 p.m. Dinner isn't until six. While I don't have much time to hang out here sound asleep, drooling on the pillow, it's not like I'm late for anything. I toss the blankets aside and drop my feet to the floor to stand as the pounding grows furious.

"Everly!" The whisper-shout further motivates me to dash to the door. I twist the handle slowly, cautiously drawing it open. Pressing a cheek against the crack, I spy my visitor. Hayes. I jump back and yank the door wide enough for him to rush inside.

"Everly . . . what took . . . you so long?" His pale cheeks flush crimson. His narrow chest heaves as he struggles to catch his breath.

"I'm sorry. I fell asleep, but it's not like I expected anyone to show up. Dinner isn't for another twenty minutes. What's going on?" I cross my arms, unsure why I just apologized. He's the one who just woke me up.

He grasps my shoulders, urgency tightening his grip. "I wouldn't have come here if it wasn't an emergency."

My eyes and nose scrunch in disbelief. "An emergency?"

"Everly, listen to me. Vanen is gone. He disappeared sometime between when we got back to our rooms and now." He pushes his glasses along the bridge of his nose.

"Are you sure? How would you even know that? Maybe he just went for a walk or something." If any of the girls just disappeared, I would have no idea until we all met for dinner. And even then, she could just be running late or feeling sick.

"We . . . we were supposed to meet to talk and he never showed. So I went to his room and there's no answer." Hayes' eyes shift nervously.

"Maybe he's just a heavy sleeper! He could be in his room right now, completely oblivious. Kind of like I was until you woke me up." The words come out harsher than I intend, almost accusatory. And honestly, I'm glad his knocking pulled me from that dream. I'd rather not return to it anytime soon.

"No." He shakes his head slowly. "You don't understand. We've been meeting every afternoon before dinner. Before everyone else meets up to walk over together." His gaze drops to the patterned carpet.

"Why?"

"Wellllll, it's . . . just," he stammers, clearing his throat. Throwing his shoulders back, he tilts his chin with a renewed confidence. "We've kind of made some more progress with our research."

My mouth drops open before I can stop it.

"More progress? When did you stop telling me about what you were finding?" *I thought he trusted me. I thought both of them did.* The sudden exclusion stings.

"When did you and Beckett start having secrets?" His response comes too quick, leaving me momentarily speechless. He's right. We have our own secrets now. And Beckett and I didn't see a reason to tell him or Vanen about them yet. I swallow my pride and nod.

*He's trusting me now, asking for my help.* I lead him over to the bed and motion for him to sit. When he slowly lowers himself onto the mattress, I do the same.

"Where was the last place you saw Vanen?" I figure that's the best place to start. He pinches his eyes closed and drops his head back.

"On our floor. We walked from Centrel Hall together, came up the elevator and both went to our rooms. At least that's what I thought."

"So you didn't hear any weird noises – like a struggle or anything?" Vanen couldn't have just disappeared without someone seeing or hearing anything. *Could he?*

"Doors banging closed, voices in the hallway, but nothing out of the ordinary." He shrugs. "It was all just the usual sounds of the guys coming and going."

"So you think he never made it to his room?"

"I think that makes the most sense." He adjusts his glasses. "I think if someone came and got him from his room, he would have made some noise."

"But who would take him and why?"

"Vanen found a way to break into the Societal Order's network. That's highly illegal and now he's missing. That's not a coincidence. We have to find him." His tone turns pleading, as if I have any skills that will help track down his missing friend.

"Look, I'll help any way I can, but I don't even know what to do. I mean, where do we even start?"

He raises and drops his shoulders in defeat. Shaking his head, he pinches the bridge of his nose. "Maybe we go to Centrel Hall and see if he's there?"

"It's practically dinnertime anyway, so that's a great place to start."

***

We slip into the hallway and gently tug the door closed, cringing when the automatic lock engages. We zip past the other doors with quiet steps and race down the stairs, avoiding the elevator altogether. The rest of the group would just slow us down.

After we enter Centrel Hall, Hayes rushes to the cafeteria. Disappointment deflates his last shred of hope as our usual tables sit empty. A few workers mull around the kitchen area. Muffled conversations and clanging pans echo throughout the open space.

Suddenly footsteps approach from the way we just came. My heartbeat spikes, reverberating with doubt and dread. *Please let it be Vanen.*

Disappointment washes over me when I meet Beckett's piercing blue eyes. "Everything okay?" he asks. "I saw you two running over here and figured something was up."

Hayes immediately launches into a panicked explanation. "Vanen's missing. Have you seen him? I think they took him! We have to find him!"

"What?" Confusion twists Beckett's features. "What do you mean he's missing?"

Hayes presses his palms together, almost in a pleading gesture. "Look, we might have taken it too far. Our snooping. They must know and they just . . . they took him." His fears tumble out in a fountain of regret. "He figured a way into their servers and found references to . . . experiments . . . happening in all three Territories."

His gaze drops to the floor as Beckett turns to me. "You knew this too?" he accuses.

"No!" Maybe Hayes was going to tell me, but until the moment he thought Vanen was in danger, he kept it all a secret.

"What kind of experiments are you talking about?" Beckett demands, his fury laser focused on Hayes.

"There's no time to explain now. We have to find Vanen!" Misery fuels his plea, but Beckett's features seem to sharpen with the challenge.

"I'm not doing anything until I know exactly what we're talking about here."

Indecision tugs at my common sense. We should act fast if Vanen is truly in danger, but I also want to know how risky this is. *If we uncover some truth to what Hayes claims, will we be in danger too – even more so than we are already?* Sneaking around the buildings is a punishable act of defiance. Beckett and I have done it enough.

"Fiiiiine." Hayes' voice cracks. "As far as we can tell, the Territories started implanting chips in babies' brains. At the hospitals when they were born." He eyes us, pausing as if we'll express disbelief or question his words. Beckett and I face each other briefly, jaws dropped, awaiting more information. "It started around 2080, so it only impacts younger people, like us."

"And what exactly do these chips do?" Beckett's harsh tone is misplaced. It's not like Hayes or Vanen did any of this, they simply uncovered it. If they're even right.

"We didn't get too far into the data before our access was blocked, but it looks like each Territory was different." Hayes' green eyes lose their focus, as if he's retreating to a memory. "Almost like they each tried something different to see which would be the best."

There've always been rumors of a competitive edge between the leaders. Maybe when you're that driven to oversee a whole population of citizens, the hunger for power grows stronger until it consumes you. Maybe a pledge of peace between regions is just for show, a thin shroud of trust for locating and leveraging weaknesses to capitalize on.

I place a hand on Hayes' shoulder. "You've told us enough and you're right, we don't have time to waste."

"If he's got actual proof of any of this, I'd say he's pretty dangerous to the Societal Order. If we could expose—"

"If we don't have Vanen, we don't have proof. It's that simple." Hayes cuts Beckett off, circling back to his only goal.

Before any of us can say anything else, drifting conversations of familiar voices reach our ears – the delegates are arriving for dinner.

"I should find Kiera and ask if she knows where Vanen is," Hayes whispers, covering his mouth with a hand.

"No!" Beckett and I blurt out at the same time, our one-syllable refusal bouncing off the walls of the still-empty room. I glance toward the hallway, sucking in a ragged breath as the others draw nearer.

"Let's get dinner and if Vanen doesn't show up, we'll ask if anyone saw him," I reason. "Maybe someone knows something we don't." Hayes tilts his chin and chews on his lower lip, contemplating my suggestion. "Wouldn't you rather ask any of them instead of Kiera?" I cross my arms. He adjusts his glasses and starts to mutter a half-hearted "Okay" just as the first of the delegates reaches us.

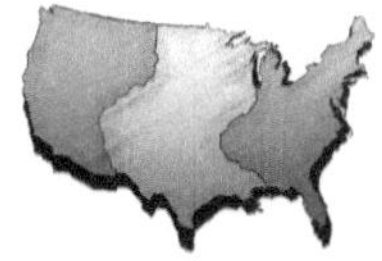

# CHAPTER 13 ~ EVERLY

## UPPER DIVISION, CENTRESTATES

"Hey! I was looking for you!" Saya calls as she beelines toward me, looping an arm around mine and leading me away from the guys. I peek at Beckett behind my shoulder but don't want to make a scene. I mouth a quick "sorry" to him before turning my attention to Saya.

"I just came over a little early. I was really hungry." *How do lies pop into my head so easily anymore?*

We just start through the food line when Beckett squeezes in behind me. He practically presses up against my back. Not even a sheet of paper could squeeze in between us. My heart flutters as my cheeks flush with heat. "We have an idea," he whispers. His warm breath tickles my ear. It sends a tingling wave all the way to my toes.

When she notices him, Saya's eyebrows jump as a smirk crosses her face. "Oh sorry, do you two need a little alone time?" She watches us as if she's happy to be part of some huge secret we just shared with her.

"I just need her for a minute and then you can have her back," Beckett promises. *At least this probably helps us seem like we're a couple.*

"Okay, I'll see you at the table." She faces forward again, scrutinizing tonight's options before sliding a few small plates onto her tray. As soon as she takes a few steps ahead of us, he quietly explains what he has in mind.

"Hayes and I will sneak into Kiera's office after dinner. You go on the grid tour. We need someone to cover for us." He gulps and squares his jaw, probably waiting for an argument. *Maybe he's right though. If I go on the tour and someone asks me where they are, I'd be so nervous that I could easily pull off confusion. I'm pretty sure I'd be fumbling for words if Kiera was the one questioning me. The nerves she rattles turn my brain to mush.*

But before I nod in agreement, a streak of defiance flashes through me. Sure, the tour would be the safer option, but also the one that completely excludes me from knowing what's happening. I should help find Vanen too. I consider him a friend, and if he is somehow in danger and needs us, then any secrets hiding in Kiera's office may be the only thing that can help us find him. Besides, I'd just spend the whole tour worrying about Beckett, Hayes and Vanen anyway.

*Nothing has come easy since I got to Centrestates, so why start now?* I shake my head. "I'm not doing it! I'm going with you!" I keep my voice low but stern. His nostrils flare as he plunks a small plate of steaming carrots on his tray.

"It would be easier and faster, not to mention quieter, if you went with the group," he hisses.

Fighting the urge to argue, I turn to him and declare, "I'll get someone to cover for all three of us!" Before he can respond, I grab the closest bowl of saucy noodles, swipe a drink from the cooler and stomp over to the table. My curt movements draw Saya's attention as I drop down into the seat beside her.

"You okay?" she asks.

I paint a smile across my face and nod, forcing the annoyance to fade. I can't exactly spill my frustrations to her, and besides, there's a much more important topic to discuss. After a few minutes of harmless chitchat, I nudge my closest friend here and lean toward her. "Hey, I need a favor."

"What is it?" Saya twists toward me, excited by the prospect. Her eyes grow wider by the second.

"Tonight . . . a few of us are going to skip the power grid tour," I pause for her initial reaction, knowing she won't hear the rest of what I'm about to say until she processes this part. Her posture immediately stiffens, the curiosity in her gaze fades to suspicion. She shakes her head feverishly and turns back to her plate.

"You can't! You'll get in trouble." Her eyes narrow as she forks a pink cube of meat. Before shoving it into her mouth, she mutters, "We'll *all* get in trouble."

"You won't get in trouble, I swear." *Of course I can't promise that. All I can do is hope it isn't another lie.* "We just need a little time and then we'll catch up with the group."

"Time for what? Why would you want to skip the tour?" She throws her arms in the air, the pitch rising in her voice before realizing she's drawing attention to us. Turning her attention back to her meal, Saya nervously pushes a heap of green beans around on the plate.

I blow out a calming breath and fold my hands together. "Saya, it's like twenty minutes, probably, and then we could catch up. And that's *only* if anyone realizes we aren't there. Maybe no one will even notice?" I hitch my shoulders up and tilt my head to the side innocently.

"There's not *that* many of us, Everly. If three delegates are missing, everyone will notice." She rubs her temples and pinches her eyes shut. "I don't understand what's so important that you can't just go with everyone else. You've changed so much these last few days. I don't get it . . . is it because of Beckett?" She nibbles on a cuticle and watches me, her eyes swimming with disappointment.

"I can't . . . I can't really say." I'm out of lies for the moment. I definitely can't tell her we want to break into Kiera's office. Or that we think she's responsible for Vanen's sudden disappearance. Or that, by the way, we might even want to find more evidence that Centrestates is plotting to take over the Divided States. If we could get it to the Uprising, maybe we could trade it to them for safe passage home.

"Everly, I want to help you, I really do." She shakes her head slowly and pauses. "And I won't tell anyone about you skipping the tour . . . but I think it's a really bad idea and I can't be a part of it. I'm sorry."

Her expression turns to stone before she focuses on her tray again. Reality delivers what feels like a punch to my gut. *I haven't exactly been a great friend and this was a lot to ask of her. And honestly, pretty unrealistic when I stop and think about it. How could I be mad at her for refusing to make excuses for us when I can't trust her enough to tell her why?*

"It's okay, really, I totally understand." I nudge her shoulder with mine. "Let's just pretend we never talked about this, okay?"

"Now *that's* a great idea!" She flashes me a small smile and turns her attention to the others.

I spend the rest of dinner barely listening to the conversations floating around me. For the most part, my mind is consumed with how all three of us are going to get out of the grid tour. The only thing I do know is that I'm not wasting a second there while Beckett and Hayes stay back to look for answers.

***

"So?" Beckett and Hayes flank me as we leave the cafeteria. Neither one notices the disappointment in my eyes as I shake my head.

"Saya won't cover for us," I admit. We're free to speak since she didn't wait for me when she was done eating. "Did anyone know anything about Vanen?"

"No." Hayes' shoulders slump. "No one saw him since we went to our rooms before dinner."

"Yeah, and no one seems too concerned," Beckett adds. "I guess you can just disappear around here without anyone noticing." A stinging pain cleaves its way into my chest. I can't remember a time I ever felt as helpless as I do now.

Within a few minutes, we catch up to the group. They all swarm around Lisum and Wynter in the lobby. Excitement radiates off the delegates, most of them anyway. Maybe it's the prospect of doing something other than sitting in their rooms for the night that has everyone buzzing with anticipation. Even Kinsley and Ryland, who mocked the trip to the grid just moments ago at dinner, whisper animatedly and cast eager glances out the windows and doors every few minutes.

When she notices the three of us join the outermost edge of the huddle, Wynter speaks. A smile blazes across her face as enthusiasm pours out of her. She claps her hands together lightly as she addresses us.

"I hope you're all ready for an exciting evening! The power grid isn't that far, so we'll all walk. You'll get a nice view of the city along the way." Before she says another word, Hayes' hand shoots into the air. When Wynter throws him a curt nod, he slides his glasses up his nose and asks the question burning on my mind.

"Do you know what happened to Vanen? He didn't come to dinner." Wynter and Lisum exchange a look before answering.

"We got word that Vanen wasn't feeling well and that he wouldn't be joining us this evening," Lisum explains, clutching a clipboard to her chest. She glances at it before adding, "He's being treated in the health center, but it's nothing serious. He should be back with us in the morning. But since everyone else is here, we should get going. We have a schedule to keep."

Once we hit the sidewalk, renewed chatter swirls through the group as we follow our hosts. Hayes, Beckett and I hang toward the back, silently evaluating any possible escape route. We look past each other and every building we pass, hopelessly searching for some walkway or corner we can sneak into and disappear.

"I say we just put a little more distance between us and them and then turn down an alley. With any luck, they'll keep going and not even notice until they get to the grid," Beckett mutters. "We can't go much farther or we could end up getting lost trying to find our way back."

I hadn't thought of that but he's right. It's not like any of us really knows our way around here. Even on our night out with Callan and the others, Beckett and I took a few wrong turns before we found our way back to Centrel Quarters.

"Agreed," Hayes says, watching for my reaction. I face each of them and nod. After a few minutes, I spy a side street that looks empty.

"Up there, on the right. How about that one?" I jut my chin toward it when the guys turn my way. Just as they both agree, I hear someone mention Hayes' name. The delegates' heads turn in search of him. The group parts as Wynter squirms through them.

"Hayes! There you are! We were just talking about how power is transferred from division to division and I remembered you had some interesting theories in your notes. Why don't you come enlighten us on what you think?"

Panic flashes through me. Is our one chance disappearing right before our eyes?

"Be right there," Hayes calls before turning toward us. "As soon as the group moves again, go. Find the health center and find Vanen. I'll sneak back as soon as I can. You just get a head start."

With that, he sprints down the sidewalk toward Wynter and the others, swinging his arms enthusiastically. His voice rings out above the others. *He's causing a distraction so we can sneak away.*

Beckett slips his hand around mine, gently tugging me closer as we approach the side street I pointed out. We both keep our eyes on the group, but no one looks our way. Hayes does a fantastic job of holding everyone's attention. Even he doesn't look back. Knowing this is our only chance, I squeeze Beckett's hand once. He licks his lips before mouthing, "Let's go."

# CHAPTER 14 ~ EVERLY

## UPPER DIVISION, CENTRESTATES

My instinct screams to run as fast as my feet can carry me. But I'm also aware that we just snuck away and the last thing we should do is look suspicious – like we're trying to escape. With a nervous gait and stiff posture, I match Beckett's hurried pace. As we frantically head back toward Centrel Hall, a thought crosses my mind, filling my legs with lead.

"How are we supposed to find the health center?" I ask Beckett. "No one's ever mentioned it before today."

Those blue eyes turn intense as his gaze drifts past me, bouncing from building to building, up and down the street.

"We need to ask someone." He rubs his chin. "But we don't know who we can trust and who would turn us in if they had the chance. Maybe the old man? We know we can trust him."

"But we have no idea where he is or how to find him. We can't waste time wandering around the city." I chew a nail as my mind attempts to conjure a solution.

"You saw him when we first got here, right outside Centrel Hall, right?" When I nod, he continues. "And the time we saw him, that's where he was. Let's start there."

"And hope by some miracle he just shows up?" None of this is Beckett's fault, but rising frustration carves a sharp edge in my tone.

"What else can we do?"

I huff out a breath and hitch up a shoulder in a half shrug. *I should have asked Saya about the health center. She'd probably know where it is. Too late for that now.*

When the massive capitol building comes into view, we both slow. Beckett motions toward the bushes flanking the entranceway. Before we can slip behind them, movement catches my eye. My gaze tracks a single silhouette pushing a wheeled cart. Squeaky wheels churn over the paved pathway until they come to a grinding halt just before what looks like a large metal box. The shadowy figure reaches into the cart and raises a bag, swinging it up upward, launching it into the box. Although he's no more than a shadow, a molecule of hope tugs at me. *Could it be?*

"Beckett!" I whisper urgently. When his head snaps toward me, I point to the figure. "I think that's the man we talked to in Kiera's office! If it is, I bet he knows where the health center is!"

His eyes widen when they land on the stranger. He gulps. "I need to get closer. Stay here."

Maybe I should be insulted that he's delegated me to just stand here and wait for him, but mostly I'm relieved. Two of us would definitely be more noticeable than one. And if that isn't who we think it is, we certainly don't want him to see us. My heart pounds as I watch Beckett practically hug the building, pressing himself into every shadow and crevice that may hide him. Tearing my eyes away, I scan our surroundings every few seconds. Thankfully it's pretty quiet.

By the time Beckett's positioned himself a few yards away, the man has tossed the last bag into the giant trash bin. He swivels the empty cart back toward the building, pushing it from behind. Beckett waits in the shadows, rocking on his heels. My heart skyrockets as I watch, jolting at the exact moment Beckett steps into the man's path. He must have found a surge of confidence that I can't comprehend.

Their lips move but I can't make out any part of their conversation. The man's eyes shift back and forth, as if anyone could be watching. The thought makes me retreat farther into the foliage lining the building. After a few minutes, Beckett casually backs away before continuing down the sidewalk as if he's on a leisurely stroll.

"What happened?" I hiss as soon as he's close enough to hear me.

"That was him," he says. "We lucked out. I asked him where the health center was and told him we were looking for Vanen. But he doesn't think we should go there."

"What?" I twist my hands in a nervous jumble. Of course Beckett's going to explain, if I give him the chance. Biting my lip, I swallow the questions buzzing in my throat.

"He said . . . " Beckett leans closer, his warm breath tickling my ear as a shiver slides down my spine. "Something's up in Centrel Quarters. Whenever people stay there, staff clean their rooms each day. But today, they were told to skip one of the delegate rooms. He couldn't remember which one, but I bet it was Vanen's!"

"That means he could be in there right now!" With that realization, my throat constricts. *Has Vanen been right under our noses all along? That can't be. He would have come out of his room for dinner. Unless he wasn't able to.*

"Yeah, I think we need to find out. It sounds to me like they're hiding something in there. And even if Vanen isn't there, we might find a clue that could help us find him."

"That's too big of a coincidence." I shudder at the thought. "The same day Vanen goes missing, the cleaning people aren't supposed to go into one of our rooms?"

Just as he turns to Centrel Hall, I tug Beckett's elbow, pulling his attention back to me. Even though we have a lead, there's one very clear obstacle waiting for us.

"How are we supposed to get into his room? Can't that guy come with us and unlock it?" Before I even finish asking, Beckett scrunches his face and drops his jaw to say something. Before he can disagree with me, I continue.

"Look, it would probably be good to have him there anyway . . . depending on what we find." My stomach lurches at possibilities of the unknown. I hope Vanen's okay but the longer this takes, and the longer he's missing, the less likely that seems.

"He can't." Beckett grabs my shoulders and meets my gaze head on, our faces just inches apart. "They told him not to go there but besides that . . . " He pauses, glancing around us for any unwelcome guests. "The Uprising is coming! Tonight!"

"What?" A lump forms in my throat, suddenly making it hard to drag in air. "What does that mean for us?"

"It sounds like they're getting ready to strike, and they need every ally we have here ready. So he needs to stay at Centrel Hall." The old man's face flashes through my mind. I wonder if he knows. My head swivels back and forth instinctively. *Is he around here too?*

"So what do we do?" I'm suddenly lightheaded. *Is the Uprising going to war with Centrestates tonight? Nowhere is safe. Not for us, at least.*

"We go to Centrel Quarters and try to find Vanen, just like we planned." His words are slow and his eyes are wide. He watches me like I'm about to slip out of his hands and run away. If that was an actual option to get out of this mess, I might. Guilt slithers through me as I think of Saya. *Is she okay? But how can we save her if we can't even save ourselves?*

"Okay," I say hesitantly. Before either of us can change our mind, we scurry back to the shadows cloaking the perimeter around Centrel Hall. We stop in our tracks the few times we see a lone person exit the building, probably someone working late. Which reminds me once again that a day dweller would not be permitted out of their home at this time of night. At least not in Eastates.

Just as we reach the last few yards of sidewalk leading the way to Centrel Quarters, a figure darts down the street toward Centrel Hall. I grab Beckett's arm and point toward the faceless person, who seems to gain speed with each step.

"Let's just go, we're close enough. They probably won't even notice us." He gently shrugs his arm away and steps forward, but a gnawing in my gut roots me in place. *Something isn't right.* The longer I watch, recognition washes over me. I know that posture. That lanky, awkward gait.

"It's Hayes! It's Hayes!" Anticipation races through me. Beckett looks at me before squinting at the approaching figure.

"Looks like he's about to bust into Centrel Hall," he mutters, cocking his head to the side as if he's trying to understand what's happening. Without another thought, I sprint toward Hayes. Or at least, who I believe is Hayes. When he sees me, he stumbles, momentarily distracted by the threat of someone barreling toward him.

"Ev . . . erly?" His feet clumsily slap the sidewalk as he slows his momentum, trying to stop. After a few steps, he drops his hands to his knees, gulping in air as his chest heaves.

"You did it? You got away from the tour?" I can't help but smile at my friend. The last time I saw him, he was the center of attention in the sea of delegates. He looks up at me, nodding.

"Hey!" Beckett whisper-shouts. "That's not a great place to have a conversation. Unless you're trying to get caught!"

"He's right." My eyes shift around the darkness stretching in every direction as Beckett's warning freshly awakens my paranoia. Light spills out from Centrel Hall and other nearby buildings, and streetlights throw off their own glow, but it only stretches so far. Anyone could be just about to turn around the next corner.

Hayes nods again and stands up straight. Once he's steady, we hurry to join Beckett in the shadows. Before Hayes can even ask, Beckett fills him in on what we know and where we're headed.

"Okay, so we're checking Vanen's room . . . again," Hayes states uncertainly. I know he knocked on Vanen's door before dinner and got no answer, so he's probably thinking this is a total waste of time.

"It wouldn't hurt to snoop around while everyone else is out," Beckett says. "Even if he isn't in his room, maybe he's somewhere on the floor."

Hayes hitches a shoulder up and without another word, the three of us dash into Centrel Quarters.

***

My nerves relax slightly from the knowledge that none of the other delegates will be back for hours. It's almost a relief to focus on just one problem right now – finding Vanen. It pushes all my other worries aside. At least for the moment.

When we reach Vanen's door, Hayes lightly knocks, his head swiveling back and forth as if we could be caught at any moment. Waiting no more than ten seconds, Beckett blows out a breath and pounds his fist on the door, trying the handle with the other hand. It doesn't budge.

"Vanen! You in there?" The three of us press our ears to the smooth surface, searching for any hint of an answer. It's quiet. Beckett repeats himself, pounding his fist even harder, making the door shake on its hinges.

"Did you hear that?" Hayes asks, wide-eyed. I shake my head no while Beckett narrows his eyes. Guess I'm not the only one who didn't hear anything. As we look at each other in suspended silence, a thud echoes in Vanen's room. It's muffled, but it definitely came from the other side of this door.

"I told you!" Hayes huffs indignantly before striking the door with the heel of his hand. "Is that you, Vanen?"

Another thud. Someone's in there, but whoever it is isn't answering us. Hayes frantically grabs the handle, which we already know is no use. An idea flashes through my mind.

"Guys! Remember when we first got here, they had a stack of room keys . . . the cards . . . down at that huge desk? Maybe there are extras! Maybe there's a key to Vanen's room down there right now!"

"Yes!" Hayes turns to me and nods, but he's clearly distracted. Turning his attention back to the door, he tries talking through it, attempting to coax whoever's on the other side to unlock it.

"That's a good idea. Can you go check? I'll stay here and keep an eye on him." Beckett motions to Hayes. "And I'll start looking for something we might be able to use to pry that door open if you can't find a key."

I nod once before saying, "I'll be back soon."

*At least I hope I will be.*

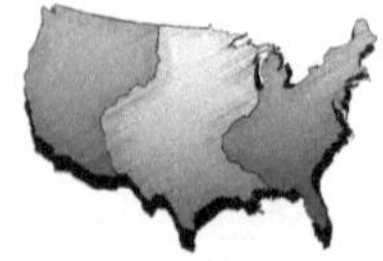

# CHAPTER 15 ~ EVERLY

## UPPER DIVISION, CENTRESTATES

I tiptoe down the hallway and push through the door to the stairwell. It feels like the best option right now. If I need a quick escape, I could slip into the safety of another floor. The elevator would feel like a cage, leaving me at the mercy of anyone who showed up on the other side when those giant metal doors parted.

My footfalls echo, bouncing off the concrete walls that seem to be closing in. My heart thumps frantically. Each step I take seems louder than the last. *Please don't let anyone hear me.*

When I reach the bottom floor, I crack the door open and hold my breath, listening. After a minute of silence, I scurry through the threshold and dash toward the enormous desk. It sits there undisturbed, as if we aren't on the verge of breaking into Vanen's room. As if the Territories aren't about to go to war. As if it's just another ordinary day in Centrestates. *Maybe all this is ordinary for here. It's nothing like what happens back home.*

I can't remember exactly which drawer held all the key cards. The first time we entered Centrel Quarters, I was focused on the extravagance of it all – the lush carpets, the beautiful decor and the televised information broadcast. Initially, everything about this place was such a stark contrast from anything I grew up around. But now, over a short amount of time, I've grown used to it. Maybe even come to expect food with flavor, and going outside any time of day that I want.

*How can I go back to the rules and rations that were all I knew for all those years? Centrestates has twisted my opinion of the only home I had.* Snapping out of my wandering thoughts, I focus on the moment and why I'm here.

When I reach the desk, I start with the drawers on the right side, sliding each one open, working my way left, from top to bottom. My trembling hands reach inside each one, shuffling through its contents. The first three hold nothing useful – notepads, pens, paperclips and a simple medical kit with bandages.

I release an audible sigh when the fourth drawer reveals the treasure I've been searching for – the stack of key cards Lisum and Wynter produced when we were first assigned our rooms. I thumb through them, slowing when I reach the small stack of duplicates for the fourth floor. *What was Vanen's room number again?* Squeezing my eyes shut, I try to force the answer from my memory. *I was just up there, and we all met in his room. Was it 410? Maybe 412?* I grab both keys, along with one for room 414, just in case. *At least I know it's one of those.* Sliding them into my pocket, a brief smile crosses my lips. A moment of relief washes over me. *We can do this.*

Just as I turn back toward the hallway leading to the elevator, the outer door swishes open. I drop to my knees, landing hard. The soft carpet barely stifles the sting. *That's going to leave a bruise.* Footsteps thud as someone enters the building. I roll beneath the mammoth desk. At least it's big enough to hide me. Scooting into the farthest corner, I settle between the wooden panels and hold every muscle perfectly still.

"What do you mean you don't know where they are?" Kiera snarls. Her voice sends a jolt of panic through me. "You should have eleven. How can three be missing? The two of you were supposed to make sure they were all there! How hard is it to follow directions? Simple directions!"

This isn't an accusation, it's a verbal attack, and I have a feeling I know who's on the receiving end. Her fury instantly consumes the air. I gulp silently as a shiver washes through me and goosebumps erupt across my arms. Squeezing my eyes shut, I force every cell in my body to freeze. I can't hear the voice on the other end of the phone, but I'm glad it's not me.

She stomps to the elevator. "So you're telling me you couldn't handle the one simple task I gave tonight?" The ding announces the car's arrival. She releases an overexaggerated sigh before I hear her footsteps again. I envision her charging through the thick metal doors as if they could swiftly jump out of her way.

When the electronics churn and I know the doors have sealed shut, I slump forward, releasing the breath and stiff posture I was holding. My fists are clenched tightly, stretching the skin over my knuckles. I flex my fingers, dropping the key card on the floor. It bounces, landing at my feet, catching a glare from the overhead light.

The key card. Vanen's room. Kiera must be heading to our floor or the guys' floor. Either way, Beckett and Hayes are up there and they have no idea what's headed their way. A fresh wave of panic washes over me.

*There's no way I can sneak up there. I can't reach them before she can.* My brain volleys between hopeful reasoning and utter defeat. *They'll hear the elevator moving and hide, right? What if they don't? What if they get caught and I don't? I'll be completely alone, with no idea what to do. I can't be anyone's last hope for help.*

My only option is to hide, and hope they do the same. They'll understand. Even if Hayes is too dazed to realize that Kiera's here, Beckett will figure it out and get them both out of harm's way. It's the only option we have.

***

An agonizing ten minutes later, the elevator announces its return. I wait in my new hiding place – crammed between the desk and the wall behind it. I figured that was safer than staying under the desk. If Kiera decided to grab something from a drawer, she'd find me in about a second.

"He's the only one up there," she says, apparently talking on the phone again. "So the other three are still missing. Just proceed with the plan. With any luck, they'll show up on-site and join the rest of you. Until then, I'll alert a few key members of our security detail. If anyone can find them, they can!"

She charges out the door, likely headed to Centrel Hall. I wait a few minutes before sprinting to the stairwell. I'm out of breath by the time I reach the guys' floor. Confident no one else could be here, I don't bother to quiet my steps or proceed cautiously.

"Beckett! Hayes!" I call as I force my legs to move faster.

"Everly?" Inwardly, I relax. Slightly. I'd recognize that voice anywhere. Beckett materializes at the other end of the hallway. He must have been hiding just around the corner. He rushes toward me.

"Kiera was just here!" His face is flushed. He runs a hand through his dark hair.

"I know. She came in while I was looking for Vanen's key." My gaze drops to the floor and my throat feels tight. "I didn't know how to warn you."

"Did you find it? The key?" Hayes asks, suddenly appearing at Beckett's side. I hold it out to him. He snatches it from my hand and turns toward his target. With just a few giant steps, he's within reach. With one simple swipe across the keypad, the little round light glows green, confirming access. Hayes twists the handle and pushes the door open, charging through it.

"So what happened?" I ask as Beckett and I follow him.

"We hid when we heard the elevator. We couldn't see much but she went straight for Vanen's door and opened it, went right inside. We heard voices but couldn't get close enough to hear what she was saying." He pauses as if he needs to explain. "We didn't know if anyone else was with her or on the way, so we just waited for her to leave."

"You were smart to stay hidden." More quietly I mutter, "That's what I did." Guilt weighs in the pit of my stomach. *Maybe I should have tried to warn them.*

"That's all we could do. We're just lucky she didn't see any of us." He grabs my hand and squeezes it gently. That small hint of comfort is exactly what I need right now. A hushed conversation breaks through the momentary silence between us.

As we push through the door, I stop in my tracks. Vanen sits before us, strapped to the wooden desk chair. His left cheek bears a purplish bruise. Hayes leans over him, frantically shaking him. His body slumps in the chair as if the bindings wrapped around his chest and arms are the only things holding him upright. His eyes are glassy and unfocused. Beckett and I rush to his side.

My hand flies to my mouth, covering my dropped jaw. "Wha . . . what happened to him?"

"Go get a washcloth. Run it under cold water." Beckett commands, kneeling in front of Vanen. I'm not sure who he's talking to, but Hayes reacts faster than me. He dashes to the bathroom and returns seconds later with a dripping cloth. Beckett grabs it, running it across Vanen's forehead. He flinches and blinks several times as Beckett pats down each cheek.

"Vanen! Snap out of it, man." His touch appears gentle but his words are impatient. "Look, we're your friends. We can help you, but you have to tell us what's going on."

"We need something to cut the straps!" Hayes mutters as he flits around the room, yanking drawers open. He's frantic, on the verge of spinning out of control. My mind reels with questions but no answers. *How can we cut that material? What's wrong with Vanen? Is Kiera about to walk through that door at any moment?*

Vanen blinks a few times. I move to his side and rest a hand on his shoulder.

"Just keep talking to him," Beckett says as he rises. Joining Hayes, he searches the room.

"Vanen, we're here now and we'll get you out of here! Please just answer us!" Hunching down to meet his eyes, I lose my balance, knocking both him and the chair to the floor. Before I know what's happening, the guys close the small gap between us. Beckett helps me to my feet as Hayes turns the chair upright. It rocks unevenly. One of the legs wobbles. Vanen squeezes his eyes shut and slowly opens them. A distant recognition, clouded by confusion, overtakes his scrunched features. He shakes his head, his eyes narrowed, as if he's working something out in his mind.

"Everyone okay?" Beckett asks.

"Yes, but look what it did to the chair." His gaze follows where I point. "It started to break. Maybe instead of cutting the ropes, we break the chair."

"That could work!" Hayes slides his glasses along the ridge of his nose. "We just have to be careful we don't hurt Vanen in the process."

Vanen's eyes track our every movement now. He's growing more aware by the minute. A low moan escapes his lips. It's like he's slowly waking up. He watches as the guys turn the chair on its side and basically bash it with their feet. Hayes focuses on Vanen while Beckett unleashes fury on the wooden legs. With just a few kicks, they crack and snap. Hayes helps maneuver Vanen out of the line of impact when Beckett takes aim at the arms.

As they work to free Vanen from his seated prison, I check the hallway for any activity. Thankfully, all is quiet. I return to the room to find the guys dragging Vanen to the bed. They lay him down and shimmy the straps out from around him. He coughs and motions with his hands toward his mouth.

"Water! I think he wants water!" I dash to the bathroom and fill the small white cup on the counter. The clear liquid sloshes around, spilling a trail on the carpet as I rush it to Vanen. He reaches for it eagerly. I help him guide it to his mouth and tilt it back. He gulps down every drop before releasing the cup and letting his arm drop to the bed.

After a few minutes of breathing heavy, he blinks his eyes a few times fast. When he finally seems to settle, it's like he's truly noticing us for the first time. We all watch him as if he's a specimen under a microscope. Hayes is the first to break the silence.

"What happened? We've been trying to find you for hours."

"Water," Vanen croaks. "More water first."

We watch him chug another glassful. After a hearty cough, he tells us everything that happened.

# CHAPTER 16 ~ EVERLY

# UPPER DIVISION, CENTRESTATES

With plenty of pauses to clear his throat and several more sips of water, Vanen explains that he went back to his room as usual after we were all dismissed from Centrel Hall this afternoon. Soon after, someone knocked on his door. He figured it was Hayes, but it turned out to be a Centrestates worker, saying he had to check the room's cooling unit.

Not knowing how long it would take, and wanting to avoid the awkwardness of waiting around while the man worked, Vanen said he would just go hang out in another delegate's room. He started walking to the door when a sudden sharp pain pierced his thigh. When he reached down to feel what it was, the man grabbed his shoulders and led him to the bed, telling him to sit down on it.

"I don't know what happened," he says, squeezing his eyes shut as if he's reliving the moment. "The room started spinning. I could barely walk. It felt like the floor dropped out from under me and my vision was blurry. I remember falling on the bed, but my arms and legs were hanging over the sides."

He pauses, gulping down what must be a lump in his throat. "I tried to lift my legs and raise my arms, but they were so heavy. I just gave up. The man who came in my room, he must have flipped me over because somehow I ended up on my back. I wanted to ask him what he was doing but my mouth wouldn't move."

Vanen shakes his head as his eyes focus on an invisible memory. His voice grows shaky. "He was just standing there, staring down at me, with some stupid smirk on his face. All I could do was lie there until my eyes got so heavy that I couldn't keep them open."

He must have stayed that way for hours, basically the whole time Hayes had been looking for him.

"I finally woke up when I felt a stinging pinch. I cracked my eyes open to see Kiera standing there in front of me. And I was tied to the stupid chair." He nods toward the wooden desk chair.

"So that's why you didn't answer when I knocked on your door," Hayes says softly, almost to himself.

"I don't know what they gave me, but whatever it was was strong." Vanen rubs his head.

"Well, I'm glad you're back," I say, leaning toward him. "We were really worried about you."

"And speaking of that, we have no idea when Kiera or someone else might check on him," Beckett says, glancing at the door. "We should probably get out of here." A jolt of anxiety strikes me. He's right.

"Why did they do this to you?" I ask as the guys help Vanen stand on unsteady legs.

"We walk and talk." Beckett motions toward the door. He and Hayes each prop an arm under Vanen's armpits and lead him through the room. I peek into the hallway before holding the door open for them to pass through. Unbalanced and struggling, they cross the threshold and attempt to pick up speed. In between the low grunts of three people clumsily trying to gallop down the hallway in unison, Vanen answers the question left hanging in his room.

"I think Kiera was . . . tired of me . . . figuring out what's . . . going on here." He clears his throat and gulps down a deep breath. He uses our brief ride in the elevator to elaborate.

"She wanted to know exactly how I was able to access their server, and confidential information that was supposed to be classified, in such a short amount of time. It comes down to her wanting to know how I beat their security. She knows about everything I found, but she doesn't know how I did it."

"But why did they only take you? I was part of it too," Hayes asks quietly.

"She said my login was the only one responsible for the breach." Vanen hunches up a shoulder. "She blamed me for everything. Didn't say one word about you. You know what I think?"

Considering we're all hanging on every word he says, he didn't even need to ask that question. All three of us stare at him, waiting.

"I think she genuinely likes you. I don't know what that means, or if it saved you somehow, but she has to know that we were in on this together." Vanen shakes his head slowly. Based on what I know about him, I'd guess he's rarely wrong.

"That has to be true," I agree. "You two were constantly together and whispering, and handing out the computers. You wouldn't do something like that and keep it to yourself. It was pretty obvious how close you two became."

"So what do we do now?" Vanen asks. "Because I sure don't want to be caught again. Kiera wants me out of the way and I'm sure she won't make the same mistake twice."

We reach the bottom floor and cautiously check the lobby area for any movement. It's quiet. Beckett motions for us to go. "Let's get the hell out of here."

"I think I can walk now." Vanen straightens his back and takes a shaky step forward. Beckett and Hayes share a glance, silently questioning if they should insist on helping. Both hesitate though, letting our friend stand on his own, slowing their pace to match his. We barely make it five steps before Vanen stops. He stares straight ahead for a moment before facing us to meet our questioning gazes.

"I just remembered something," he says quietly. "Something else Kiera said, the last thing she said, actually, was that she should have just sent me on the tour because that would have made this so much easier."

*The tour!* My eyes lock with Beckett's and we share a panic-fueled realization.

"We forgot all about it after we saw Hayes and then found you." Words tumble out of my mouth almost as fast as the thoughts pass through my brain. "But we found something in Kiera's office! There was this whole list of things in that red notebook she always carries around!"

"You went through her office?" Hayes scrunches his face in disbelief.

"Just a little bit. But we found her notes. She's planning something big. Something that would cause an . . . act of war." I swallow my trepidation. Just saying the words leaves a bitter taste in my mouth. I look to Beckett, who rushes to explain more when I hesitate.

"We had to find proof that she was up to something. And we got it." Beckett grits his teeth. "She had a list, like steps for what she planned to do. It started with the delegation and how they'd watch us and how we interacted with each other. Then it said something about eliminating some of us through an act of war."

"You sure she said it like that? An act of war?" Vanen's eyes widen, searching both of our faces for confirmation.

"I saw it too." I nod and glance at Beckett. "But it gets even worse."

"There was something about planting evidence to make it look like the delegates did something and that Centrestates had to defend itself. One of the last steps was about military attacks." Beckett blows out a deep breath, as if sharing all this somehow lightens the load of carrying that knowledge.

"And there was something about uniting under one leader," I add.

"Wait." Hayes paces back and forth. "An act of war would be an invasion or an attack. How could anyone try to make it look like we invaded or attacked anything?"

"Or it could be an attempt to overthrow the current leader." Vanen stares past us, into a nonexistent distance. "Which is crazy. Imperant's barely paid any attention to us. It's not like anyone even cares. I guarantee you none of the delegates could be plotting to take him down."

"What else would be considered an act of war . . . " Hayes trails off as he taps his temple. He stops for a moment before resuming his pacing.

"Kiera was pretty angry when she got here, just before she went to Vanen's room." I'm not sure why, but it feels important to share. "She was on the phone with someone, it had to be Lisum or Wynter, and she was saying that they were supposed to make sure all the delegates were on the tour tonight."

"We knew that. They said it a bunch of times." Hayes tries to brush off my comments, but something nags at the back of my mind. *I've got make them understand.*

"She knew three of us were missing, and she knew Vanen wasn't there." *What else? There must be something I heard that is useful.*

We fall into a contemplative silence that stretches for minutes but feels like hours. Just as he's about to wear the carpet down from incessant pacing, Hayes stops mid-step. His jaw drops and he nervously gulps down air.

"If they're staging some kind of attack, the capitol building would make an ideal target. And we've spent most of our time there, other than Centrel Quarters. They could say we've been planning it since we got here."

Vanen stumbles back a step, his eyes shifting to the side then the ceiling. I sense that he's processing Hayes' thought process and calculating his own interpretation. Slowly, he raises his finger in the air, as if he's cutting into a discussion.

"When she woke me up and demanded to know how I got into their servers, she said it was my only chance to tell her." He pauses, narrowing his eyes. "I kept my mouth shut, which infuriated her. She asked me again and when I ignored her, she said she should have just sent me on that tour because it would have been easier. Yeah, I remember the snarl on her face when she said that. It has to mean something."

"So, think about it. Why would they do something here, at their capitol building? It's too valuable." Beckett's eyes slide to each of us in turn. "The tour *has* to be her cover. Do you remember what Callan said in one of our meetings about an alternate power source?"

"Yes, he did say that," Vanen agrees, chewing his lower lip. I don't remember, but that doesn't mean it didn't happen.

"So if Kiera wants to get rid of the delegates and blame them for an act of war, she could sabotage the whole thing. If the grid was damaged during this tour, Centrestates has an alternate power source anyway, so it's a low risk for them. And the grid is so valuable that if she could make it look like the delegates damaged it, and succeeded, that makes the case for Centrestates having to defend the Territory. And it gives them more control because this alternate power source hasn't been shared yet."

His words echo in the silence. I realize we all stand like statues, completely caught up in our thoughts. A shiver dances over me, making the hairs on the back of my neck rise. *Could he be right? Because if he is . . .*

"We've got to tell the Uprising!" Beckett growls, practically baring his teeth. "They're the only ones who can stop it!"

"The Uprising?" Vanen balks. "Made-up stories from when we were kids won't help us now."

"Everything Beckett told you about the Uprising is real." I hold their doubting gazes. "I've met a few of their members." *No need to reveal that Beckett just happens to be one. And the fact that my mother is one of their leaders.*

Hayes crosses his arms. "If the Uprising was real, we would have heard about it before we came to Centrestates."

"We don't have time to debate this!" Beckett's impatience boils over, with good reason. He takes a step closer to the guys. I'm caught between two sides – one completely confident in his assessment and what needs to happen while the other two weigh logic and sense.

"I know this sounds hard to believe, but it's true. Please, just listen," I plead.

"Fine, but I don't know how you can prove it," Hayes mutters.

"Let's just get out of here." Beckett turns and hoofs it toward the entrance. We follow, bounding over the last stretch of tiled floor in a stomping, echoing clamor. The glass doors slide open and we burst into the humid night air. As we charge forward, my mind continues to process what's happening.

At first I thought Kiera's list was a collection of ideas. But knowing that it's actually a formula weighs heavy on my conscience. She outlined a list of actions that would serve as dominoes, unraveling the Territories as we know them, capitalizing on their vulnerabilities. Just so that she and Imperant can seize control of everything.

They want to unite the Territories, not because it's in the citizens' best interest, but because they crave power. *How would that change life back in Eastates? No matter what happens, it will never be the same for me. Not after all of this.*

# CHAPTER 17 ~ CARO

## UPPER DIVISION, CENTRESTATES

We dart through the tunnels, clinging to the shadows. Other than the occasional stray stone that connects with one of our feet and skitters off the path, the stretch of darkness is eerily quiet. It feels like we've been running for hours, but it's closer to minutes. After we disembarked the train at the Xone wall, our only mode of transport was foot. It doesn't matter; the adrenaline rush is more than enough to power me through this. Each step I take brings me closer to the daughter I lost too many years ago. And that's just the start. Once the Uprising gains control, I'll have my whole family back. That can't come soon enough.

"It's dark but I think we take the next exit. According to our contact, the power grid's only a few miles from the third one. I think we've passed two. You up for a run like that?" Zai asks. Sometimes it's hard to believe we're on the same team.

"I'm ready for it, and anything or anyone else we come across along the way." I didn't suffer at the hands of this government for years just to give up now. Someone, somewhere, decided that they didn't like me stating the truth about the Societal Order. Rather than accept any constructive feedback to right any wrongs, they decided to shut me up.

As if I was nothing at all, they plucked me from the life I knew, the family I loved, and tossed me in another Territory to start all over again. And I was just supposed to forget everything I was forced to leave behind. Their callousness only motivated me to take my life back, no matter what I needed to do.

A scraping sound echoes in the distance a moment before voices rise. Their words are muffled as they bounce off the walls. I can make out two shadows. Hopefully that's all there is.

Our mouths close as our eyes widen. We both slow our pace to a stop. Shuffling toward the dingy walls, we press ourselves against them. The harsh scent of urine stings my nose. I noticed it when we first entered the tunnel, but now that we've stopped moving, it hits me full force.

We strain to listen. Someone's down here with us. The question is whether they are friend or foe. And unfortunately, by the time we can figure it out, it may be too late.

Zai motions toward the other side of the tunnel, directly across from our current position, then points to himself. I nod once in agreement. He hunches as low as his six-foot frame allows and soundlessly inches toward his destination. Once he makes it to the other side, we won't be able to see each other but it's not like it matters right now. Neither one of us is moving until these people are gone.

A trickle of sweat runs down my back. I press my palms flat against the wall behind me and squeeze my eyes shut, concentrating on staying immobile. I flick my finger when a slight tickle brushes over my knuckles. Opening my eyes, my pulse rockets when I catch a glimpse of a mouse. Without a thought, I fling it off me.

While I manage to stifle the scream clawing at my throat, the force of de-mousing myself causes me to stumble. My boot strikes the uneven concrete in a crunch that echoes well beyond the small amount of space I occupy. I can sense the others suck in a startled breath.

"Did you hear that? There's something down there." Feet rush toward me as two streams of light sweep along the wall. There's nowhere to hide. I meld into the wall but it's useless. Squinting, I search the darkness for Zai but see and hear nothing. *Good.* No reason for him to get caught. Besides, I can handle this on my own. With any luck, they could be Uprising insiders looking to help me. And maybe even lead me right to Imperant. *Yeah, right.*

The flashlight beams grow stronger, and dangerously close. They bounce along the wall, rolling closer and closer until one lands on my face.

"You there, halt!" The men come to a sudden stop. The one who yelled raises his hands in a commanding gesture.

They've seen me. There's no point in trying to run. I'm sure they have weapons, and they've been trained to use them. I turn toward them, raising my left arm to block the blinding flashlight. My right hand hovers just over my pants pocket and the loaded pistol snugly tucked inside it. One lowers his flashlight to reach for a revolver he promptly aims at me.

"Come closer, with your hands up. Nice and slow."

I oblige, raising my hands in the air, instantly regretting putting any distance between my trigger finger and a gun. *They wouldn't just kill someone they caught down here, would they?* I'd be more valuable to them if they could interrogate me to find out how I got here and how I know about the tunnels. Banking on that logic, I choose what I hope is an unexpected approach.

"I am part of the Uprising." I pause just enough for them to comprehend my words. "Are you enemy or ally?"

"The Uprising," one of them snickers. He turns to his comrade and elbows him. "Boss is gonna love this." They both turn to me with hungry eyes. Their hatred is obvious. I was hoping it wouldn't come to this. As if on cue, two shots explode from behind the men. Even in the dismal lighting, Zai doesn't miss. Their bodies drop in succession. Neither one knew what hit him.

"Hell!" Zai complains. "Didn't think we'd have to drop anyone so soon." He scratches the dark stubble on his chin and turns his head from side to side. I imagine he's looking for a place to hide the bodies.

"Looks like it's all straight and narrow," I comment. "Do you know of any offshoots?"

"Not this close to the city. No."

"Then we find the darkest stretch of shadows and dump the bodies there. We don't have time for anything else. And if someone else shows up to check on them, we don't want to be anywhere close."

He nods and sidearms his weapon. "You go ahead, make sure it's clear. I'll drag these two back a few hundred yards."

Grasping my pistol, I slip past Zai and stalk forward. I'd much rather scout ahead on our trail than dispose of dispatched bodies.

About ten minutes later, we meet up where the two men first saw me. Silently, we charge toward the next junction, where Zai claims is an exit.

***

The exit door blends into the stone walls. If Zai weren't here, I'd never have found it. He hauls a shoulder into it before it barely budges. I flinch as its shrill squeal announces our presence to anyone who may be nearby. Luckily, no one jumps out or commands us to stop what we're doing.

As soon as we push through the heavy barrier, the peaceful night breeze stirs my senses. Lights define the city clearly. Buildings rise beside their shorter brethren, seemingly in no specific pattern other than what looked aesthetically pleasing. Whoever designed it did it right. It's beautiful.

"First time here?" Zai asks.

"I traveled through when I was first exiled, but this is the first close-up look I've gotten. You?"

"Been here a few times. Still not used to all the lights at night in an upper division. Guess that's what you get when you own the power grid." He huffs. For once we're in agreement.

"Well, I think it's a good sign if everything is as usual here," I say. "So we'll make our way to the power plant and watch. Wait for whatever is supposed to happen tonight."

"Watch and wait?" he snorts. "We didn't come all this way to sit around and do nothing. We go there and find the delegates and evacuate them before anything happens. We eliminate anyone who tries to get in our way."

*How does his wife deal with this guy?* He is nothing like my own husband. I just have to keep reminding myself that the reason I'm here is so that my family can be whole again. This is temporary frustration for a permanent fix.

I release a sigh and gesture for him to lead the way. "To the power plant."

Our steps are brisk. We survey our surroundings as we rush by them. We stick to the outskirts of the city, but the power grid soon comes into view – it rises above the landscape like an almighty force. It feels more like a solitary entity than a cluster of electronics controlled by people.

After about thirty minutes, Zai calls over his shoulder, "Not much farther."

Our compatible silence is extinguished by a sudden thundering boom. The ground, solid beneath our feet just moments ago, trembles. A flash of blinding light ignites the sky. I cover my eyes to block what must be brighter than a thousand suns. The air sizzles with excess energy. Terror surges through my veins. *Are we too late?*

"What the hell was that?" Zai roars. He knows as well as I do. Without another word, we both bolt toward what is sure to be chaos.

---

# CHAPTER 18 ~ EVERLY

---

## UPPER DIVISION, CENTRESTATES

"Where're . . . we going?" Hayes asks, gasping for breath.

"The grid!" Beckett answers over his shoulder, not even slowing his jog. "We have to warn them."

I glance at Vanen, who stumbles as he tries to keep up. He's probably still weak from whatever they injected him with that knocked him out. Lisum and Wynter made it sound like the grid wasn't too far away. I hope that's true. Then Vanen would just have to make it a few more blocks.

It's hard to tell how close the smokestacks are, but at least they serve as a guide. The smoke-chugging pillars are dwarfed by the skyscrapers we rush past. From everything I've learned about the grid, it should be the biggest structure here. By far. But there's no time to contemplate that now.

My lungs scream for air as my feet slap the sidewalks that appear to be the most direct path to our destination. Beckett easily outpaces us, remaining several yards ahead. He stays within our sight, craning his neck every few feet, taking stock of when we need to turn or veer in a different direction. He radiates confidence and determination, almost making me believe that we can stop whatever may happen. Every cell in my body feels charged, fueling a fresh surge of energy.

*I was selected to be a delegate. I came here to ensure a peaceful coexistence between the Territories, and if I can help prevent a war, then that's exactly what I'll do.*

Just as a ripple of relief washes over me, the sky flashes a blinding white. A blast of fury rips through the night as if the Earth itself has snapped in two. The ground rumbles and buckles, knocking me to my knees. Realization replaces determination with terror. Instinctively I curl into a ball and cover my head.

For a moment, I can hear only the beating of my own heart. It throbs in my ears, louder than a train churning on its tracks. My mind struggles to comprehend where I am and why. A murky fog washes over me, stinging my eyes and throat. *The others. Are they okay?*

An unsteady figure pushes himself up onto his feet. *Beckett. He twists back and forth, taking in everything around him.* Tears prick at the corners of my eyes. He barrels toward me, urgency fueling his clumsy steps. His arms stretch out to me before he's even within reach. It's enough motivation to force my legs to work. He helps me up and wraps me in a tight hug.

Resting my head on his shoulder, I crack my eyes open and spot Hayes. Just a few feet away, he presses a hand to his ear and squints his eyes. His jaw hovers open wide in disbelief. Raging flames billow, reflecting in his glasses. That reflection promises danger bristling within seething dark clouds that conquer the sky. I swallow the bile rising in my throat.

The surrounding buildings block most of the damage from our view, but it's clear that the blaze in the distance harbors death and destruction. My stomach churns as I stand, forcing my unsteady legs to work. A burning tickle sparks at the back of my throat as tears pool in my eyes, blurring my vision.

"My God." Vanen stares, rubbing his hands up and down his arms as if brushing away a chill.

"Is everyone okay?" Beckett asks.

Hayes shivers but nods slowly. Vanen and I confirm our agreement.

"We have to find the Uprising and Harley's our best chance. Everly, you know where to look for him, right?" Beckett doesn't even wait for me to answer. "Take them there and tell Harley everything that happened today. He's got to make sure the Uprising knows. I'm going to the grid. If the delegates were still there, they could be hurt and need help. And that's if we're lucky."

"We should all go see this Harley—" Hayes starts.

"No," Beckett cuts him off. "I already know the Uprising is real. And I think we all know what that explosion was. Kiera targeted the grid and she's not getting away with it. Not as long as I'm still here. I'm going to find the delegates. If the Uprising can help, great. If not, I'll do it myself."

Beckett's posture stiffens as if his whole body is coiled, ready to strike. His nostrils flare and his jaw clenches. A fierce intensity rolls off him in waves that threaten to envelop the rest of us. I sense he may run off at any moment, ready for a battle we all know is coming.

After a momentary silent standoff, I explain what I know to the guys.

"Vanen, remember that old man we met on our first day here? Right outside of Centrel Hall?"

"That crazy guy who was talking nonsense?" he asks, his eyebrows knitted together.

"Yes, that's Harley. But it wasn't nonsense. Everything he said was true. He's part of the Uprising."

Vanen narrows his eyes and scratches his head. Hayes purses his lips in what may be an attempt to hold back the doubts running through his mind. Neither of them says it, but they don't believe me. I look to Beckett for backup, but he huffs out a grunt before his impatience runs out.

"I'm going. Come with me or not, but I'm not waiting one more second." Beckett rushes around us. I shoot him a pleading look, but I know he's right. He sprints down the street, toward the undoubted wreckage that was once a powerful electrical grid.

Without thinking, I turn and shuffle in the direction he just went. *I'm going with him.* I've never felt more certain of anything in my life. I call over my shoulder, "I know it sounds crazy, but go find Harley. Tell him we sent you. He's usually hanging out right around Centrel Hall. We'll be back soon and we'll find you."

"Everly, don't go. It's too dangerous. Stay with us," Hayes pleads, lunging for me. I back up, slipping just out of his grasp.

"It's probably already too late," Vanen mutters with defeat before a hacking cough overtakes his words.

"It can't be," I whisper through gritted teeth. Although they can't hear me, urgency sharpens my tone. Even though it's only for my own benefit, I add, "We have to try."

Those four words say it all. We've got to warn the others and we may already be out of time. But if there's anything we can do, it's worth a shot to try to help them. Somehow. Turning my back on them, I sprint toward where I last saw Beckett. He's not going without me.

***

The now-familiar storefronts and skyscrapers rush past me in a hazy blur. Each step brings me closer to the destruction and the resulting cloud of toxins it released. I have no choice but to inhale the poisoned air.

Sirens wail in the distance. Red lights flash urgently, bouncing off the predominantly glass exteriors. Small clusters of residents huddle together on the streets. They must have been inside the businesses still open. We haven't exactly ventured too far off the main roads though, so there could be homes tucked away a few blocks from here. Once again I consider that in Eastates, at least in the Upper Division, everyone would be home at this time. No one would dare come out after 6 p.m., especially if there was some sort of emergency or disaster. The default directive would be to shelter in place.

Of course they don't have that here. Instead, a reassuring male voice flows through the streets, growing louder when we near light posts. There must be some sort of voice amplifier within each one, programmed for announcements.

*"We are experiencing a temporary emergency. Please return to your homes for your own safety as well as the safety of our responders. Refer to the information broadcast for more information and updates as they become available."*

As the message plays on a continuous loop, repeating every few minutes, citizens gawk or clumsily stagger about, their unanswered questions caught in the choking air. We're all seeking answers that no one has. One figure catches my eye, weaving through the shadows swiftly, deftly. He's the only one who moves with purpose. My eyes lock on him as my feet scramble to catch up. *That's where I need to be. With him.*

I push past the others. Like us, they're drawn to the commotion, but they're at the mercy of their own curiosity. I become a nameless face floating through the gathering crowd. Confusion and horror etched in their features, they grasp for some explanation of what's happening. Consumed by a split-second event that shattered their sense of safety and control, no one seems to notice me.

My chest heaves with exertion as the gap between me and Beckett begins to narrow. As if sensing my presence, he looks over his shoulder. When our eyes meet, relief seems to flash within his. He slows to a jog before stopping completely to wait for me.

"I thought you . . . were staying back . . . with Hayes and Vanen." He catches his breath and crosses his arms, not exactly radiating happiness to see me.

"I wasn't . . . letting you go . . . by yourself," I huff out between gasps for air, my tone more ragged than his.

Those eyes, with emotions running as deep as the ocean, lock on mine. The tiniest hint of a smile plays across his lips. I swear they form the word "thanks" but it's so faint that I can't be sure he actually said anything.

He takes a step closer and squeezes my hand reassuringly before saying, "Let's go."

Matching his determination, I nod. *We've got to do this.* When he turns and takes off toward the grid, everything else fades to the outskirts of my senses – thick smoke smothering the sky, shrill voices crying out in panic, a round of silencing booms spewing from the collapsing structure. I center myself and focus on Beckett's back. I'll follow him to the awaiting inferno. He has my complete trust.

It's not long before we reach the wreckage. Pristine buildings yield to a stretch of rolling hills that serve as a barrier of sorts between the city and its energy workhorse. What I never realized is that the hills rise around the grid. While the smokestacks stand tall, the accompanying buildings merely peek out from the steep embankments. No wonder the city's buildings looked taller – they're built at ground level. The land must have been dug out to form a giant pit or a valley, and Centrestates dropped its energy grid right in the center of it.

I remember pictures of the components from lessons at school. It looked so perfect on paper – four massive curved towers, their base and top flaring out wide while the thinner middle seamlessly connected the two ends. The tops were completely open, like giant mouths facing the sky, puffing out their own version of bloated white clouds. A dozen thin towers flanked their much wider, curvier brethren. Crisscrossing metal poles connected to form enormous steeples that surrounded the towers. Twin boxy buildings, at least a dozen stories high, stood at attention, flanked by clusters of much smaller buildings.

But that's not what lies before us now. Images on the pages always showed perfect symmetry, strong angles and solid foundations. This vision could qualify as a nightmare. Beckett and I stand in shock, shoulder-to-shoulder, our minds trying to comprehend the unreal scene unfolding before our eyes.

Everything I'd expect is there, including the two main buildings. Their size alone commands authority. Each one is as long as the street

I live on. And probably just as wide. I sense that whatever happens within those walls is clearly key to the entire operation.

And one of them is sliced open right down the middle. It looks as if it's been smashed by a giant fist that rained down on it, tearing away every wire, wall and floor that crossed its path. Black smoke pours from its busted gut. Deafening alarms scream while shocking red and white lights flash from somewhere inside the now-torn-open building.

Craning my neck, I watch the tall towers belch puffy white plumes. It's supposed to be steam, a harmless by-product of the cooling units, but the rising noxious gases invade it.

Thick black cables droop between the crisscrossed steeples. Some rest on the ground, their snapped ends glowing an electric blue. A few flick back and forth erratically like an electrocuted snake that's no longer in control of its own body.

I struggle to remember what we learned about the power grid, other than what it looked like. We memorized the different parts of it – the cooling towers, distribution lines, substations, the reactor. I shudder, thinking about the last one – the reactor. Squeezing my eyes shut, I seek any sort of memory hiding in the cobwebbed corners of my mind. *What did we learn about the reactor? Are we standing in front of a ticking bomb that could blow up at any minute?* No answers surface, and I'm in no frame of mind to concentrate.

Panic courses through me as I stand, staring at where I was supposed to be tonight. *If Kiera had her way, Beckett and I would have been inside there. Along with Hayes.*

# CHAPTER 19 ~ EVERLY

## UPPER DIVISION, CENTRESTATES

"Come on." Beckett tugs me from my useless thoughts. He points to the fiery opening. "Stay close to me. We should look for them in there."

My survival instinct begs me to run away. To leave this place and return to the safety and comfort of home. It may be monotonous, but at least nothing like this ever happens there. As I numbly follow Beckett, reality reminds me that home isn't safe anymore either. Nowhere is. There's no going back, not after this. Kiera will never let us set foot outside of Centrestates again. We know too much. And besides, as I discovered on the train ride here, we don't even have a way home. Kiera never intended for us to leave here.

"Everly, snap out of it." Beckett waves a hand in front of my face. His patience evaporated half an hour ago, and having to coax me out of my wandering thoughts is only aggravating him even more. I shake my head, willing away the distraction. *If we're going to make it out of here alive, I need to be alert.*

Under his scrutinizing gaze, I'm suddenly hyperaware of the beads of sweat clinging to my forehead and scurrying down my back. Swiping them away, I focus on Beckett and bark out the only thing I can think of. "Lead the way."

We trudge up the last barrier between us and the power station – a sprawling hill with an escalating slope. As the climb grows steeper, every step we take is calculated as we dodge rubble – from splintered chunks of wood to sharp fragments of metal. Random pieces of the once-powerful grid litter a wide radius around the damaged building. We reach the top only to take in the entire scene.

While the outer walls still stand, the rest of the main building crumples inward where the roof has caved in. The random scatterings of rubble grow into small mountains around the split opening. But before we can even reach that, we have to pass the downward incline on this side of the hill. It's like a minefield of the grid's broken and battered innards. It makes the side we just climbed look like an easy stroll. My shoulders slump as gravity seems to drag me into an infinite exhaustion. *How are we going to do this?*

Beckett stares at the mess before us, his conviction seemingly deflating. When I wrap my fingers around his hand, he stirs and motions for us to move. We carefully pick our way through the mess, sidestepping every sharp edge and splintered board. Every few minutes, a metallic screech or a shrill snapping warns us that this whole area is unstable.

Beckett peers at me over his shoulder a few times, probably making sure I'm still following him. The closer we get to the ruins, the more apparent the level of damage is. It's like the steeples carrying the thick cables to each other were ripped right out of the ground. Several of them lie crumpled in a mangled mess.

A wall of heat brushes over my skin, instantly releasing a fresh layer of sweat. Air shimmers between us and the flames eating away at what's left of the structures. My curious gaze alternates between watching where my feet land and keeping an eye on the wreckage for movement. As the building gasps what could be some of its last breaths, an eerie calm descends for just a moment.

Flickering flames lash out from cracks and piles, but so far I don't see any sign of anyone trying to escape. Hope stings like a dagger twisting in my chest. Saya came here tonight with the group. I could have warned her, but didn't. *Please don't let us be too late.* By the looks of it, if the delegates were here when this thing exploded, there's no way they all survived. It's probably unlikely any of them did.

After what feels like hours, the hill levels out and we reach the bottom, only to reveal our next problem. The only way to get inside, what is now also outside, is to climb on top of the newly-formed piles of stones, cement, glass and wood.

"Be really careful," Beckett says, as if it weren't obvious. "There could be poles or sharp edges in there. I'll go first but we can't go too fast."

Together we scale the shifting pile, gravity trying to tug us under. It's like swimming in a pool of quicksand, except the sand is primed to impale you if you make one wrong move. I fight every urge to freeze and let the pile consume me. This was where I was supposed to be tonight, if Kiera had her way.

"Come on!" Beckett calls, rescuing me from a wave of self-pity. Before I realize it, he's reached solid ground and motions for me to join him. Offering a hand, he helps me slide out of the mess and stand on my own feet. Now that I don't have to focus on each movement, my senses are bombarded by the destruction surrounding us.

A stringent odor burns my nostrils. I press the back of my hand to my nose in a useless attempt to staunch the smell. Untamed electricity sizzles in the air as shattered glass crunches beneath our shoes. Tears sting my eyes and acid swirls in my stomach. For a moment I watch the acrid smoke rise, considering all that it carries. Besides the melting electronics and scorched steel, it must be polluted with charred flesh.

A low moan sends a shiver down my spine. I turn to Beckett, but his eyes are already searching, scanning the rubble for movement.

"I hear something . . . over here." His hand reaches for mine and squeezes, tugging me along behind him. Draping the other arm across his face, he presses his shirt sleeve to his mouth. While I doubt it will make breathing any easier, I do the same.

We inch deeper into the damage, dodging wires and toppled electronic panels. We alternate between dashing and cautiously stepping around the debris, eager to reach a possible survivor without injuring ourselves. He leads me toward a corner where two walls once met. Now, fractured chunks of gray bricks are scattered around the floor, spilling outward where they were neatly stacked on top of each other less than an hour ago.

A thunderous boom sends my heart into a wild gallop. Flames burst from metallic cylinders as if fury boils in each molecule of air. The hair along the back of my neck rises. *How long until this whole place blows?*

Beckett lowers his elbow and points. "Someone's right there." He drops my hand and dashes just a few feet away, toward the quivering figure on the floor. I follow him, stumbling. When we reach the faceless lump of sprawled arms and legs, we both stop abruptly.

Petite legs peek out from a blackened, torn skirt. Every inch of skin is dusted in a thick gray ash. Beckett carefully lifts a cracked piece of panel and tosses it aside. Beneath it is a face I recognize. Her short, dark hair is plastered to her pale face. A cut stretches from her left eyebrow all the way down to her chin.

"She's breathing!" Beckett frantically digs into the pile entombing her. The movement jostles her body and her eyes flutter open. They search up and down, left and right, unfocused before they land on us. Her forehead crinkles in confusion. It takes her a moment to speak.

"Beck—" A cough racks Lisum's whole body. When she stills, she reaches a trembling hand toward us. "It's not . . . safe. You have to . . . go."

I suck in a breath, immediately regretting the influx of smoky air. An uncontrollable cough erupts from my throat.

"We're not leaving you here," Beckett grates through his teeth. His head swivels back and forth, those blue eyes searching for something. *But what?* He shakes his head in defeat. "Everly, help me clear all this away."

I drop down and join him in clawing through the remnants of smashed bricks, sharp slices of tile and feather-light fragments of foam. Dust and dirt coat my fingers and forearms as I seek out anything light enough that I can lift or push away. I let out a sharp yelp whenever an unseen jagged edge catches my skin. Pressing my lips together is the only way to prevent the involuntary reaction.

*These little scratches are nothing compared to what Lisum is going through.*

We finally clear away the last bit of debris that was covering her, but any relief we may have felt is quickly dashed away. What we uncover twists my stomach in knots. Beckett presses a fist to his mouth and his eyes cloud with pain.

A metal rod pokes through her abdomen as a crimson pool swells beneath her. It's much worse than we thought. On the surface, she looked bruised and cut. But underneath it all, a six-inch stake impales her. That's where all the blood is coming from. There's so much of it.

Dropping to the floor, I smooth her hair down as tears sting my eyes. *Can anyone help her? Can she be . . . saved?* I feel Beckett beside me before I see him. He crawls closer and cradles her head, supporting her neck.

"Shhhh, it's okay. We'll get you help." The genuine concern radiating from him clenches my heart. This is a side of him I've never seen.

She shakes her head. "There . . . is no help . . . for me. But you . . . you have to go. Help is . . . coming . . . for you." A deep cough rumbles from her throat. She presses a shaky hand over her mouth. When she lowers it, a trickle of blood dribbles down her chin. Without a thought, I swipe it away, only to find my own hand trembling.

My eyes meet Beckett's. His deep blue irises brim with hopelessness, and I'm certain mine reflect the same. Her skin pales with each passing minute. Again he turns his head back and forth, searching, but anything that might be of any use is buried beneath piles of snapped wood, shards of glass and slices of metal.

"We pick her up and carry her out of here at least." His words have a sharp bite. I know he's instantly shifted from caring and concerned to furious and vengeful.

"Nnno . . . you can—"

Ignoring Lisum's cut-off plea, Beckett gently snakes an arm under her and wraps the other around her torso.

"Grab her legs. We stand on the count of three."

I grasp her ankles but she writhes and twitches from the touch. She shakes her head as the puddle of blood surrounding her spreads like lava seeping from a volcano, flowing dangerously closer to us with each passing minute.

"Leave . . . me." Her chest heaves with effort. "If they . . . find you . . . " She coughs, rattling her whole body in a tremor. "I should ha . . . have known."

I shake my head as tears well in my eyes, blurring my vision.

"G-go," she pleads. "Centrel . . . Hall. Take the . . . elevator . . . to the . . . T level."

"We'll take you with us. We're not leaving you here, besides—" Beckett tries to stop her again.

"No!" she barks with more fervor than I thought possible. "Listen." She shudders, curling into herself as another cough overtakes her. When she stills, determination and fury radiate in her eyes. "There are . . . tunnels. Take the . . . elevators. T . . . level." She pauses, gasping. When I rest a palm on her shoulder, she flinches and shakes her head.

"You need . . . you need . . . the code. It's . . . four digits." She gulps from the effort, drawing in rapid breaths. When her eyes shift between us, I sense the life draining from her.

Beckett leans closer. She presses a palm to his shirt and squeezes it into a fist. "It's one." She stiffens before continuing. "Three."

If I do anything this night, it's memorizing these numbers. Each passing minute sends my heart into rapid fire beating. *One, three, what's next?* The destruction surrounding us fades to the background as I focus on Lisum.

"Ni—" She chokes out, keeling forward. Sliding a hand over her sliced skin, she shudders. I can't tell if it's from the pain or the realization at how severe the wound is.

"Don't worry about that right now," Beckett whispers, cradling her head again. "We're gonna take care of you. It'll all be okay."

His promise is empty. We all know that, but somehow it fuels her will to continue. She gives him a shaky nod as her eyes swim with tears. Her lips quiver as she struggles to form words.

Her eyes drift closed as her body slumps to the floor. My last shred of composure snaps. I wildly shake my head no as hot tears erupt into ugly crying. My nose runs and my mouth hangs open in anguished sobs. Beckett squeezes my shoulder. "Everly." I hear him. I hear the gentleness, laced with concern, in his voice. But I can't pull my eyes from Lisum. *She has to wake up. She has to be okay.*

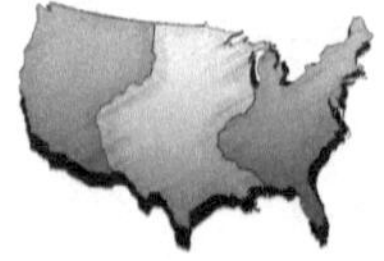

# CHAPTER 20 ~ EVERLY

## UPPER DIVISION, CENTRESTATES

A chaotic blend of sirens roars in the distance but every shrill sound and acrid scent fades away as I contemplate the enormity of this evening. What was supposed to be a boring trip to the power grid turned into a nightmare with no waking end in sight. Lisum is gone. Forever. We don't know if anyone else survived.

A hand wraps around my shoulder, tightens and shakes me roughly. "Hey, are you hearing me? We have to go!" My gaze slides to meet Beckett's, but sorrow slows my reaction. When I numbly nod in understanding, he wraps his arms around mine and guides me to standing. With one final nod, he captures my hand in his and turns toward the caved-in opening we entered through. Tugging me along, we dodge fractured fixtures and heaps of pulverized remains.

When we break free of the fiery inferno, Beckett leads us to a patch of grass hidden in the shadows. We both drop to our knees to catch our breath, gulping in the air. It's thick and hazy but my lungs welcome it compared to the choking smoke pouring from the dying grid.

"Beckett, what if someone else is still . . . in there? We didn't even look." Tears cloud my vision as my heart drops with hopelessness.

"You know we couldn't help Lisum," he says. Pointing toward the wreckage, he adds, "If anyone else is in there, they need a lot more help than what we can give. And besides, by the sounds of it, someone's on the way now."

My lower lip trembles as I scan the surrounding area for movement. *We can't be the only ones out here, can we?*

"Didn't she say help is coming?" My voice cracks on the question. He squeezes his eyes shut and mutters, "I thought she said that too but she probably just meant the emergency services." He shakes his head. "Maybe she said *hell* is coming. She was pretty clear that we need to get out of here."

"But who else . . . is here that we haven't found?" Agony sweeps through me, dense as the chemically saturated air.

"Everly, I swear, if I thought we could do something, we'd stay." He wraps a hand around mine and meets my eyes. "But those sirens are getting closer. Close enough that they'll find us if we stay here much longer. You know we were meant to be in there when it blew up." He points to the once-powerful energy source.

He's right. Dread strangles my throat and all I can do is nod again. Beckett's intense gaze bores into me. My heart jumps in anticipation of the unknown. *I don't know what to do.* Before I can contemplate any other thought, Beckett grates through his teeth, "We have to get out of here before anyone shows up. No one can know we were here." His resolve awakens my survival instincts. Hand in hand, we turn back toward the city, two worn souls not yet ready to give up.

"You two! Stay there, we can help you!" a female shouts as two figures dash toward us. They're camouflaged by smoke and dust, but I don't recognize the voice. It's not Wynter. *Or Kiera, thankfully. Whoever it is, I'm sure the last thing they want to do is help us.*

Sharing a wild-eyed yet knowing glance, we break into a run. Neither one of us looks back.

## ~ CARO ~

Those have to be delegates up ahead.

"You two! Stay there, we're here to help!" I call. They don't acknowledge me, but they definitely heard. Jumping to their feet, they dodge any wreckage in their path, racing like a tornado tearing through a field. *Damnit.*

"Why'd you do that? Of course they'd run!" Zai barks. "And if anyone else is around, I'm sure they know we're here now too."

"Obviously I was hoping they would recognize that we aren't officials." I know it was a long shot given the haze and conditions, but they were about to leave anyway. If they could have clearly seen us, they'd know that we aren't representing any Territory. Our clothes are a dead giveaway. We decided to wear tan pants with green shirts, the left sleeve bearing the former united country's colors – one stripe each of red, white and blue.

"Since you've blown our cover, let's see if we can recover anyone from this mess!" Zai tears off through the destruction, dodging downed wires and crumbling stone. I follow at a slower, more cautious pace. We're of no use to anyone if we get injured by being careless.

Goosebumps erupt over my arms as we near what was the inside of the power plant just moments ago. Just as I slip on an uneven stack of cracked ceiling tiles and nearly tumble to the ground, Zai calls out.

"I found someone!"

The smoke stings my eyes. Each cautious step I take is weighed down by dread. Debris crunches beneath my boots as I maneuver through split steel and smoldering wood. Warning flares in my mind the further we burrow into the waning structure. We dodge sparking wires and protruding metal rods.

When Zai suddenly drops to his knees, I lose my footing and nearly careen into his back. I start to ask if he's okay before catching sight of a small foot resting on the ground beneath him. I step beside him, covering my mouth with one hand and ducking beside him to examine the unmoving body.

Her narrow frame lies still, nestled among the wreckage. Blood spills from a metal rod that gouges her stomach. Her short dark hair is plastered to her head. Her porcelain features rest peacefully.

"Any idea who this is?" Zai barks. I startle, swallowing the queasiness churning in my gut. My brain refuses to accept what my eyes see.

"I said, can you identify her?" His impatience flares. I know him. He's not angry with me. He's furious that someone had to die and at the hands of Centrestates' leaders.

"Yes," I mutter. If it's too soft for him to hear, he must see it on my face because he doesn't ask again. "That's Lisum. She's . . . she's one of us. She was my key contact here." My eyes drift across the wreckage. As pockets of smoke slightly clear, I can make out other figures. Not moving.

"Oh great, just great! Maybe they knew she was feeding us information."

"I don't think that was it," I admit. "This was much bigger than her. And like she told me, this was about the delegates. She tried to stay close to them . . . to protect them . . . and it cost her." I press a fist to my mouth and bite back the emotions threatening to spill out. There's no time for this now. We've got to act fast if we're going to help anyone who's still alive.

"Well, by the looks of her, the delegates probably aren't in much better shape. We need to find them! My son is out there too, you know!"

*Yes, I know. Luckily your son is much more tolerable than you.* The immediate response that comes to mind is best left unsaid.

"I'll search this section." I point deeper into the smoldering carnage. "You take the opposite side. Make a quick sweep and meet back up in the middle. We need to check as many sections as possible before Enforcers arrive, or whoever Imperant sends to clean up his mess."

With that, we part ways and scramble through the destruction. As I suspected, others are nearby, but we're too late for them. A slender arm reaches out from beneath a cracked pillar. The dark skin is coated in white powder as if layers of dust have collected on it for years. It requires no closer investigation to know that anything attached to that arm has been crushed beneath the merciless weight of concrete and stone.

I push through a pile of splintered wood and frayed wires, both eager to leave the corpse and find someone who can be saved. In the distance, alarms screech through the murky night air. Soon enough, they will roar as they approach their destination.

"I found one!" Zai yells.

I rush to his side. Even through the cloud of chemicals separating us, I easily make out his struggling form. With one arm wrapped around a petite, curvy body, he uses his other hand to wrap the girl's arm around his neck for support. I quickly do the same, helping to support the dazed, bleeding teen. *She must be a delegate.*

"Who . . . who are you?" she asks, coughing. *Does she realize that we aren't from Centrestates by our mismatched clothing?* I can't tell if she comprehends anything that's happening or if she's just asking whatever question pops into her mind.

"We're here to help you!" Zai answers. "Are there any others around here?"

"I . . . I don't know," she answers slowly. "I . . . feel . . . dizzy." Her eyes scan the immediate surroundings, but they don't land on any one place. It's like she doesn't recognize where she is. "What . . . happened? This place . . . it's destroyed."

"There was a big explosion here but you're very lucky to be alive." Zai glances toward me, worry evident in his features. "Let's get her out of here."

I nod and we take our first step. The girl sways, clearly unable to find balance, even with our support. Our motion is erratic, and we both try to adjust to her unsteady gait. I suspect she has a concussion or some other head injury. She's probably in shock too.

We move carefully, trying not to jostle her too much, but the threat of spending too much time here chases every step. And we're not even remotely able to move stealthily in our current situation. We've got to stay ahead of the Enforcers or medical workers, whoever's on their way here, to avoid getting caught.

Zai leads us back the way we came, at a painfully slow pace. We stop at a patch of grass for a breather. I take a closer look at the girl. Her clothes are coated in a gray powdery residue. Tears mar the fabric and a few blackened spots must have been scorched. I can't even tell which Territory's color she wears. She's banged up, but she's alive. And with some medical attention, she may be just fine. *If she survived the collapse, others may have too.*

"You two stay here. I'll run back in and see if I can find anyone else." I turn to go but my feet fumble when Zai unleashes incredulous fury.

"Absolutely not!" he booms. "We can't stay! We're an army of two!" His wide eyes are wild and his chest heaves from exertion. Most of what he says is barked like a gruff command. It still grates on my nerves every single time. I know he's right, but my heart begs me to stay here until I claw my way through every last bit of debris and retrieve anyone who has even a remote chance to survive.

In that last moment of indecision, the sirens scream their warning and flashing lights bounce off the dust cloud hovering around us. They're getting close. When the girl shudders and nearly knocks them both off balance, I rush back to her side. The most I can give Zai is a curt nod. *We can't be caught here or the whole mission is compromised.*

# CHAPTER 21 ~ EVERLY

## UPPER DIVISION, CENTRESTATES

I follow closely as Beckett darts through alleys and side streets, leading us right back to where we started. Tears flood my eyes and bile stings my throat. We push our bodies to move as fast as they can, knowing our lives may depend on it.

By the time we pass a few familiar buildings, my mind is numb from overanalyzing the implications if we're right. We were supposed to be touring the power grid when it blew up. Kiera planned our deaths. And I'd bet Imperant would have rewarded her for destroying any remnants of truth we might divulge.

But who would we even tell? Our local Enforcers have always served in an authoritative role, not one that welcomed criticism or input. I never had a reason to seek their help before, but this is also entirely different. I don't even live here, and whoever is in charge of the Enforcers probably works in Centrel Hall, with Kiera. And she is right there at the top with Leader Imperant. They even meet at night when nearly everyone else is gone. I've never met our Territory's Societal Order leader, Tage Ault, in person. He's addressed us all on the information broadcast, but it's not like I have a direct connection to reach him.

My feet tingle with numbness as they pound the pavement. I've never felt so lost, so empty, so unsure of what the next five minutes holds, let alone any sort of future. We don't even know if any of the other delegates are alive. Their faces flash through my mind. Saya, who brought us all together for a slumber party to get to know each other and just have some fun. Kinsley, who always had something to say and rarely held any thoughts back. Callan, whose opinions I rarely agreed with, or even wanted to hear. And the others, the only ones in this whole world I've shared this experience with. Not one of them deserved this.

At least we know Hayes and Vanen weren't there. Hopefully they found Harley. *Who could have guessed that we'd be seeking out the old man who tried to warn me about this place outside Centrel Hall that first day?* Back then I didn't even know the Uprising existed. And that my mother was a part of it.

My gaze shifts between the ground before me and Beckett's back. I mindlessly follow him as memories float through my consciousness. Twelve strangers came together, tasked with dusting off a decades-old peace treaty. As we settled into a daily routine, conversations began to flow naturally.

Somehow I grew comfortable with these people. Some a little more than others, but still, it feels like a world away from when we all arrived, strangers desperate to impress and outshine each other at any opportunity. At the same time, it was our first experience separating from the comforting confines of home. That awakened insecurities that may have dampened the spirit of competition. For some of us, it forged a connection.

No matter how many details I ever shared with Josli, she could never understand everything that's happened here. No one could, not even those who watched or listened to the perfect portraits that the information broadcast tried to paint of us. The other delegates are the only ones who truly know what this experience has brought – pride, indulgence, deception, shame, sorrow, fear.

And now, in the span of a breath, they tried to eradicate us. I blink back the endless tears and swallow the scream clawing up my throat. They made us come here. They made us leave our homes and our families. And now they're done with us.

Just as we turn the last corner, a sharp ache spreads through my side and my nose bubbles with mucus. Beckett slows and I match my pace to his, eager for a break. If we hadn't just been running for our lives, a sense of relief might overtake me at the sight of our temporary home. *Is it even safe to go inside Centrel Hall?* We have nowhere else to go.

"Could we get a message to someone in the Uprising?" I blurt out, expecting that I already know the answer.

"There's a chance but only if we could find someone who's part of it," he admits. I think back to Kiera's office, when Beckett wanted to find a list. And it's not like we even know if she has one. Still, that's our only hope.

"How do they . . . you . . . even communicate?" Obviously electronic methods are possible but not exactly secure. Vanen and Hayes proved that. Beckett's gaze slides over me as if he's evaluating how much to share. After a moment, he blows out a breath and leans closer, speaking quietly. "Mostly by phone. We have members everywhere. Some are transport overseers, some work in production factories and some are even educators."

My eyebrows jump at the realization. *Could any of the educators who taught my classes back in Eastates be members of the Uprising?* A shiver dances through me. How would I have ever known? I shake my head. It doesn't matter. All that matters now is getting out of here.

"So we try for the tunnel?" I ask meekly. The thought of going back into Centrel Hall twists my stomach into knots.

"Yes." Beckett says confidently. "Lisum said to take the elevators down to the . . . I think it was the T floor."

The closer we get to the familiar entrance, the stronger my body reacts. My heart thunders and my throat constricts. It feels like I can't catch my breath.

"Beckett, we can't do this." My voice wavers as I slowly step backward. The fear coursing through me spills out in each syllable. "What if they're waiting for us inside? Ready to finish whatever they started at the power grid? And we have to find Hayes and Vanen." I'm a useless, shuddering mess.

He plants his palm to his forehead, his voice rising in tandem with his frustration. "Hayes and Vanen probably found Harley."

"But what if they didn't? What if they got caught?" I couldn't live with myself if we left them behind. "Maybe Harley can hide us and help us get home?"

"Everly, we have to go to the tunnels. That's probably all Harley would do anyway. It's the most direct way out of here, and Lisum told us how to get to them."

The dam of emotions bursts and a fresh wave of tears spills down my cheeks. "We don't even have the code to get there. She . . . she .

. . couldn't tell us." Before I collapse into a slobbering heap, Beckett wraps his arms around me. With his chin pressed to the side of my head, he speaks softly in my ear.

"We'll figure this out. Getting to the tunnel is the only chance we have right now." He runs his hands up and down my arms. It's more comforting than he could ever know. After a few shuddering breaths, I calm down. I'm numb, and so ready for this nightmare to be over.

Beckett's facial features blend together through the blur of tears. He grabs my hand and leads me toward Centrel Hall's grand entrance, stopping a few yards away from the automatic doors. He points to the bushes.

"Hide in there. I'll peek around and look for Hayes and Vanen."

Panic flares in my chest. "No, don't leave me. What if you get caught? Then what do I do?"

He raises a hand toward me, a physical command to stop. I clamp my lips shut, afraid they'll spill every single worry I've ever had if I don't stem the flow.

"I won't get caught. I'm a noct, remember? I can sneak around better than anyone else here." He shoots me a sly grin, which somehow eases my anxiety a notch. *How can he be so confident when I'm one sniffle away from a total breakdown?* I guess what he says makes sense. When I chew my bottom lip, he rests a palm on my shoulder and leans closer.

"Trust me. It'll be faster and less noticeable if it's just one of us. I swear, I'll be right back. Just hide here for a few minutes." His eyes plead with me to understand and cooperate. I release a huff of breath. *We're wasting time arguing.*

"I can do that. Just hurry up." Before I change my mind, I part some branches and wedge myself into the foliage. Stubby twigs scratch my arms, alternating with silky leaves that tickle as they brush the rising goosebumps. *How is it that I'm hiding in a bush again?* Once I'm settled, I search the entrance for one last look at Beckett. One last reassurance. But he's already gone. At least he was right about one thing – he is good at blending into the night.

I close my eyes and inhale slow, deep breaths. A tiny corner of my mind dares to believe that we will find a way out of this. Somehow. I don't feel like I'm meant to die here tonight, but Lisum probably didn't either. And the other delegates, where are they? Just as my eyes flutter open again, a twig snaps to my right. I freeze and try to tame my heart, which thunders in my chest. My eyes shift from left to right but I'm too scared to turn my head.

Footsteps approach. I'd never notice the faint sound if my senses weren't fine-tuned to every hint of danger nearby. The movement is quiet and cautious, which means someone is trying to sneak up on me. Which means they know I'm here. Dread crawls through my gut. *It can't be Beckett, he'd know better than to approach like this.*

I'm suddenly hyperaware of my aching muscles. Holding the same position, contorted between branches, is taking its toll on my body. I can't move though, I'm paralyzed with fear, and praying that whoever this is will walk right past me. Maybe they're here for another reason and I just happen to be close to their destination.

The footfalls stop. I can't tell how far away the person is since I don't dare turn my head. Just when I'm about to crack with anxiety, a hand shoots through the bush and taps me. I clamp my lips together to stifle a scream. *This is it, they caught me. There's no hiding or pretending that I'm invisible.*

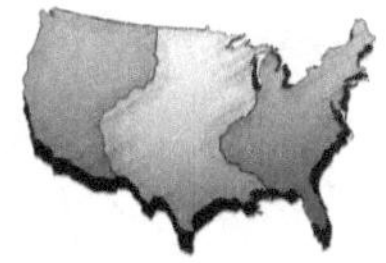

# CHAPTER 22 ~ CARO

## UPPER DIVISION, CENTRESTATES

The three of us shuffle as one awkward, uncoordinated unit. As we go, Zai tries to gain intel from the survivor weighing us down.

"What's your name?" Zai asks when the girl raises her head to look around.

"Ki . . . Kinsley." She squints her eyes closed and presses her lips together for a moment. "I don't . . . feel so good."

Zai and I share a worried glance. We have no medical equipment or even any real training. We have to get this girl to someone who can help her. And we have to hope they will be too distracted by the emergency to notice us. Our goal was to prevent any harm from coming to the delegates. Obviously we were too late – that plan literally blew up in our faces. Now, instead of extricating the ones from other Territories, we're trying to pick up the pieces, with no idea how many delegates may have survived.

"And are you a delegate, Kinsley?" Zai prods the girl.

"Yeah . . . yes." She doesn't offer any more information than what we ask, but she's also obviously in pain.

"Were there other delegates with you before we found you?" I ask gently, trying to keep eagerness from my tone.

"I . . . yes," Kinsley admits, pinching her eyes closed. "We all . . . we went . . . on a tour." A whimper escapes her and she bites her lower lip. "But then . . . it was just . . . light . . . heat . . . pain . . . smoke." She drops her chin to her chest and sobs. I gently rub her arm with my free hand as my motherly instinct kicks in. Luckily, my survival instinct is stronger. We're not going to get any useful information from her, so there's no point in prodding. I shift gears.

"Zai, where do we go from here?" I have to rely on the only one of us who's been here before. We can't drag this kid through the tunnels in her condition. Besides, she'd probably pick up some sort of infection from the filth and rodents that reside there.

"There's a safe house, just outside of Centrel Hall," Zai says as his eyes shift from me to Kinsley. I know what he's thinking – the same thing I am – then what do we do with her? Our best case is if this safe house has medical supplies, which I imagine are pretty hard to come by. But we can't reveal the location of a safe house to her. Especially one that close to the capitol building. As cold as it sounds in my own head, I wonder if we could leave her somewhere. Outside a medical building and hope someone notices her soon and takes care of her?

I share a knowing look with Zai. There's nowhere else to go – we've got to pierce the heart of the city. It's the belly of the beast. Imperant's castle. But it's our ultimate destination anyway. Maybe

Kinsley knows a way to get in other than blazing through the front door. *If only she was coherent.*

With each passing minute, her body grows heavier. I think she's shifting more of it to us as her muscles go limp. If we do reach Centrel Hall, maybe dragging in a wounded citizen would serve as a distraction and we could disappear into the shadows as people tend to her. We could subtly back away and put distance between us and this emergency before anyone even realizes we brought her in.

*I keep my mouth shut but slowly shake my head. It's just wishful thinking. All of it.*

# CHAPTER 23 ~ EVERLY

## UPPER DIVISION, CENTRESTATES

"Everly, it's me!" a deep voice whispers urgently. With my heart battering my chest and my lower lip trembling, I turn to the voice and squint through the branches. Familiar glasses and a mop of curly hair come into view.

"Hayes!" I exhale his name on a sigh of relief. Peeling away from the bush's clutches, I emerge from my hiding place. "What are you doing here?" I crash into him with a hug. It's awkward and stiff, but it's confirmation that he's real and not just a trick my mind is playing.

"I've been waiting here, watching for that old man," he says, dropping his eyes to the ground as if he's ashamed, or trying to find the right words. "We never saw him though. As soon as we got here, the streetlights flashed and then everything went dark for a minute before backup lights came on. Then I could really see the giant dust cloud, hovering right over where the power grid is. Or I guess I should say *was.*"

"Wait, where's Vanen?" I twist back and forth, searching for our friend.

"Vanen was . . . not feeling good. He couldn't stay here." Hayes cringes.

"What do you mean he couldn't stay? Where is he?" The words spring past my lips before I can stop them, accusatory with a hint of anger. *We just got him back, and Hayes left him alone somewhere?*

Watching me intently, he slides his glasses up the bridge of his nose. "He seemed like he was getting better but after you left, he collapsed and started throwing up, all over the sidewalk. He just kept heaving . . . and I didn't know what to do. When he finally stopped, he was dizzy and weak. He could barely walk." Hayes presses a palm to his forehead as if the memory makes his head ache. He seems too lost in his own thoughts to say anything else.

"So where is he now?" Although his anguish is palpable, I need to know more and Hayes is the only one with that information.

"I didn't know where else to hide him so I took him to the gardens. No one really goes there and it's pretty dark. And right now everyone's distracted by the explosion."

As if that triggers his memory of why we separated in the first place, he asks, "Did you find anyone there?" His eyes shift past me, undoubtedly searching for the other delegates.

My shoulders slump. "We found Lisum but . . . we couldn't . . . we couldn't help her. And we had to leave . . . people showed up and started yelling at us. We just took off and ran here."

"Yelling at you? Did they chase you? What about Beckett?" His voice rises on a wave of panic, as if he suddenly realized I'm here alone. Like him.

"No, we got away from them. And he's fine. He's sneaking around, trying to see if we can get inside Centrel Hall."

"For what?" He gulps, his face growing pale. Before I can explain anything else, Beckett returns, out of breath.

"Hayes, I'm glad you found us." A relieved smile crosses his face. Beckett's never been happy to see my counterpart from Eastates. Maybe that's what a life-threatening situation does to you. "Did you find Harley?"

"No, we didn't. And Vanen's gotten worse since you two left." Hayes wrings his hands together nervously. "He needs to go to the health center, but we can't exactly do that since there seems to be a target on our backs." He runs his hands through his hair, clenching a fistful of reddish-brown curls in each hand. His frustration is clearly mounting. "What are we supposed to do?"

"We have to get out of here," Beckett says coolly. "We know the explosion was on purpose, to target the delegates. Kiera wanted us all there. She's not about to let any of us just walk right out of here. We have to leave before she realizes we know what's going on."

"Did you find anything at the grid that would help us?" Hayes asks softly just before his foot twitches. I'd guess he's on the verge of pacing.

"We talked to Lisum but we didn't have much time with her. She told us to leave Centrestates." Beckett presses his lips together.

"And how are we supposed to do that? Did she say how?" Hayes demands. "What about Wynter? Was she there?"

"The only one we saw was Lisum and she could barely even talk! She was in pretty bad shape," I snap. His questions ignite a rage within me. My voice cracks as fresh tears sting my eyes. "What does it matter? They're all probably dead and you're asking about stupid details that don't matter!"

I squeeze my eyes shut and press both palms to my face. *This isn't the time to melt into an emotional blob.* I know that, yet I can't stem the tide of tears that flow. A strong arm wraps around my shoulders, tugging me against a warm chest. A fresh woodsy scent invades my senses.

"Look, when we first found her, she said something about how she should have known," Beckett says, clearly better equipped at controlling his emotions. I bury my face into his shirt, squeezing my eyes shut, blocking out everything but his voice. Our brief encounter with Lisum replays in my mind as he explains. "And she said we had to go before they find us."

Hayes gasps. "She warned you . . . she was trying to help you. If she was in on this plan, she wouldn't have said that." His voice rises and fades as he continues. *He must be pacing.* I'm not willing to tear myself from the comfort of Beckett's rising and falling chest to find out. I sync my breaths with his, savoring this simple connection.

"So she didn't know that the explosion was going to happen but she wasn't surprised about it either." Hayes' thoughts spill out freely, a stream of calculated theories churning through his mind. "She expected it, and she tried to warn you that you were still in danger."

"And we know that the only ones who could pull off something like this are Kiera and the almighty Societal Order leader!" Beckett interrupts, tightening his grip around me. "They were willing to destroy the most valuable resource they have. Something that supported everyone across all three Territories. And now, what's happening back home? Are they all sitting there, waiting for the power to come back on, thinking this is just a blackout or a minor glitch?"

"How about we talk about this when we're out of here? Like, really far away from here?" I lift my head to meet Beckett's gaze. Rage boils just beneath his surface, all of it justified. But it isn't helping us right now.

"She's right." Keeping his eyes locked with mine, he addresses Hayes. "Lisum told us to take the tunnels below Centrel Hall. The only problem is, there's a code we need to access that floor. Lisum was able to tell us three of the numbers before she . . . was gone . . . but she said it was four numbers."

"Okay, first we get Vanen, then we crack the code." Hayes turns on his heel and bolts down the sidewalk, glancing back once to make sure we're following him.

Beckett releases his embrace, tilts his chin down to meet my eyes and gently asks, "You ready?" When I nod, he scoops my hand into his and we barrel after Hayes.

***

Within minutes, we reach the gardens behind Centrel Quarters. At night, it looks like an impossible maze of hedges and brush. Although there are way too many places someone could be waiting to jump out and attack us, Hayes was right – it's a good place to hide Vanen. Two right turns and one left turn later, Hayes stumbles to a stop just before a wrought-iron bench. My heart drops when I see that it's empty. Dropping to the ground, he reaches beneath the seat, his hand disappearing into the shadows.

"Vanen!" he whispers. "We're back. Wake up!"

As Beckett and I crowd around him, my eyes adjust to the dimness. At the other end of Hayes' prodding fingers is a lump curled into a ball. It's not moving. Just as a knot tightens in my stomach, Vanen releases a low moan. Beckett hurries around the other side of the bench and reaches for our friend.

A few minutes later, the guys hoist Vanen up onto the seat and explain our plan. Shouting interrupts our quiet conversation. The echo of stomping feet bounces off the nearby buildings, honing in on us like a boomerang that could strike at any moment. We pause to listen, recognizing a systematic pattern in the footfalls. This isn't just random people running throughout the city streets. The stomping is organized, in unison. Beckett and I share a worried glance.

"Sounds like they're sending their security forces to the grid," Beckett mutters. "This may be a good time to sneak into Centrel Hall."

Vanen pushes off the bench, takes a wavering step and motions for us to go. Hesitation sweeps over Hayes' features, but Beckett turns his back on us and charges back the way we came. The three of us follow him, with Vanen leaning on Hayes for support. Beckett winds through the gardens until we pop out near the side of Centrel Quarters. From there, we sneak along the back of the building, clinging to any patch of darkness in our path.

Beckett stops a few feet away from a nondescript door. The single bulb dangling above it flickers in time with a low buzz. What a contrast from the front entrance. Where that one is glass and shiny silver, this one looks like an afterthought. *Maybe we'll catch a break and it's so forgotten that it's unlocked.*

Casting a hopeful glance our way, Beckett steps forward and grabs the handle. Squeezing his eyes shut, his arm pushes down but it's met with immediate resistance. Locked.

"Great. What now?" I mutter.

"We keep going," Hayes answers. "There's got to be a way in, other than the main entrance."

"You're right. We just keep going." Beckett nods toward Vanen. "You good, man?"

"I can do this," Vanen replies, standing a little straighter.

Without another word, we continue our search for a way into Centrel Hall. We pass two more doors, all locked. By the time we round the last corner of the building, we're out of options.

"Stay out here. I'm going in," Beckett announces. He raises a hand in the air to stop the immediate flurry of arguments Hayes, Vanen and I sling his way. "This is the only way. There's no chance four of us can sneak in there, but there's a chance one can."

"And then what?" I ask, my tone edging toward hysteria. "We just wait out here for what?"

"I'll get you in there. I promise." He takes my hands in his and wields those blue eyes at me. "All of you. I'm not leaving here without you."

Before any of us can protest, he turns and darts toward the main entrance.

"I sure hope he knows what he's doing," Hayes mumbles, pressing his fingers to his temples. Beside him, Vanen bends over, resting his hands on his knees. I can't tell if he's tired or about to retch.

"Yeah, me too." My foot taps the ground, fueled by the nervous energy fluttering through me.

The three of us wait, staying close to the mighty structure. We're technically out in the open, but with the flurry of activity happening just blocks away, we're less noticeable, gaining invisibility simply by staying put. We hear more than we see, but the frantic voices and screaming alarms confirm what we already know.

The city is falling apart. Lives are lost, and we all face an uncertain future. I can't – and don't want to – imagine what chaos could be erupting throughout the Divided States right now. *Are Dad and Easton okay? And Josli?* My heartbeat skyrockets as my anxiety surges. *We need to get out of here. And everything hinges on luck.*

After a few minutes, a uniformed man strides out of the building. His eyes sweep back and forth before landing on us. Satisfaction washes over his features as he raises a gun and points it at us. He quickens his pace, watching us intently as he approaches.

"You three! Stay right there!" he barks. He grabs the radio clipped to his collar and raises it to his mouth. "He was telling the truth. I got them."

# CHAPTER 24 ~ CARO

## UPPER DIVISION, CENTRESTATES

In the distance, vehicles barrel through the streets. Alarms scream and red lights flash, cascading over the surrounding buildings. Citizens clutter the sidewalks, gawking at the plume of smoke that draws emergency responders and, likely, Enforcers.

Avoiding any risk of interaction, we turn down a dark alley, hoping to evade the crush of activity. A few steps in, we nearly trip over a crumpled body face-down on the street. Zai mutters an obscenity under his breath. He untangles himself from his half of the human crutches we form around Kinsley. I slide my leg out farther for support. I can hold her up on my own, but I'm not sure for how long.

Zai cautiously steps toward the figure, leaning in for a better look. As he hovers just inches from the man's face, an eye flies open. "Help!" It's a throaty whisper but there's determination behind it. Streaks of crimson paint his blond hair, which clings to his head. His left ankle turns inward at an odd angle.

"What happened to you?" Zai looks him up and down. The man flinches as he tries to roll onto his back. His light hair is a rumpled mess and clothing is torn and marred by dark patches. *Burn marks?*

"I'm a . . . delegate," he breathes out. It's enough of an answer for Zai to respond. He plants a knee on the ground and helps the man turn to face us. I realize "man" isn't the right word. Cuts slice across his smooth skin and an inky bloodstain marks his right shoulder. He's still a kid, like the one who's been leaning on me for what feels like hours. I shift more weight to my other leg, but it does little to relieve the strain on my muscles.

"Can you walk?" Zai asks, easing the kid to his feet.

"I think so." He slowly rises on shaky legs, leaning on Zai for support. That's when he notices me, and my extra weight.

"Kinsley. You made it out. I didn't think anyone else survived." I squirm under the growing weight, but Kinsley doesn't respond. *Maybe she's unconscious.*

"She's in pretty bad shape," Zai says, nodding our way. "Let's get you both somewhere they can help you."

"I was trying to . . . get to Centrel Hall," the kid starts, cringing as he tries to find balance. "My leg . . . I think it's . . . broken."

"What's your name, son?" I ask, even though he hasn't even acknowledged my presence. I'm curious to know who he is, and if he knows his way around here better than we do.

"Callan," he grunts. "I'm a citizen here but I'm also a delegate . . . or what's left of them."

"You got that one?" Zai asks, jutting his chin toward the body currently weighing down mine.

"Not really," I admit. He chews his bottom lip. At least he knows better than to interject a snide comment. I know my capabilities, and bearing the weight of someone else won't be possible when we have blocks to cover while trying to avoid attention.

"All right then," Zai announces. "We make a line. Callan, you're on my left and Kinsley is on my right. We're stronger together, so use each other's strength."

"You said you were going to Centrel Hall, Callan. Can you guide us on which way to go?" I ask.

He nods. Once we start moving, at an awkward, uncoordinated gait, he calls out directions. "At the next street . . . turn right."

Of course he has no qualms about taking a direct route, leading us right through the gathering crowd. I share a side-eyed glance at Zai. We're way too noticeable. Besides carting around extra bodies, our mismatched clothing colors stand out.

*Why did we not wear Centrestates tan to come here?* We've scavenged more than a few Territory-assigned sets of clothing, so we have the supplies. It would have provided us some camouflage for situations like this. Instead, we all agreed to declare our loyalty to the Uprising by wearing all three Territory colors at once. While it easily identifies us to our undercover allies, it also clearly alerts our enemies that we aren't typical citizens.

We barely make it one full city block before Zai's patience grinds to a screeching halt. He stops abruptly and we all nearly topple onto him as the motion pulls us along like an accordion of paper dolls. Kinsley lifts her head slightly, but her eyes blink feverishly as if she can't possibly keep them open. Her posture relaxes again as her body goes slack.

"We need another way!" Zai grumbles before turning to Callan. "We can't get through all those people." He nods toward the city blocks ahead that buzz with curiosity and concern. "In case you didn't notice, we take up a lot of space, hauling your asses and all."

"Okay, okay . . . sorry," Callan says, shifting more weight onto his good leg, wincing from the movement. He takes a deep breath and repositions again, seemingly a little more relaxed. "We can take some side streets instead. That way." He points to an alley that looks dark and deserted compared to the hive of activity we were originally heading toward. The hint of a smirk plays across my lips. For once Zai's gruff impatience is going to help us.

As we skirt through the empty side streets, I notice the golden hue just beyond most of the windows we pass, even in the distance. It seems normal here – lights shining at night. But we're in the upper division, where energy is supposed to be conserved beginning at 6 p.m. I tuck that observation in the back of my mind and make a note to ask the others if they find the same during their missions.

Before I left Eastates, every neighborhood for miles was dark at night, conserving energy like ideal Societal Order citizens. But here, that doesn't seem to exist. And beyond that, the power source just exploded. How are all these buildings still powered with no interruption?

"Hey, you notice how the electricity still seems to be flowing even though the power source just collapsed?" My question is meant for Zai but Callan can't resist answering.

"It's the generators," he says proudly, even as he struggles to keep pace. His pain seems to fade as arrogance replaces all else. He looks back and forth animatedly before continuing. "Aaaaannnddd there just might be a super-secret alternate power source that they're testing. That may have kicked in."

The air rushes from my lungs. *Alternate power source?* I'm betting whatever this thing generates isn't being funneled to the other Territories. What's happening in Eastates right now? And Westates? Blackouts happen but are usually planned. If I'm right, it's just a matter of time before the other Territories realize they've been cut off. But how long?

"How would you know? That something they told the delegation about?" Zai asks casually. If I didn't know him, and that the questions running through my mind are mirrored in his, I'd actually believe he was just making conversation.

"My dad works in defense. He tells me stuff sometimes." Callan's back straightens as obvious pride washes over him. "I'll be working there too when I finish school."

We both feign being impressed. Inside my heart rockets. Makes me think of an ancient saying about keeping your friends close but your enemies closer. In this case, we need to make an exception, and quickly. The closer this kid is to us, the more danger we're in of being discovered. Zai shoots me a knowing look. I nod once before we lead the injured delegates to a bench that sits amidst a small patch of yellow flowers.

"Hey, what are you doing? We're almost there!" Callan demands as Zai guides him to sit while removing himself from being the kid's shoulder support. Without answering, Zai reaches for Kinsley's limp arm and wraps it around his neck, hoisting her off me and toward the bench. The momentary ease on my back and neck is quickly replaced with what feels like a thousand pinpricks. Pain radiates down to the small of my back.

"I asked you what's happening!" Callan's impatience soars. In the short time we've known him, he's gone from grateful to arrogant to demanding. His type is easy to recognize – volatile and selfish.

There's no way he'd help us sneak into the capitol building. He'd be too intent on announcing his presence, eager for the attention his injuries would warrant.

"We have to go," Zai says with finality. "Stay here. We got you close enough that someone will find you and help you." With a quick tilt of his head, I rush to his side and we continue toward Centrel Hall.

"Come back here and help us!" As we break into a jog, Callan's demands are swallowed by the urgency and confusion descending upon the city. His words fade away as we put more distance between us and them.

# CHAPTER 25 ~ EVERLY

# UPPER DIVISION, CENTRESTATES

Hayes, Vanen and I all wear the same look of shock – eyes wide, jaws dropped, lips poised but unable to form any sounds.

"All right, you're gonna line up single file and you're gonna walk through those doors nice and orderly, got it? And don't even think about trying anything. You run, I'll put a bullet in your leg. You try to attack me, I'll put one in your chest. You think you can outsmart me, I'll put one in your head."

*This is it. There's no way out this time.* Shooting me a look of utter misery, Hayes goes first. I follow with Vanen close behind. We trudge to the entrance. None of us wants to see what's awaiting us on the other side of the doors. It can only be a march to our extermination.

Kiera's probably waiting inside, giddy with eagerness to complete what she started tonight.

"Straight to the front desk!" our captor orders. My feet know exactly where to go, which allows me a moment to search the room for Beckett. I don't have to look too far. He leans against a chair behind the desk with his arms crossed. He watches with mild amusement as a Centrestates worker darts around him, maneuvering back and forth from one counter to another, answering phone calls and alternating between giving and receiving orders.

This must be their command center. Besides a couple of phones, half a dozen radios are scattered across the counter. The man turns toward us when he notices our approach. I immediately recognize him as the guard who caught us when Beckett and I snuck into Centrel Hall the last time.

His gaze rakes over Hayes and Vanen before it zones in on me. *He must recognize me too.* His eyes narrow, but before he can say anything, a radio beeps behind him. He rushes to answer it. As soon as he starts talking, another radio beeps, just a few feet away. When the guard finishes his conversation, he faces the man who brought us in.

"They need backup at the corner of Centrel and Seventh Street," he huffs.

"Where do you want these kids?" the man behind us asks.

"I can't babysit and answer all these lines!" The guard throws his hands in the air.

"Okay, so who can?" Although our captor's tone remains even, a twitch in his cheek tells me his patience is wearing thin.

Although I'd love to suggest that they just let us go, I save my breath. The guard scratches his chin and raises the radio clipped to his collar. "Could you come down to the first floor? I need your help with something."

He dismisses our captor with a stiff nod and tells Beckett to wait with the rest of us. Just as he squeezes in beside me, the elevator pings, drawing our full attention to the doors sliding open. *Please don't let it be Kiera.*

Relief smothers my nerves when the person who was just summoned steps off the elevator and heads in our direction. I curl a finger around Beckett's pinky and squeeze. He squeezes back. Taking a deep breath, I paint a neutral expression across my face. The smile trying to creep along my cheeks has to stay hidden, for now.

The janitor we met in Kiera's office, who's part of the Uprising, casually approaches the guard. He acts like he doesn't even notice us.

"Security is a little short-staffed right now, as you can probably figure," the guard says. "Could you take these four up to Miss Saign's office? Stay with them until I can alert her that we've located some of the delegates."

I shudder at his words. It feels like a tight band is wrapped around my throat, constricting my breathing. Of course he can't wait to tell Kiera that they have us. *The question is, how soon will she know and how long before she comes to see us? Hopefully long after the Uprising can get us out of here.*

"Sure, I was cleaning on that floor anyway. I'll keep an eye on them while I work." He shrugs, feigning disinterest. If we hadn't met him before, I'd believe that he either had no idea who we were or didn't care that we were delegates.

"Make sure you keep a close eye on them!" the guard calls as the janitor motions for us to follow him back to the elevator.

***

The smooth ride up is charged, but silent. We all share nervous glances, but none of us dares to speak. Our escort stares straight ahead. When we reach the eighth floor and the doors part, he charges into the hallway, raising a hand to motion for us to follow him. Lights spill out in patches from a few offices, but otherwise the hall is dark.

Without a word, he leads us to a door. Pulling it open, he tilts his head toward it. As we shuffle inside, my senses are assaulted by the stringent tang of chemicals. He flicks on a light and tugs the door closed behind him. Squished into the tight space, surrounded by buckets and brooms, I allow myself a quick exhale of relief. Only then do I notice Hayes and Vanen.

Vanen's face is scrunched and his fists are clenched. His stiff posture suggests he's in pain or in fear of what's to come. Hayes wrings his hands in a repetitive fidget. Both watch the janitor as if he's a venomous snake that could strike any second. They have no idea that this guy actually wants to help us.

"You guys, we're okay." I nod toward the janitor. "He's part of the Uprising. He can help us."

Confusion and distrust lurk in their narrowed gazes, which jump from me to Beckett to the janitor.

"It's true," he says, raising his hands innocently. "Otherwise, I would have taken you directly to Kiera's office, like I was told."

"If he was on their side, he'd have no reason to try to hide us," Beckett adds.

"Up until now, I've kept a low profile but tonight my cover gets blown. I'm getting you out of here." He slips his hand into his back pocket and digs out a folded piece of paper. "I found something in Kiera's office and I want you to take it."

Carefully unfolding it, he holds it up so we can all see. It's like a written version of the information broadcast. The headline immediately grabs my attention. And churns my stomach with nausea.

**Invited Delegates Double-Cross Divided States:** *Plot to Destroy Grid Uncovered*

What follows is a lengthy article with our names and photos – everyone but Saya and Callan. *I guess Kiera decided to paint them as innocent in all this.*

Hayes gasps, raising a trembling hand to cover his mouth. Vanen squeezes his eyes shut and massages his temples. Beckett's lips tighten into a thin line.

"This had to be printed before tonight's trip to the grid even happened." I spit the words out before pressing a fist to my mouth. The others must feel the same fury as me. There's no sense in rehashing it over and over. We all know that Kiera's plan all along was to set up a bunch of kids. And everyone will probably believe her.

"There's more," the janitor says. He reaches for a shelf just behind me that holds an army of spray bottles, each one brimming with a bright purple liquid. He retrieves a small stack of papers and fans it out before us, urging each of us to read what they say. My eyes skim the words, breezing over paragraphs and catching a few phrases, but I'm not sure what it is.

"This is just a small sample of what I found in Kiera's office," he explains. "I couldn't take much or she would have noticed." He shakes his head. "She has records of everything you've all said since you got here."

*How is that even possible?* With a renewed interest, we all take a few papers from him, studying the contents much closer. *Sure enough, he's right.*

Pages and pages of our conversations are documented in black and white. Some jump out, marked with an urgent yellow highlight, demanding immediate attention. Like when Callan told us about Centrestates having another power source. When we talked about seeing our INDs. When all the girls went to Saya's room to gossip. Anxiety coils through my stomach. They were listening to us this whole time.

Hayes and Vanen thought it was possible. We even tested it. Or thought we tested it. Kiera was smarter than that. Of course she wouldn't fall for some trap a couple of kids tried to set. This new layer of deceit makes my head throb and my stomach churn. Beckett's cheeks flush with fury while Hayes and Vanen whisper to each other.

"This is proof, all of it," the janitor says, reclaiming our attention. "And I'm sending it with you. We're getting you out of here. Take this to Eastates. We have a contact waiting there to intercept you. It's too dangerous for you to stay here any longer."

He motions to Beckett. "You see that brown box in the corner? Open it. Inside is a bag – a messenger bag. You wear it across your chest so it's always right under your nose, protected. No one can tear it off your back. There's also a weapon in there. It's just a knife, it's all I could manage, but it's something. Hopefully you won't need it."

Beckett slides the black, rectangular pouch out of the box and hands it to the janitor. He promptly snatches the pages out of our hands, returns them to his pile and slips them all inside the bag before zippering it closed.

"You should be the one to wear this." He thrusts it toward Beckett, who promptly grabs it, slipping it over his head and around his shoulder. "The rest of you are in Eastates blue, so you'll blend in better, but my contact can definitely keep his eyes open for a Westates citizen."

What he doesn't say is how easy it will be for anyone else to notice that Beckett's out of place. Until this delegation, I never saw a Centrestates or Westates citizen in person. *I just hope no Enforcers see him when we get there. If we get there.*

"Here's the plan." We all huddle closer together, hanging on every syllable the janitor says. Our bodies radiate heat in the cramped space, the stuffy air swelling with humidity as minutes pass. This closet was never meant to serve as a meeting room for five people. Swiping away the sheen of sweat coating my forehead, I listen to his plan.

When he finishes, he asks if we all understand. Four heads nodding serve as confirmation. He raises a finger to his lips in a "shhhh" gesture before cracking the door open. A glorious draft of air rushes inside, just enough to make my lungs crave more. After a glance up and down the dark corridor, he tiptoes out into the hallway. One by one we follow him.

We jog through the eerily quiet hall bathed in shadows. Our feet touch down softly but steadily. We're on a mission and our lives depend on it. We quickly reach the stairwell and push through the heavy door. Every creak and squeak bounces off the walls in an amplified echo, but we press on.

Racing all the way to the ground floor, the janitor stops and turns to us. Waving his hands to draw us closer, we converge into another huddle. "Once we're through this door, it's a straight shot to the underground subway. The entrance is locked down. Access is very limited down here."

"You can get us through?" Beckett asks.

The janitor nods. "Yes, there's a keypad and I have the code."

"A keypad?" I ask, a recent memory striking me like lightning. "Lisum tried to tell us a code but—"

"It doesn't matter, I know it." He cuts me off, raising a hand in the air in a silent "stop." "Now let's go!"

With a lump in my throat, I watch as he dashes through the door. Too soon, the others pass by and it's my turn.

# Chapter 26 - Everly

## Upper Division, Centrestates

"So what happens after we get past the door?" Hayes asks as we scurry down the corridor.

This is the first place I've seen in direct contrast to Centrestates' perfect image. It's like a blemish they prefer to keep hidden. Rough gray bricks run from floor to ceiling, forming worn walls that look as if they could crumble if one of us bumped into them. Shallow puddles of water pool on the uneven concrete floor every few feet. I scan the ceiling in search of the source. Half a dozen rusty pipes hover overhead, drops sneaking out of them, lazily jumping to the ground. White light pours from rectangular cages affixed to the walls, each holding a single bulb wrapped within thin metal bars.

"You're gonna hop on the high-speed train. It'll take you right into Eastates in about an hour," the janitor says casually, as if this is as simple as grabbing lunch in the cafeteria.

"How are we supposed to do that?" Vanen asks sharply, limping along as if his last bit of energy is draining out of him. "We can't just walk onto some train without someone seeing."

None of this sounds possible.

"Not many people know about this train," he promises so passionately that I almost believe him. "It runs back and forth all night, but there are only a handful of transporters each way and they're mostly caught up in shipments they're delivering and receiving because of their tight turnarounds. You'll see them securing doors, checking inventory lists. But even so, they only load the first two or three cars. The last ones are empty most of the time."

"So how do we get on one?" Beckett presses.

"Every two and a half hours, another train goes. Just climb onto the last car when you hear the engine start up. It's a skeleton crew. At that point, they'll be settling in for the ride while a driver is setting the controls. There are small windows, keep watching and when you start to recognize your neighborhood, jump."

"Jump?" He can't be serious.

"Once they get closer to the neighborhoods, they slow way down. But since it's night there now, no one should be out."

The four of us stare at him. *This is his plan?*

He drops a hand on my shoulder and leans toward me. "Go home. My contact will meet you outside your house."

I gulp as a shiver dances along my spine. *How much do these people know about me? Will the Enforcers in Eastates be looking for me too?* Before I can ask, we reach the last barrier separating us from the tunnels – the locked door. The janitor charges up to it and punches four numbers on the keypad. I can't see what they are but it really doesn't matter. Once I leave here, I'm never coming back.

A red light flashes once and a low buzzer grumbles from the keypad.

"Must've punched it in wrong," the janitor mutters, raising a hand to strike each number with more force than needed. The red light flashes twice this time and the buzzer sounds longer. Just then the radio attached to his hip beeps, startling all of us.

"Stay quiet," he mutters. As if any of us would dare speak. "Yeah, this is Joe."

"Joe, where the hell are you and those delegates?" an angry voice barks.

"Just getting them settled in the Unity Room. That's where you said to take them, right?" His tone is steady but the slight twitch in his cheek gives away his nervousness.

"I just checked the whole floor, Joe. No one's there."

Panic flashes through me.

"One of them had to go to the bathroom. Couldn't trust her to go alone. Soon as she's done, we'll be right back."

The line remains silent. My own shallow breathing fills my ears. The anticipation is worse than if the person on the other end said something. Any sort of acknowledgment. We all wait, so tightly wound that the next word spoken could shatter the thin veil of calm we only pretend to control. Staring at the radio, the janitor shakes his head.

"They already know," he mutters. "Stay here. I need to find the code!" Just before he barrels down the hallway, Hayes and Vanen protest, begging him to stay. He either ignores their pleas or doesn't hear them. The four of us watch as his silhouette is quickly swallowed by the shadows. We're alone.

"Maybe we can figure this out." Beckett turns to the keypad. "Lisum started to tell us . . . "

His reminder yanks me out of my thoughts. I focus on him, ignoring the fear rising within me.

"She said it was one, three . . . "

"Nine." Beckett completes my thought. "But we didn't get the last number."

"That's easy!" Hayes says. "We just enter one-three-nine and then start with zero and try each number in order."

The rest of us nod excitedly, eager for an escape. Hayes marches to the door and types in 1-3-9-0. This time the red light stays on and the buzzer sounds for a solid ten seconds. The buzzer and light stop abruptly.

"Warning. One attempt left before security lockdown is deployed. Warning," a robotic voice announces. Only then do I notice the small cluster of holes just above the keypad. It must be a speaker.

"Great . . ." Beckett mutters, pressing a palm to his forehead.

"That means we have to figure it out," I say. "Think! What could one-three-nine mean? Is there a pattern?"

Hayes and Vanen trade thoughts and guesses. "They wouldn't just pick random numbers. It must mean something."

A shout echoes in the distance, followed by the rhythmic thudding of heavy footfalls. My heart beats wildly as panic overtakes my whole body. Beckett silently jogs down the hallway, where the janitor just disappeared.

I steal a glance at Hayes and Vanen. Hands raised in frustration, they quietly argue. I can't make out anything they say, but it doesn't look like they're any closer to figuring out the code than the janitor was. Going against every instinct I have, I tiptoe after Beckett slowly.

He stops at the first bend in the walkway. Pressing his side up against the cold stone, he stares straight ahead, focusing all his energy on listening. His fingers flex around the strap of the messenger bag, tightening their grip.

"Never figured you for a traitor, Joe," a deep voice growls. "Now, tell us where those kids are and we'll go easy on you."

"They got away from me," a familiar voice answers. "I don't know where they are."

"We all know that isn't true." A few others murmur, echoing the same sentiment. *Isn't anyone else there from the Uprising? Can't someone help him?*

A single click splinters the rising tension.

"Put down that gun, Joe! Right now!"

Beckett's wide eyes slide to mine. His face is a portrait of misery and defeat. Dread coils deep in my core. *What are we supposed to do?*

"Last chance!" The guard barks the words out impatiently.

"Go to hell!" Joe shouts a second before the deafening burst of gunfire erupts. I drop my head and cover my ears instinctively. Beckett backs into me, stumbling for a second before he grabs my hand and tugs me into a run back to the guys. They both look up as we skid to a stop just inches from crashing into them.

"I've got it!" Hayes blurts out. "Three. It's three. One, three, nine, three!"

Vanen punches the numbers in and the light above the keypad flashes green. Hayes yanks the door open and they both rush through it without hesitation. As it starts to leisurely glide closed, I pass through the door, holding it open for Beckett. He pauses, catching my eyes for a moment. I narrow mine in confusion. *Why's he stopping? We finally got through.*

The bellow of stomping feet reverberate through the narrow space. And they're definitely growing louder, closer. Just as I motion for Beckett to hurry up, he unzips the bag clinging to his chest and shoves a hand inside, clearly scrambling for something. A moment later, he raises a knife – the only weapon we've got. Grasping the sharp edge, he rams the handle into the keypad. It's like he's channeling every ounce of fury he's ever felt into each hit. Blood drips from his clenched fist, the knife's blade slicing into his palm. He pounds the keypad half a dozen more times before I grab his free hand and drag him away. He pulls the door closed just as a group of guards charges toward us, demanding that we stop.

They shout and bang on the door as we tear away from the only barrier standing between us and them. At least it's still holding. If it wasn't, they'd already be out here cuffing us by now. A chill rushes over my skin and the dank, heavy air floods my nose and lungs as we spill into the tunnel. Its earthy scent and rock-laden walls that meld into a high arched ceiling confirm that we're underground. The massive passage extends behind and before us indefinitely. Luckily, our target is clear and straight ahead.

Three sets of tracks sink into the ground, one serves as a temporary resting place for a sleek white train that sits at the ready. It's nothing like the one that carried Hayes and me here. Its sleek, rounded nose and curved edges look like it was designed for pure speed. There can't be more than ten cars, each one with a mere four windows. The train that brought us here was mostly glass, offering views of everything before, beside and behind us.

"Come on!" Hayes whisper-shouts from several steps ahead of us. His shrill tone carries along the chilled breeze. A slight echo seems to spill into every pocket of air within the tunnel system. *Please don't let anyone hear us.*

He and Vanen stop so we can catch up. When we reach them, I notice how Vanen's face pales and his chest heaves. Even in the dim light, his forehead glistens with a sheen of sweat. *It's freezing down here.* I watch him closely, wondering if he's still feeling the effects of whatever they injected him with. He should be shivering, like me.

"I can't," he says. "I can't go any farther. It's too narrow, too close. I just can't." His shoulders slump and his gaze drops in shame.

As he clasps one hand around Vanen's shoulder, Hayes' intense gaze conveys more than his words. "This is our only chance. If you stay here, you're dead. I don't know what's going through your head, but you have to push past it. There's no other way."

"We have to keep going. Now," Beckett grinds out through his teeth. Hayes turns to us. "Go ahead. We'll catch up."

"N–" Before I can even object, Hayes raises a hand in the air. He grabs my shoulders and meets my eyes. "I can get through to him. I know I can. But you two need to go." When Beckett and I stare at him in disbelief, he adds, "I promise, we'll be there. But it's too much for him with all of us. Just leave us be. I can talk him through it."

Beckett's lips fade into a thin white line but he says nothing. He turns on his heel and continues along the dark path, cradling the hand that gripped the knife blade against his side. Hesitation tugs at his pace, but self-preservation pushes his feet forward.

Before following Beckett, I pause and try one last time. "We're almost there. We just have to get on that train and it'll take us home. I don't want to leave you behind, but we can't stay here."

Vanen squeezes his eyes shut as his lower lip trembles. Tears sting my eyes as I scurry away. We can't force Vanen to come, but I'm not giving up the only chance I have to escape this place. The janitor died and it can't be for nothing. In a burst of unhinged fury, I sprint to

Beckett, catching up to him. Relief washes over his features when I tug on his shirt to stop him. He motions toward the last car on the train, which is also the one closest to us. A panel of lights runs along its ceiling, illuminating the inside, and how empty it looks from our vantage point.

"Let's just sneak up to that one and hope the door's unlocked."

I nod. Before we take one step, the train's engine rumbles to life, signaling that our time to act is slipping away like sand in an hourglass. With one last glance in every direction, Beckett grabs my hand and we race to our target, climbing the few steps leading to the car's entrance.

Beckett presses his face to the narrow window and scans the car. His shoulders drop in relief. *No one's in there.* His hand lands on the handle and twists. Shoving the door open, he motions for me to slip inside.

# CHAPTER 27 ~ CARO

## UPPER DIVISION, CENTRESTATES

We slip through the shadows in near silence. Sounds in the distance – alarms, voices, machinery – stifle any noise we make, like the soft thud of our footfalls. This is one of those rare times when Zai and I are completely compatible. Every wink, nod and gesture speaks when we are unwilling to utter a sound. Nonverbal communication is a skill every Uprising leader learns. It's saved us many times over. Today is no different.

When Centrel Hall's main entrance falls into our line of sight, we stop and crouch down to evaluate the level of activity at each entry point. Zai raises a finger, pointing to a dark path that winds around the back corner of the building. I nod once, only to cringe when a voice calls out from behind us.

"You there. You lookin' fur trouble?"

*What did we walk into now?* In unison, Zai and I slowly stand and turn toward the voice. My eyes narrow as I take in the person it belongs to. A scraggly old man smirks at us, his knowing gaze tracking up and down our bodies. He recognizes the Uprising's informal uniform. With as little movement as possible, I dip my right hand toward my pants pocket, inching my way down. I'd feel better having a weapon within grasp before verifying if this guy's friend or foe.

Zai raises his hands in a non-threatening manner, and takes a step, approaching the old man. "Harley?"

"That would be me." The man flashes a smile, minus a few teeth, and nods to Zai. "Ya look familiar."

"Zai. I believe we've met before." They close the gap between them and Zai extends a hand, which the old man grasps and shakes.

"And who ya got with ya?"

"This is Caro Scott. She's one of our leaders. You can trust her."

*I never thought I'd hear those last few words pass Zai's lips when it comes to me.*

Harley silently evaluates me. I can sense his distrust even after Zai's vote of confidence. Without being asked, I hike up the pants leg on my left side and spin in place to show him my tattoo. The U symbol demonstrates my conviction to the cause. He bends down, inspecting it closely. Once he's satisfied, he straightens and turns away from us, throwing a hand through the air in a "follow me" motion. With exactly no other options, we do.

I wish we found this guy sooner. Or rather that he found us sooner. He leads us through walkways so narrow we have to form a single-file line. He must have been planted here for many years. It's obvious by his ease in navigating through parts of the city that are obviously less traveled. Although we pass no other souls, his head constantly swivels back and forth and side to side. I appreciate his cautious nature.

Finally we reach a building at least two dozen floors tall. He leads us inside. The hallway is lined with doors, each labeled with a number-letter combination – 1A, 1B, 1C, and so forth. These must be dwellings. We take the elevator to the top floor. When the doors part, Harley winds through the hallway until we reach the door labeled 12E.

He knocks on the door – six dull raps in quick succession. Someone on the other side mimics the sound and Harley responds with three sharp knocks. The handle twists and the door slowly swings open. With no hesitation, Harley slips through it, guiding us inside.

As soon as the door closes, he announces, "This's our comms center." He pauses, letting us survey our surroundings. It's not the typical living space I expected, although you would never know from the outside.

The walls are covered in large gray squares. They're some sort of foamy material. Patterns of lines rise and fall across each square. *Maybe it's some sort of soundproofing material?*

Centered in the main room are three curved desks spaced about a foot apart. If there was one more, they would make a complete circle. Instead, that opening appears to be an entrance and exit point for whoever uses the desks. The flat surfaces are loaded with electronic devices, some I recognize – like two-way radios – and others I don't. Lights flash on some, frantically demanding attention, while others appear to simply collect dust. A cluster of monitors sits directly above each desk.

Two women and one man occupy wheeled seats within the configuration. Their backs are to us and they ignore us completely. But they obviously know we're here. Someone opened the door. Whoever it was must have rushed back to their seat.

The man and one of the women alternate between talking and listening on handheld radios. Their conversations overlap each other and mingle with intermittent static when it's their turn to listen, so I can't make out what anyone is saying. The third one, another woman, types on a keyboard as her eyes shift from one screen to the next in front of her. This one room must account for more than all the power my old neighborhood back in Eastates was allotted during their twelve dwelling hours each day. And yet it goes unnoticed here.

A hallway leads to a few other open doors, but since no noise comes from them, I assume the only occupants are the ones we see. I look at Zai, but his expression is unreadable. As it should be. I hope my own is too, but beneath the surface a rush of pride sweeps through me. This is all part of our mission, and these people believe in it enough to defy their own Territory.

When we both turn to Harley, ready to make our next move, he leads us into what looks like a small kitchen. Two windows are just above the sink. Various equipment litters the counters, including a telescoping lens aimed at the glass. Harley motions for us to take a closer look. Zai leans forward and peers into the smaller end. A smirk plays across his face as he pushes back and steps aside so I can look.

This little apartment, with its devices and flow of information pouring in and out, also happens to be positioned directly across from Centrel Hall. And I'm guessing the office we're staring into belongs to Societal Order Leader Kirill Imperant.

# Chapter 28 ~ Everly

## Upper Division, Centrestates

As soon as we push through the opening, we both drop to the floor. Even though we haven't seen anyone near the back of the train, it doesn't mean they won't show up any second. The engine's churning grows louder, bouncing off the stone walls encasing the otherwise subdued underground station.

Beckett points toward a seat but instead of sitting on it, he crawls beneath it, contorting himself to fit in the confined space. I tuck myself under the seat next to him. Guilt over leaving Hayes and Vanen behind douses any relief I might have felt for making it this far. Although I watch the door, willing them to walk through it, my eyes are drawn to a trail of crimson drops. The erratic line they form stains the scuffed tan flooring and leads right to Beckett. *His hand!*

"We have to wrap that up with something. You're bleeding everywhere," I whisper, scanning the cabin for anything useful.

"Wait until we're in motion," he says, waving me off. "Just want to be sure no one's planning to check this car before we go. Besides, Hayes might still need help to get Vanen on here."

A grinding squeal blares from the front of the train just before the floor vibrates. *This thing's ready to take off.* The door swings open with so much force that it slams into the side wall. My heart stops. It takes every ounce of self-control within me to swallow the scream clawing at the back of my throat. I scrunch into the tiniest ball I can manage beneath the tan cloth seat, bracing to be captured.

But no one shouts or hurls threats or accusations at us. I peek at the approaching figure's legs to find that it's actually two sets of feet, clumsily shuffling inside the car. Leaning forward to get a better look, relief strikes me like a bolt of lightning. Peeling myself out of my hiding spot, I jump up.

"Hayes!" Terror flashes across his features before his mind comprehends that it's just me. He visibly relaxes for a moment, even as he struggles to regain his footing. That's when I notice that he's not just helping Vanen, he's supporting all our friend's weight. In a flash, Beckett pushes past me to help them. Wrapping an arm around Vanen's waist, he leads the guys to a seat.

Beckett mumbles something to Hayes before they lower Vanen's body to the floor and drag him under the seats across the aisle from the ones Beckett and I claimed. Once he's settled into the best hiding place we can offer, Beckett and Hayes promptly drop to the floor. Suddenly feeling exposed, I follow them, retreating back to my piece of the floor.

"What happened to him? Is he okay?" I ask.

"Fine. He just passed out again." Hayes slides his glasses off and pinches his eyes closed for a moment.

With one last screech, the train starts rolling. After a few minutes, Hayes explains that he just kept trying to convince Vanen to get on the train. But claustrophobia froze him in place and no words could make him budge. Vanen begged Hayes to leave him, but Hayes refused. Their loyalty to each other stabs at my heart. Shame washes over me. *I was willing to leave them both behind.*

When the train's engine started rumbling, Vanen's breathing skyrocketed until he was hyperventilating. Hayes was trying to get him to calm down when he just crumpled like a rag doll. Hayes caught him before he hit the ground, but it was a struggle to get onboard.

"Sorry we left you. I thought maybe he'd come once he saw us go," Beckett mutters, cringing as he wraps his fingers around his injured palm. Once again I search the cabin for something, anything, we can use to wrap the cut.

"Where's the knife?" I ask. Beckett's eyes narrow before he unzips the pouch again and presents the bloodied blade to me. I snatch it from his hand and promptly dig it into the seat closest to me, tearing into the smooth tan cloth. Both guys watch with interest as I slice a strip about twelve inches long. Brushing off a few specks of lint, I set the knife down and gently lead Beckett's injured hand toward me. I carefully wrap the cloth around his hand and attempt to tuck the end under a crease. I doubt it will stay, but at least something is there to stanch the bleeding. With that taken care of, I focus on Hayes.

"We should have been there to help you," I mutter.

Hayes runs a shaky hand through his auburn curls. "Honestly him passing out was the best thing that could have happened. He never would have left that tunnel." Just as the words pass his lips, we burst out of the confined passage, breaching the night. All three of us fall silent as the enormity of everything that's happened engulfs us. *Are we the only delegates left? Does the weight of our innocence fall on our shoulders?*

As we gain momentum, I crawl out from under my seat and kneel on it, pressing myself to the window. I allow myself one last look at Centrestates and what I hope to never see again. A haze of fog distorts the city skyline. The rising column of smoke where the grid used to sit is clear even in the darkness. The buildings are nearly all lit again, the benefactors of whatever alternative power source Kiera had waiting.

Red lights flash, bouncing off the tunnel walls we just screamed past. I didn't notice them before but they're impossible to miss now. Turning away from the disappearing Territory, I yawn and return to my little nest, letting my eyes rest closed for just a moment.

"You should try to sleep," Beckett says. "I'll stay awake and watch for signs that we're getting close to a neighborhood."

"You've never even been to Eastates! You won't know when we need to get off the train!"

"But I will." Hayes sits between two seats, resting his arms on his bent knees. His gangly limbs would never fit in the small space I've crammed myself into. "Get a little rest, Everly. That way you'll be fresh when we get to your house."

I gulp past the knot in my throat. That's right, the janitor said someone from the Uprising would meet us at my house. *I wonder if they're at the house right now, if they've woken Dad up.* The rocking movement tugs me into a lull. Just as my mind starts to drift, a question springs to mind.

"Hayes!" Both guys startle when a memory sparks unintended urgency in my tone. A past conversation with Beckett returns, insisting that I ask the question we were both unable to answer at the time.

"What? What is it?" Hayes twists his neck back and forth, searching for a threat his eyes wouldn't locate until it was too late anyway.

"Sorry! I just remembered something I wanted to ask you." Beckett's hunched shoulders drop slightly, relinquishing their defensive stance with my confirmation of a false alarm. He rolls his eyes, slowly shaking his head.

I turn to Hayes. "How did you figure out the code? What was the last number?"

His shoulders drop and he releases the breath he was holding. I can tell what he's thinking: "That's what you just had to know at this exact moment?"

"So the first three numbers, the one-three-nine, those could also look like letters." He smirks, unable to contain his pride. At least it helped him forget the panic he felt just a moment ago. "Like an I, M and P, as in Imperant. So I thought maybe the next letter would be an E. If you twist that around, it could be another three. And that's what it was."

"You really are brilliant, and you saved our butts back there." My own lips part into a smile. Of all the people I could have come here with, I was lucky it was Hayes.

"Yeah, nice going," Beckett adds. With that, we fall silent, the weight of everything that's happened finally taking its toll. Hayes stretches his arms and yawns before lying down on a seat. It looks almost comical. He's way too tall to fit – his long legs form a bridge across the aisle, his feet resting on those seats.

I curl into a ball and use my arm as a pillow. As my eyes drift closed, I watch Beckett press his back to the wall behind him, pulling his knees in to rest his elbows on. His hands dangle in the air, slightly swaying with the train's rhythmic movement. It lulls me into a false comfort and I surrender to exhaustion.

***

"You guys, wake up!" As my eyes flutter open and my mind returns to consciousness, I recognize the voice. Hayes darts between me and Beckett, going back and forth, shaking each of us until we respond.

"What's going on?" Beckett asks, his voice scratchy.

"Yeah, what?" I yawn and rub my eyes. When they adjust to our surroundings, I notice Vanen sitting in a seat, awake. "Hey, good to see you alert. You are alert, right?" He runs a hand through his dark hair.

"I am. Thanks for getting me out of there." His gaze shifts to each of us, a mix of appreciation and comprehension. Maybe the drugs are finally wearing off, whatever it is they gave him.

"It was no–"

"There's no time for this right now!" Hayes cuts me off. "We're moving in the wrong direction. And we're going much slower." He gulps before continuing. "I think they know we're on this train and they're taking us back to Centrel Hall."

"What?" The last remnants of grogginess fade as panic shoots through me.

"Just look out the window. This isn't the way we were going when we left. I bet the guards who chased us into the tunnels just radioed to whoever's driving this train and told them to come back so they can look for us." Hayes paces, rubbing his temples. "We're sitting ducks."

Beckett jumps to his feet and scrambles to the door. He grabs the handle and pulls. Nothing happens. He tries again, grunting with exertion. Vanen rises and joins him. Together they try at the same time, struggling to keep their footing. The door doesn't budge.

"It must have a locking mechanism that's controlled in the main car," Hayes mutters. "Great. Just great."

Beckett turns from the door, his wild eyes searching. His gaze slides from the window to the back of the compartment. He nods toward Vanen and Hayes. "Help me rip that pole out of the floor. We'll use it to smash the window."

I don't say it but the last thing I want to do is jump off a moving train, even if it's slow. That could break a bone or who knows what else. We don't even know what's out there. What if we're on an incline right now and the only thing surrounding the tracks is a cliff that drops into a never-ending chasm?

I must be the only one thinking that because all three guys grab hold of the pole. They count to three and pull. It groans and shifts a little but holds. They huddle together for a moment before each of them plants one foot on the ground and presses the other to the pole. On the count of three, they all push once again, this time with the force of their legs.

After a few minutes of straining, the shiny silver pole buckles. It spurs their motivation. All three wrap their hands around it and pull, channeling their strength into one fluid motion. They yank it free. When they pause to catch their breath, I notice that the crude bandage wrapping Beckett's hand is soaked with blood.

"Your hand!" I point. He flinches, as if he just noticed the pain. "I'll cut another strip of cloth." I wish we had something to clean the cut with.

Vanen steps forward, claiming the downed pole and rushing to the other end of the car. "Take care of his hand. I'll break the glass."

I rush back to the seat I already damaged to cut another strip of fabric, stealing glances at Vanen every chance I get. Grasping the pole like a baseball bat, he winds up and strikes the window with deadly force. I wonder if he's fueled by pure adrenaline, and a drive to escape. Not too long ago, he was completely unaware we're even on a train.

The pole bounces off the glass, leaving a small spiderweb of cracks in its wake. Vanen repeats the process, three more times, targeting the same spot, trying to capitalize on its weakness. But it doesn't break through.

"It must be shatterproof." Hayes winces as he paces up and down the aisle. "Unbreakable."

His chest heaving, Vanen drops the pole in defeat. It smacks the floor with a loud clang and rolls sideways away from us. I squeeze my eyes shut and sink to the floor. There's no escape. We're not getting out of here. I'm never going to see home again.

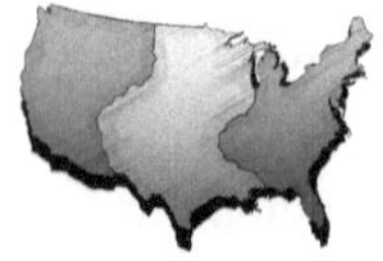

# CHAPTER 29 ~ CARO

## UPPER DIVISION, CENTRESTATES

"That there's Imp'rent's office." Harley points to the exact place my eyes focused on. "We don't jest watch, we hear too." He flashes us a toothy smile, which is actually more gums than teeth.

"You've got his office wired?" The question spills out before I can stop it. Zai turns his head, sliding his narrowed eyes my way. I know what he's thinking: *Let the man explain.* My excitement got the better of me. I clamp my mouth shut and listen as Harley explains their setup here and all that he's seen and heard since they perfected the configuration.

While the communications center has been running for nearly a year, the surveillance on Imperant's office is new. They've been testing and tweaking it for several months and just got everything functioning within the past few weeks. I want to devour every last detail, but time is ticking away.

After he's told us what we need to know right now, he asks, "Did yah come here ta act'vate us?" His eyebrows jump in anticipation. I exchange a look with Zai. It's time. This guy is a loyal member of the Uprising and if we're going to ask him and others to risk their lives, he deserves to know.

"Yes," I answer, quickly adding, "Although we're hoping it doesn't result in casualties."

"I doubt that's possible," Zai grunts. "Imperant's the problem, and if the other two Societal Order leaders aren't willing to get on board with us, then we won't have any other choice but to make them all disappear."

Genuine pleasure slides across Harley's face, in the form of a wide grin that reveals a few missing back teeth in addition to the ones I noticed earlier. *This man does not fear violence.* I understand Zai's drive to end the Societal Order altogether, but if he had his way, too many innocents would pay for his impatience. I'm not willing to have that blood on my hands. And in the end, I think he'll be grateful to avoid that too. *If we both make it out of here in one piece.*

"There's a few things we'll need and I'm hoping you can help us out, Harley. First thing is more bodies. You got any connections here?" Zai asks Harley. "Any recruits who are loyal to the Uprising?"

Harley flashes us another grin. "I can round 'em up. Whad yah have in mind?"

"For my plan to work, we need a small army along with a few, very specific connections."

"Cons'der it done." The old man crosses his arms and raises his chin. Any hesitation I may have felt about him is gone. He's key to this plan succeeding. And he's clearly committed.

"Harley!" one of the women seated at the monitors calls out. "We're picking up a communication from the high-speed train." She presses a small black device to her ear and holds it in place. Her eyes widen as she listens to whatever conversation is happening. "They believe three delegates attempted to escape." Her eyes shift nervously as she focuses on what she's hearing in order to convey it to us. "They were headed for Eastates but they turned it around and they're coming back. They believe the delegates are on board that train. Security forces will meet them at the tunnel station to take them into custody."

Zai and I practically pounce on Harley, barking out our thoughts at the same time.

"We have to go now!" Zai booms.

"Where?" I demand. "Where can we intercept the train before it reaches the station?" Emotions rattle my nerves but my mind is sharp enough to form the only question that matters. If they truly are delegates and they were hitching a ride to Eastates, I bet they were trying to get home. And if that's right, there's a good chance Everly is one of them.

"Jest inside the tunnel," Harley calls as Zai and I head to the door. "Ye want help?"

"Not yet," Zai says confidently. "We can get there. Just be ready for us when we get back. Everything we talked about, what you can provide, be ready to go."

"Aye, aye," Harley says, saluting us both. "I'll have the team ready an' waitin'."

# CHAPTER 30 ~ EVERLY

# UPPER DIVISION, CENTRESTATES

"You are not authorized to be aboard this train," a voice booms from the ceiling as yellow lights flash along the inside walls of the car. We all duck as if we're under attack. "Sit down and remain seated until this train comes to a stop. There are consequences for damaging Centrestates' property."

"What are we gonna do?" Hayes asks, his voice cracking like a brittle branch in a harsh wind. He presses both palms to his head and paces. "We're done. This is it for us."

"No it's not," Beckett mutters before he retrieves the knife. Holding it flush against his leg, he lowers himself into the nearest seat. I scramble to sit beside him while Vanen ushers Hayes to the row across from us.

Time slows to an agonizing pace as the train decelerates. We sit in silence, awaiting our capture. Our only defense is Beckett lunging at someone with a knife. I'm sure they have guns and outnumber us by a lot. I bite back the tears as pressure builds behind my eyes. A lump catches in my throat as my heart batters my chest. When we finally roll to a stop, I let my head drop forward and my shoulders slump in defeat. The door clicks before it whooshes open. I don't even look.

"Put your hands over your head, stand up and walk over to me," a gruff voice barks. Like obedient robots, we all rise and do as we're told. Beckett cuts in front of me, motioning for me to stay behind him. I understand. If he decides to use the knife, he wants a clear path to his target.

We step cautiously toward the man and the gun he wields, aimed directly at us. As we draw nearer, his eyes narrow and he leans closer. Dropping his voice to just above a whisper, he asks, "Did Joe make it out?"

When none of us answers, he asks again. "Where's Joe?"

"Who's Joe?" Beckett asks. His arm twitches nervously. The glint of silver reminds me that he's holding the knife.

"The guy who got you here," the man huffs out impatiently. "Where is he?"

"The janitor," I mutter, dropping my gaze to the floor. "He didn't . . . he couldn't come with us."

"He stayed back, trying to hold off all the guards. They knew he was helping us," Beckett explains.

"Dammit!" the man snaps, taking a step back. He regains his composure quickly and holsters the gun.

"Look, you don't have much time. You're not going to Eastates. Everyone here is looking for you and they won't stop until you're in custody." His words spill out in hushed but controlled instructions.

"We're still a little ways from the station but you need to get off this train before we make it back there. You need to get to Harley. Do you know him? Can you find him?"

"The . . . the old man," Beckett confirms.

"Yes, but you have to be inconspicuous. You have to find him without drawing any attention to yourselves or him." He pauses for a moment before adding, "Now give me the knife."

Beckett and I share a glance. *How did he know?* Without questioning it, Beckett hands the man our only weapon. He's obviously on our side.

In the blink of an eye, he turns it on himself and slashes it across his chest, releasing a low grunt. Red lines seep through the sliced fabric, exposing one long gaping wound. As if nothing just happened, he thrusts the bloodied blade toward Beckett. "Take it. You'll need it."

Reluctantly, Beckett takes it from him. We all watch as the man unclips a pair of handcuffs from his belt. He affixes one around his wrist and attaches the other to the pole we didn't rip out of the floor. "We're just inside the tunnel that connects to Centrel Hall. I was supposed to secure you for the rest of the ride since you started smashing things up." We all shift uncomfortably. He's not wrong, but we also didn't exactly have many options. When no one speaks, he continues.

"I'll radio the control car and say I've got you secured. By the time they figure out you're gone, we'll be back at the station. When they find me, I'll give them a story about you overpowering me after I reported in. Now get out of here. Run through the tunnels. Take the first exit on the left to get to the street. Then find Harley. Stay out of sight."

After just a moment of consideration, Beckett brushes past him and slips out the door. Like shadows chasing after him, Hayes, Vanen and I follow. We burst through the door, spilling out at the foot of the tunnel I thought I'd never see again. Or at least hoped I'd never see.

"This way." Beckett points. That man, another member of the Uprising, just bought us some time. Not much, but maybe it's just enough to give us a chance. We run, not exactly at full throttle, but as fast as we can move without making too much noise. Especially since every time our feet touch down on the dirt floor, it sends an echo ahead, like a warning signal.

The train's wheels slowly start turning, carrying it back to the station where we found it. The sound helps drown out any noise we make. Out of the corner of my eye, I glance at Vanen every few minutes. If he panics again in the tunnel, then what? This time no one's leaving him behind.

"You think we can find Harley?" I ask no one in particular.

"We have to," Beckett grinds out. He's right. There's nowhere else for us to go. No one here is going to help us, except for the Uprising, but we don't know who is an ally until they reveal themselves.

As we near the tunnel's massive opening, Vanen cringes, stumbling. His steps slow. I'm the first to notice. "Guys, hold up!" I call to Beckett and Hayes. They both skid to a stop and turn to face me. Immediately their eyes shift to Vanen. They bolt toward him, concern and understanding washing over their features.

"Vanen, we have to do this," Beckett says before he even reaches our friend. "Just don't think about it and run." Vanen's lower lip trembles and he starts to shake his head. Before he can say anything, Beckett motions to me and Hayes. "We block him in and then we run like hell. He'll keep up."

The guys meet each other's gaze for a moment before Hayes nods. His lips disappear into a tight line, temporarily restraining his worry. Beckett slides a glance my way before turning back to the path. We surround Vanen as best we can with our bodies and awkwardly run, trying to match pace. With no choice other than to crash into us, Vanen nervously tries to keep up. Even in the dimness, his face pales. But he stays with us, the center of our little herd.

My mind wanders as we run. It feels like the train ride to get here was a lifetime ago. Hayes and I were so excited to see every inch of the world just beyond the windows. There was so much we never imagined we'd get to see, and it all felt within reach. We zipped across miles effortlessly. Back then my biggest worry was whether Hayes or I got the window seat. Now I don't know if I'll ever see my dad or Easton ever again. Or home.

We stay close, moving as one unit, through the dank tunnel. The farther in we go, the more cautious we have to be. Every hundred steps or so, Beckett throws a hand up and we stop to listen for any movement other than our own. After a few tense seconds of trying to calm my thundering heart, and confirming it's the only other nearby sound, we continue.

Yellowing bulbs dangle from the side walls. Almost every third one is out, adding to the somber, eerie calm. A sudden chill passes through me, sending a wave of goosebumps over my arms and legs. The scuffle of feet echoes behind us. A beam of light pierces the thick air just over my shoulder. Dread coils in my stomach.

"There they are!" a deep voice bellows. A man comes into view, screeching to a halt several feet away, as if we're somehow dangerous. He sweeps a flashlight across the tunnel, pausing as it lands on each of us. "We know what you've done. We found the bodies." *What's he talking about? We didn't hurt anyone . . . but maybe Kiera's set it up to look like we did. Right after we blew up the power grid.*

Another voice calls to us, his tone sharp. "You are not authorized to be here, and the Societal Order has issued warrants for your temporary custody. Come with us now. If you continue to flee, you will be considered fugitives of the Divided States, subject to apprehension in any Territory or division."

Our little formation crumbles as we each contemplate what to do. *Nowhere is safe.* It doesn't matter if we stay here or go home. My feet stumble as I stifle a sob. There's no choice really. Hayes glances at me, surrender tugging at his lanky frame. His shoulders droop and his pace slows. Vanen's deflated posture reveals his misery. Just as I'm ready to raise my hands and surrender to our fate, one word slices through my anguish.

"Run!" Beckett's strangled whisper, laced with intensity, scares me more than if he shouted the simple command. Fear sizzles in my veins. Each heartbeat pulses in my ears, amplified in a sweeping rush. It muffles the steady thump of feet pounding behind us.

I don't dare look back, even when a grunt and scuffling scrape promise to overtake me. Sure enough, half a breath later, they do. A solid mass catapults into my back as if there's a target painted between my shoulder blades. My palms and knees skid along the gravelly surface, the force raking me over every sharp rock and crack. The blue fabric of my standard wear clothing offers only a thin barrier of protection, and it shreds instantly. Burning pain sears my palms and knees, but I can't afford to let it slow me down.

Adrenaline coaxes me to rise on unsteady feet, but before I can gain a sense of balance, a hand wraps around my ankle. I twist, retracting my other foot so I can aim and launch a series of kicks at my attacker. Facing down my enemy, I recoil when I recognize the curly mop of hair and gangly limbs.

"Sorry! I tripped!" Hayes mutters. "And I landed on my glasses. Everything's a blur!" He releases me from his grip while Vanen takes this opportunity to catch up to us.

Beckett skids to a stop, kicking up a haze of small stones. "Come on!"

Shouting erupts behind us. Beckett grabs my hand and pulls me toward him. When Vanen helps Hayes up and joins us, we start running again. A blast echoes through the tunnel, chased by a scuffling sound and a cry of agony. Two more rapid blasts pierce the air.

"Get down!" Beckett yells. His command fuels our instincts as we all drop to the ground and huddle together.

"We can't outrun bullets," Hayes mutters, pulling his knees to his chest.

"He's right," Vanen grumbles. "We have to give up. We can't keep running to nowhere, not when they're shooting at us."

We stay in place as heavy footsteps thud in their rapid approach.

"There . . . they . . . are!" a woman says in between gasping for air. I squeeze my eyes shut, blocking out the reality that is our inevitable fate.

"I knew we'd . . . find them," a male adds, catching his breath.

I realize my fingers are entwined with Beckett's when he slowly starts to stand and takes my arm along with him. Opening my eyes, I watch his features, which soften instantly. That's when I look at our captors. They aren't guards though. They wear mismatched clothing that makes it impossible to identify where they're from. The puzzle clicks together when Beckett utters one word.

"Dad?"

# CHAPTER 31 ~ EVERLY

## UPPER DIVISION, CENTRESTATES

The tall, gruff-looking man with dark hair charges to Beckett and clamps a meaty hand around his shoulder. "I knew you'd make it out of there, son." Even as the darkness cloaks most of his face, I see a smirk tug Beckett's lips upward. "Of course I did. Was there ever any doubt?"

"Of course not." The burly man wraps Beckett in a bear hug. I watch with fascination as this little reunion reveals a side of Beckett I've never seen. Vulnerability and affection. I'm so caught up in the moment that I don't even notice when a woman steps forward and touches my shoulder. I jump back, startled.

My heart rockets as familiarity washes over me. My mouth drops open as I freeze in place. Her long brown hair and deep brown eyes are a reflection of my own. If I walked into a time machine and stepped out thirty years later, she would be me.

"Mom?" My heart flip-flops and my nerves tingle. With every ounce of matter in my body, I know who this woman is. And she's not the person who claimed to be my mother at the IND visit.

"It's me, Lyly." There it is. The nickname she had for me. Her lower lip trembles and her eyes sparkle with unshed tears. Locking my gaze, she throws her arms around me in a tight embrace. Somehow the hint of lilacs drifts through the narrow space between us. In a low voice, meant only for my ears, she whispers, "We'll never be separated again. I have a lot to tell you, but it has to wait. If we want any kind of future for our family, we have some work to do first."

I nod, too overcome with emotion to respond. My dad has no idea she's alive. And Easton. When he finds out . . . we have to make sure he finds out. That we're all back together again.

My mother shifts back, holding me at arm's length. "Lyly, we'll talk more later. And hug. A lot more. But right now, we've got to keep moving."

Again I nod, swiping away a fresh trail of tears. Beckett's introducing his dad to Hayes and Vanen. The four of them speak quietly. As if sensing our attention, they abruptly stop and turn to face us.

"Everly, I'm Zai." The large man approaches me, eyeing my mother as if silently seeking permission. "I'm Beckett's dad."

"Hi," I say shyly as I take his outstretched hand in my own and give it a firm shake.

"I'm glad you're still in one piece." After just a moment, he nods his head toward my mother and adds, "And now I'm not stuck with just her anymore."

Beckett releases a bark of laughter and my mother offers a small smile. Hayes and Vanen look just as skeptical as I am. I'm not sure I like this man, Zai. Still, even after a moment of scrutiny, I relax slightly, knowing we finally found adults who are truly here to help us. Ones we can actually trust to make decisions for us, choices that are in our best interest, not for their personal gain. In a span of just a few minutes, we went from running for our lives to gaining the luxury of being teenagers whose responsibility was absorbed by authority figures.

"Where were you going?" my mom asks.

"Back to the street to find Harley." Beckett motions to Vanen. "They drugged him and locked him in a room for hours. We found him but he's been passing out. We don't know what they gave him, but it's messed him up pretty good."

"And I sort of fell on my glasses." Hayes clutches his cracked lenses. "So I can't exactly see much beyond what's one foot in front of me."

"Well lucky for you, we know exactly where to find Harley," Zai says. "Follow us."

### ~ CARO ~

The city streets are relatively empty as all focus is centered on the power grid. Flashing lights beam through the rising smoke and voices echo, but we can't make out any words. Sporadic ambulances blaze through the streets, likely headed to the health center. Their urgency casts a tense pall over the city. Yet every cell in my body pulses with energy. I've been waiting six long years for this moment, and while it's not a perfect reunion, I've got my daughter back. Pure elation chases my every step. I have to remind myself to be alert and aware. We're in hostile territory and that means we're under the constant threat of danger.

With a renewed purpose, I keep a close eye on Hayes, making sure he turns and ducks when necessary. I don't remember much about him from when I lived in Eastates. He was a good kid, and I'd bet he still is. I just wish he wasn't clumsy enough to break his own glasses. It's not like we have extras just sitting around, ready for the taking.

As we scurry farther away from the Centrestates border, desperate to dissolve into the darkness, Beckett and Everly flank Hayes. Every few steps he bumps into one of them as he struggles to keep up and follow our general direction. Between his compromised vision and traveling at night, he must feel so disoriented. The instinct to survive wars with the rules we've been taught since birth – that we belong inside our homes when dusk falls.

Zai repeats Harley's series of knocks when we reach the comms center apartment, and the door opens. We lead the kids inside. They stare with utter fascination at the setup. While they observe the Uprising's technology and monitoring systems, Zai and I talk to Harley. He's made some contacts while we were gone and although our numbers can't compare to Centrestates' security forces, we have key intel and contacts that could give us the upper hand.

While we firm up our plan, another Uprising member tends to the kids. I glance over every few seconds, still somewhat marveling at the fact that we found them. After Everly's scrapes are tended to, she lingers while Beckett's bloodied hand is cleaned and bandaged. I notice how close she stands to him, obvious worry tainting her features. An ache coils in my gut. I've missed comfort and companionship, but I'm glad my daughter found it.

When it's Vanen's turn, the Uprising member leads him to another room. Hayes trails behind them, turning his glasses over in his hands. I doubt they'll be able to do anything about the lenses, but it's worth asking. Maybe they can try to smooth out the cracks. Limited medical equipment and supplies are better than nothing and it's clear that this is the best we can offer these kids.

When Harley and Zai step away to confirm our strategy with the remaining Uprising members, Everly approaches. "Mom?" She tugs on my sleeve. It takes every ounce of restraint I have to not throw my arms around her and never let go. "Can these people bring Dad and Easton here? I mean, they don't even know you're alive." Her hopeful eyes widen. And I have no choice but to extinguish that hope.

"No, not yet." I place a hand on her shoulder, attempting to offer some form of comfort. "We have immediate issues to take care of here."

"But they may not be safe in Eastates!" She crosses her arms and narrows her eyes.

"No one is safe anywhere until we can neutralize Imperant." It's more than a seventeen-year-old should have to hear, but we can't waste time arguing. It's not possible to bring everyone we care about here, and honestly this is the worst place for them right now. "We'll talk about reuniting with our loved ones later."

My tone is stern, but I only hope the look in my eyes doesn't give away the hint of sorrow and regret that weighs on the decision. Our gazes lock and for a brief moment we mirror each other – silently evaluating the other for what she is – part stranger, part family. The trance is broken when Zai returns. He must have overheard part of our conversation, because his tone and message are aimed at Everly.

"We have one mission right now and that's to gather undeniable evidence against Leader Imperant. Without that, the other Societal Order leaders won't even talk to us. Hell, they might not listen even if we do have evidence. But I guarantee you this – if we fail tonight, none of us are getting out of here alive. None of us." He pauses, letting his words sink in. We're all swimming upstream and we have to work together. Everly's eyes shift to me for confirmation. Pressing my lips together tightly, I nod once.

"This operation is bigger than just us right here." Zai waves a stubby finger around the room. "We have contacts invading all three Territories right now, and haven't been able to reach them for hours. For all we know, they're already dead." That's when I decide to cut him off. He's terrifying her. I can see it in her sudden pallid complexion.

"Everly, please understand. We're running out of time and we need your help." My approach is a little softer than Zai's. "We came to activate our allies. Every single one of them. The delegation may have started this, but the Uprising is ending it."

"You two," Zai motions to Beckett and Everly, "go check on your friends. I need to talk to Caro for a moment." Hesitantly they head down the little hallway to find Vanen and Hayes. As soon as they're out of earshot, I whisper the single thought churning through my mind.

"Tell me this is necessary." I hate to admit weakness, but I'm second-guessing our plan.

"I promise you it is." Zai drops his chin to meet my gaze. He clasps a hand around my shoulder. "We know what we're doing. Imperant's too damn cocky to think anyone could ever catch him off guard. That's his greatest weakness and tonight we use it against him."

"We just got them back." I suck in a rattled breath. This is not the time to lose control of my emotions. For the past six years, I've been a rebel first, not a mother. But seeing Everly, actually here with me, reactivates that motherly instinct to protect her. I've wanted to have my family back for so long and now it's finally within reach. As long as we don't fail.

"And if we do this right, we get to keep them," Zai continues, "but if we do nothing, they'll be hunted for the rest of their lives. You know that as well as I do. They're marked for knowing too much. Nowhere is safe so we have to make a safe place. For everyone."

I nod, biting back the emotions threatening to spill. *He's right. This is our only hope. Even if it puts our children in immediate danger.*

Harley escorts Hayes, Everly and Beckett back out to us. I'm guessing the other one, Vanen, needs more treatment. Pointing out some chairs in what would normally be the living room, Harley motions for the kids to sit. The three of them slide into seats beside each other. Zai looks at me, raising his eyebrows. I nod, silently agreeing that he's the best one to explain to them what is about to happen.

He folds his hands together and stands before the kids. "Tonight we take a stand against Imperant and we need your help to do it. We have a plan, and support from key members of the Uprising. They'll be right there with you, watching, waiting to strike, but this plan involves you being on the frontlines. We want to send you directly into the snake's pit to lure Imperant into admitting what's been going on."

"You want us to meet face-to-face with Leader Imperant?" Everly asks, her face growing more pale by the second.

"Yes, but under the premise of being caught. We'll be watching you the whole time, like we're right there with you," I explain.

"But what if they don't take us to see Imperant?" Hayes asks, "What if they just kill us on sight?"

"You're very valuable to them right now," Zai says. "Won't be for long though. From what our sources are hearing, they want to bring you in for questioning." His voice trails off when he adds, "After that they'll need to dispose of you."

"But we'll prepare you with what to say and what to do," I add.

"Are all three of us doing this?" Hayes asks.

"No," I answer. "Only two. We don't have enough reliable equipment that's portable enough to hide on more than two."

"And besides," Zai adds. "The less bodies in the way, the better. If we have to take a shot, we want it to be a clear one."

"Then who goes?" Everly asks. Even after all these years apart, I sense her dread as if it's feeding my own.

"Hayes and I'll go." Beckett crosses his arms. His square jaw and narrowed eyes dare anyone to disagree. Zai drops a hand on his son's shoulder.

"It's not about gender. It's about who they dislike the most, who can get under their skin and get them to talk."

"Well, that still means that I go," Beckett smirks. "Because Kiera hates me."

Everly laughs, one small burst before she muffles it with her palm. For that split second, her smile warms me. But that's all I'll allow myself to enjoy of the brief display. It reminds me of a young, carefree girl who didn't have to worry about risking her life to help a rebellion remove corrupt leaders from power. All too soon, reality returns, along with our next decision – *Hayes or Everly?*

"Kiera likes Hayes. Vanen told us," Everly says with somber confidence. "And I think it's safe to say that she doesn't exactly like me."

"That true?" Zai asks the guys. Beckett scratches his chin but nods once. Hayes fidgets, shifting in his seat. Zai tilts his head toward Everly. It's pretty obvious who should go. "You think you can do it without giving anything away?"

"Yes," she squeaks. No matter how long we've been apart, I know my child and I've never been more certain that she's lying.

# CHAPTER 32 ~ EVERLY

## UPPER DIVISION, CENTRESTATES

For a brief moment, I felt relieved to have adults here to tell us what to do. They were supposed to take that burden from us, but instead they swapped it with another. *We have to face Kiera and Imperant? We're definitely the most hated delegates.* Bile rises at the back of my throat. I swallow it down and clamp my lips closed in case it tries to force its way back up.

A gentle swipe tickles the back of my hand, drawing my eyes down to my side. It's Beckett. Although he sits at full attention, as if he's hanging on every word his dad and my mom say, his fingers fumble for mine. An innocent brush becomes a full entwinement as we listen to the plan to crumble Centrestates from the inside out. My heart quickens, both from the physical contact and the fear slithering through me.

"We know it's a lot to ask of you," my mom says, watching us both carefully. "But this is the only way. We would never purposely put you in danger, and we'll be right there with you, as close as we can be without giving ourselves away." Before either of us responds, Beckett's dad speaks up.

"This is it." He raises his hands in an animated gesture. "Tonight is what we've been waiting for. Maybe we aren't ready, maybe we'll never be ready. But there's no going back after this. We have to make our stand because if we don't, Centrestates will, and a war would decimate too many innocent lives in all of the Territories."

"You're right," I say, chewing my bottom lip to stop it from trembling. "I'll do whatever I can to help." The hint of a smile plays across my mother's lips. She nearly glows with pride.

Beckett suddenly sits up straighter, tugging his hand away from me. "I almost forgot." He ducks his head and slips the messenger bag strap over it. Handing it to his dad, he explains, "Someone from the Uprising gave this to us. There's some pretty interesting papers in there. Notes from Kiera's office and an article they prepared before we even went to the grid, saying how we destroyed it."

"This is perfect, son. Great job!" Zai eagerly grabs the bag and turns it over in his hands. Beckett quickly returns his hand to mine, cradling it within his strong yet gentle grip. Just then someone knocks on the door. Not a typical knock, but the same pattern of raps that Zai did when we got here.

Harley answers it and a short woman with dark skin and hair charges inside. My eyes narrow in recognition but I can't place where I've seen her before. A lumpy tan bag is slung over her shoulder. By the way it tugs the fabric tight, whatever's in there must be heavy.

Maybe she works in the cafeteria or somewhere in Centrel Hall and we passed her in a hallway? Either way, she clearly recognizes the delegates in her presence. Her eyes lock on us with keen interest.

Zai and Harley lead the woman away. They're obviously talking about us though, because she glances over her shoulder our way several times during the hushed conversation. My mother explains a little more about what's going to happen.

"Hayes and Vanen are staying here." When Hayes starts to protest, she raises a hand. "You can't see more than a few inches in front of you and he's unstable and needs to rest until the drugs are all flushed from his system. Not to mention, he clearly had a target on his back. You did a good job keeping him safe. We'll take care of that now."

"You know," Hayes starts, "Vanen's dad is some kind of technology expert in Eastates." He pauses, watching her reaction. Her eyebrows jump in interest. "I don't know if you have a way to reach him, but I bet he'd help if it would save Vanen."

"That's great information, Hayes, thank you for sharing it. I'll let the crew know and we'll see what they can do with it." She winks at him and excuses herself before striding over to a woman feverishly typing at a keyboard beneath a row of giant monitors. Just then another series of knocks sounds at the entrance door. My mother opens it and two other Uprising members hurry inside.

When I glance at Beckett, he squeezes my hand. I forgot we were even holding hands. The closeness is reassuring. At least I don't have to face Kiera and Imperant alone. The people watching the monitors rise from their workstations, slowly making their way toward a huddle the newcomers have formed. Harley weaves his way around the bodies to reach the center. He starts to speak but is cut off by two shrill beeps that slice through the air. My heart lurches. *Now what's happening?*

"That's one of our other teams!" Zai bellows. "They're making contact." Everyone falls silent as my mother and Zai both dash for a boxy black device sitting on the edge of a desk. He snatches it before she can reach it. Depressing a button, he raises it to his mouth and speaks into it. "This is Centre Team, go for report."

"Centre Team, it's Orla." The woman's breathing is heavy and fast. "My team and I reached Leader Huntsman. Had to take out two of his men, but it was worth it." Even through the radio, it's clear she pushes the last part out through clenched teeth. With each word, her tone turns harsh, steely. *This woman from the Uprising must be in Westates. And she helped kill two people there.*

"That's enough!" a deep voice cuts in. "This is Societal Order Leader Shane Huntsman. I don't know who you are and I don't really care. Your colleagues were detained shortly after they broke into my personal residence and murdered two of my staff. Her accomplices are in custody and unless you can give me a valid reason as to why they should not be executed, you can consider this your last conversation."

~ CARO ~

I suck in a deep breath as alarm strikes me like a lightning bolt. *We all agreed that killing would be a last resort. And since Orla's nowhere near as volatile as Zai, she must have had no choice. And now a very angry and retaliatory Huntsman holds our West team's fate in his hands. We cannot fail them.*

Zai's grip on the radio tightens, stretching the skin on his knuckles to a strained white. Harley gently pries his fingers away and places the radio on a counter. "Can't efford t' break dat," he mutters. No longer holding the radio, Zai presses the heels of his palms to his eyes and squares his jaw. Tension swells within the small space, consuming every crevice.

"So what's it going to be?" Huntsman taunts. "Shall we proceed with pulling information out of our captives or are you prepared to explain exactly what this little charade is?"

His threat spurs me to act. I grab the radio before anyone else can and speak. "Did you give Orla a chance to explain?" I try to keep my voice even and authoritative. Obviously he holds all the power here. Spouting off threats or demands won't get her out of this, but I also won't cower or beg.

"You may address me as Leader Huntsman. And yes, I did. According to *Orla*," he practically spits her name with clear distaste, "we are on the cusp of a war that Centrestates is preparing to launch. I take the safety of my citizens very seriously and I will intervene to prevent any and all threats of harm. But this is a sobering accusation. If untrue, it could in fact launch a war of its own."

"Leader Huntsman, what she told you is true. We are the Uprising and we have connections throughout all of the Territories. We–" He cuts me off before I can finish. It makes me instantly regret using his formal title.

"In order to be taken seriously, this so-called Uprising needs to produce proof of what you say. Without that, your accusations are baseless. I cannot simply accept the word of a murderer and her associates. Taking another's life is a significant infraction in Westates. You have my attention, but I will not allow you to waste my time. We will hold these murderers for twenty-four hours. If you cannot provide me with undisputable proof that what she says is true, then they will face punishment for their crime. And it will be harsh."

Before I register any movement, Zai rips the radio from my limp grasp. "Oh we'll get you proof! You keep hold of this radio and listen. When we're ready to share it, you'll know!"

"Twenty-four hours. That's all you've got." With that, the line silences and we know the conversation is over. Zai punches the nearest wall, leaving a fist-shaped puncture – a lasting souvenir of our brief visit. Harley paces the room, calling out an obscenity every few seconds.

I bend down, planting my palms on my knees in an attempt to clear my head. Huntsman has Orla and the clock is ticking to save her, along with everyone else. I buried all my self-pity years ago. If I hadn't, right now I'd be wondering how the weight of the world fell onto my shoulders, or rather the Uprising's shoulders.

Paranoia claws at the back of my mind. "We've got to check on the East Team," I announce. I'm the one who demanded this mission, and it will be my fault if any of our leaders die because of it. They all agreed to fight for this cause, but maybe I skewed the decision on when to strike based on my personal attachment to the delegates.

Zai clenches and unclenches his fists before grabbing the radio and changing the frequency. He initiates a pattern of keystrokes that emits three solid beeps. For several minutes, it sits there silently, uselessly, which makes me want to smash it to smithereens. Finally, another three beeps sound. We have contact. Hopefully this report will be better than the West Team's.

"East Team report, this is Centre Team." Zai's tone has an edge, as if his words are part demand and part plea.

"Centre Team, this is Welch. We're still en route but we're nearing Leader Ault's headquarters." I release a sigh of relief. *At least they haven't been caught. Yet.*

"Power grid blew here. You notice any unusual activity there?" Zai asks.

"Dark as it should be," Daxton reports. "Quiet now. We passed a few Enforcers but not many."

"All right, check in when you have progress," Zai commands. After a quick acknowledgement, Daxton wishes us luck and disconnects.

Harley spins on us, his eyes lit with accusation. He jabs a pointer finger toward each of us. "Ya didn't say nothin' 'bout yur friend who got caught in Westates." Zai's nostrils flare. I share his annoyance but remove any emotion when I answer Harley.

"With any luck, the next time we talk to them, we'll have our proof and Orla and her team will be safe. No need to distract the East Team with what might never happen," I attempt to explain. "Besides, they're all trained to conduct missions. They realize the risk, but I don't want them so paranoid about making a misstep that they end up making a stupid mistake."

"Now, about that proof." Zai drags a nearby chair toward him and drops into it. "I think I have an idea. It could get some people killed, but I guess that's just the risk we have to take."

"Sounds intrestin' to me!" Harley pounds his fist on a table. My mind races as Zai and Harley negotiate details. So far we've accomplished very little. Zai and I made it here but we weren't able to save all the delegates, or Lisum. Of the two survivors we found at the grid, one is likely being treated for her injuries in the main health center while the other is probably sharing every detail he can about us with his father, who happily leads Centrestates' security.

Orla and her small team has been captured, with no chance of making it out alive if we can't deliver evidence strong enough to convince Huntsman that his Territory is on the brink of attack.

Daxton and Welch haven't arrived yet in Eastates, but I'm sure they won't get a warm welcome there either. Somehow it all has to come together. After a few intense minutes, I tune back into the discussion before me.

"I'cn make that happen." Harley rubs his stubbly chin thoughtfully. "Yur first contact is ulready here."

"Perfect." Zai leans back in his wobbly chair. "Let's get the kids set up and walk them through the dialogue."

"Take 'em down the hallway. First door on the left." Harley jabs a stubby finger in that direction before weaving through the room, disappearing within the small group.

The clock's ticking, but so are we.

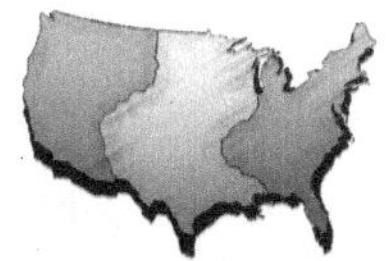

# CHAPTER 33 ~ CARO

## UPPER DIVISION, CENTRESTATES

Everly's shoulders slump as we lead her and Beckett to the room Harley pointed out. A small cot sits in the corner, but otherwise folding chairs dominate the space. Zai sets one up for each of us. A few minutes later, Harley joins us with a short dark-skinned woman in tow. She rushes over to the kids and asks if they recognize her. Beckett narrows his eyes as if trying to place her and Everly slowly shakes her head.

"I was part of the information broadcast team that documented your visit in photos. Kiera told you to pretend we weren't even there so that we could capture natural-looking images. I guess you did a good job of ignoring us and I did a good job of keeping a low profile." She flashes them a small smile and grabs one of the extra chairs leaning against the wall and unfolds it, dropping into the seat while lowering her bag to the floor. When they don't react, she continues. "Just relax while I get you both wired. It'll only take a few minutes."

"Mom, what's happening?" Everly asks nervously as the woman unzips the bag and pulls out a few wires and earpieces. Zai and I share a glance. It's time to brief the kids on their part of the mission. The woman continues her work as I pull a chair closer to them and explain.

"You two are going to be *captured* and brought to Kiera and Leader Imperant." When Everly cringes, I try to reassure her. "This is all a setup. Uprising members will be around you the whole time. You just won't know who they are, but they'll be ready to protect you if that time comes."

"What do you mean *if* that time comes? Of course it will come! You're sending us right back to the people who tried to kill us!" Everly's voice cracks with emotion as tears spring to her eyes. Beckett wraps an arm around her. She leans into his touch and drops her forehead to his shoulder, sobbing. A small part of me shatters, but I can't let it show. My child is terrified, rightfully so, and I'm not the one she turns to for comfort. I'm the one forcing her into this nightmare.

"So what's the plan after they catch us and take us to Centrel Hall?" Beckett asks. His jaw is square and his posture stiff, but I know he's already accepted this challenge. He's been a part of the Uprising longer than I have.

"You get them talking," Zai says, stroking his beard. "You get them to admit that they blew up the grid and that it was meant to turn the other Territories against them."

The woman taps on small round mouthpieces she tucks just below Everly's and Beckett's collars. "These little transmitters will pick up everything you say. They're sensitive enough to capture every voice within twelve feet of you. The worst-case scenario is we end up with a recording of your conversation. The best case is that it's broadcast live across the entire Divided States on each Territory's version of the information broadcast."

"You can do that?" Everly asks through sniffles.

"We believe we can," the woman answers. "It's never been done before so this will be a test, that's for certain, but either way, the key is getting an admission of guilt. And if I've learned anything about Centrestates' leaders in the time I've lived here, it's that they *want* to brag about what they can do. They *want* others to know that they hold all the power. Besides, once they have you in custody, you're no longer a threat to them."

"Son," Zai starts, locking eyes with Beckett. "Harley's contacts were able to track down your brother." I swallow the lump in my throat. His admission ignites both dread and anticipation. I never met Beckett's older brother. He was already gone by the time I arrived in Westates.

"It seems he was sent to the lower division of Centrestates. They intercepted one of his messages about the Uprising. In all these years, he's always claimed that no one else in the family knew anything about it. I don't know if they believe him, but one thing I do know is that as soon as this is finished, we're getting him back."

If Beckett felt any hesitation about this plan, learning about his brother just restored his resolve. He nods once as his lips disappear into a tight line. Everly sits up straighter and squeezes his hand. There's definitely a connection there and I should probably be thankful for it. When we successfully manipulated the delegate list, with Lisum's help, adding Beckett's name to it was a huge risk. It probably helped that his brother had already been detained, which made him the ideal indicator that might predict a delegate's behavior. While the Uprising's strike was always the ultimate goal, I put all of my faith in Beckett finding my daughter and keeping her safe until we got here. And now we're sending her right back to the face of danger that she narrowly escaped.

"Okay, what do we need to do?" Beckett asks as his gaze slides from Zai to me to the information broadcast woman.

***

"Can you repeat it back to us?" Zai asks after we review the plan with the kids. "You don't have to give us every last detail, but we just need to hear it in your words, that you understand how this will work."

Beckett blows out a breath while Everly twists her hands together in a nervous shuffle. They glance at each other, briefly locking eyes, before she gives him a slight nod. It's their way of agreeing who will speak.

"We play dumb," he says. "We run into Centrel Hall as if we're all scared and don't know what to do. They'll take us to Kiera. If it's just her, we pretend like we don't know about her plan for the delegation. We try to get her to brag about it. Once you hear enough evidence, the Uprising busts in and takes over."

"And if she takes you to Imperant immediately?" Zai prompts, rolling his wrist in a circular motion.

"We tell him everything we know so that the two of them can argue over what really happened. From the few times we've seen them interact, it's like she always wants his approval, and most of the time he seems annoyed by her. Or maybe he's just annoyed by anyone other than himself."

"Don't forget, besides having Uprising members in the building, our team here will be watching and listening to everything that happens. We'll be ready to move at the blink of an eye. And we will not hesitate to act the second anything goes wrong." When the room falls silent, I ask, "Any last questions?" Secretly, I almost wish they would refuse to do this. It would send us back to square one, scrambling for another plan with dwindling time and the pressure of our colleagues being executed. But at least I wouldn't be sending my child to the front lines of a war that could ignite at any moment.

Everly and Beckett shake their heads slowly and join hands. I take them both in my arms and beg them to be careful. Zai hugs them both too, whispering a few last words of encouragement to each of them.

# CHAPTER 34 ~ EVERLY

## UPPER DIVISION, CENTRESTATES

I can't believe we're doing this. Goosebumps spread over my skin as shivers dash down my spine. Realizing that I'm on the verge of hyperventilating, I drag in a deep breath through my nose and concentrate on allowing my lungs to slowly release it. Beckett's grip on my hand tightens with each step we take farther away from the Uprising's communications center. It's the only semblance of comfort we can afford.

We lurch toward Centrel Hall, both trying to relax our gait. It feels like the tiny devices tucked within the folds of our clothing are on full display. I worry that something will fall out right there in front of Kiera and she'll know exactly what we're trying to do. The information broadcast lady told us to say we went to the grid tour but got there really late. She brushed dirt and soot on our faces and tore our sleeves and pant legs so that we appear tattered.

Normalcy is returning to the city as the rush of vehicles and security forces has quieted. Beckett nods toward a pair of guards. "They're as good as any. Let's go get ourselves caught."

We slink toward the oblivious men, watching their every move. They chat casually, as if nothing unusual has happened tonight. When we're close enough that they should see us, we face each other and pretend to whisper.

Strong hands clamp down on my shoulders. A startled cry rips from my throat as my body bucks in an automatic response. Beckett grunts and struggles. Out of the corner of my eye, I see he's facing the same fate as me. Security guards. They've got us, and even though this is what we expected, it feels completely wrong.

"Now that's enough," the one holding me grumbles. "You aren't going anywhere and if you try to fight, I'll have to restrain you."

"It's that easy," the other guard adds. "You behave, and you can stand here like civilized adults. You give us trouble, and we'll have to cuff you."

I press my lips together. If silence helps me avoid being restrained, I can stay quiet. Beckett shakes the guard's hands off him before settling.

"Well, who do we have here? Looks to be delegates if you ask me," the short, balding guard squawks.

"We are delegates," I push out through gritted teeth. "We were at the power grid and there was some kind of accident. We didn't know what to do, so we came here for help."

"Oh really? Well we've been looking for you for a while, so where've you been?" the taller, thin guard asks.

"We were both knocked out in the explosion," Beckett explains. "When we came to, everything was on fire. It took some time to find a way out that wasn't a wall of fire."

The men exchange a skeptical glance. "Well, either way, we're all heading inside. There are some people who are looking for you."

"You two are going to follow me and my friend here will follow you," the shorter man says before marching to the entrance. The other guard falls into line behind us and mutters, "Now don't get any stupid ideas. We all carry weapons and rarely get to use them. But if you give me a reason, I will."

I let a defeated sigh escape. This was really our only option. Even if we had made it to Eastates, we couldn't just hide at my house. It just would have put Dad and Easton in danger too. I don't bother to let that thought fully take hold. Besides, Beckett has his own family and he wouldn't want to hide in another Territory forever. They'd find us and they'd punish our families too. *Maybe it's better this way. Maybe this will keep Dad and Easton safe.*

They lead us inside and point to two chairs in an obvious command for us to sit. One steps around the large reception desk and picks up a phone. After a brief, animated conversation, he nods to the remaining guard, who hovers just a few feet away from us.

"Looks like they're ready for you upstairs. Come with me." We rise and head for the elevators. The ride up is excruciating as I contemplate everything that could possibly go wrong. All three of us stay silent, although ours is clearly laced with defeat. Each step feels heavier than the last one. When the doors part open, Beckett and I both know where we're headed – no one needs to tell us. Imperant's office.

The guard stops just outside and knocks on the closed door. When it swings open, a face I didn't expect to see is waiting on the other side. Wynter. She steps back, out of the way, as the clack of heels strikes the floor. Kiera storms into the hallway and addresses the guard.

"Thank you for your assistance with these *delegates* who have clearly broken the very few rules we asked them to follow." She spits the word *delegates* as if it's an insult. She steps back and motions with her hand. "You are dismissed. Leader Imperant and I are prepared to deliver their discipline."

The pleasure behind her words makes me physically recoil. My heart pounds and my mouth goes dry. The guard gladly obliges, pulling the door closed behind us after we're inside. I knew he wouldn't help us, but it feels like that door is an impenetrable barrier that we'll never pass through again.

Leader Imperant sits behind his enormous desk, his hands steepled and his face painted with mild amusement. Fury blazes off Beckett. He watches Kiera and Leader Imperant with a scowl. I think I'd rather feel anger than fear in this moment, but it's not a switch I can power on and off.

"So, it seems as though you two missed the educational tour tonight. Is that correct?" Kiera asks smugly.

"We actually got there late," I squeak out, struggling to keep my voice even.

"Is that true?" Kiera turns to Wynter, who drops her gaze to the floor and shakes her head.

Kiera crosses her arms. "So you're lying. You skipped a mandatory tour and then lied about it. Quite deceitful." She clucks her tongue once.

"Deceitful?" Beckett seethes. "I would call it deceitful to invite us all here just to try and kill us!"

Imperant nearly jumps out of his seat, knocking the chair into the wall behind him. Leading the way with an accusatory finger pointed at Beckett, he practically growls, "I will not allow guests of my Territory to hurl such preposterous accusations at us!" Beckett holds Imperant's steely gaze for a moment.

"Wynter, you are dismissed." Kiera's words slice through the tension. "Start drafting a statement we can share on the information broadcast about tonight's unfortunate incident that terminated the delegation." Without even an acknowledgment, Wynter scurries out of the room, keeping her head down. As soon as the door closes, Kiera perks up.

"Sir," she chirps, "I guarantee you that these accusations will not leave this room." As if suddenly realizing how close he came to losing control, Leader Imperant turns on his heel and strides back to his chair. Hands clasped behind her back, Kiera prowls around us like we're prey.

"You were all supposed to be excellent test takers. Yet you all failed time and again." She shakes her head disappointedly, tsking as she meets each of us with a disapproving glare. "If you can't be trusted to keep minor details confidential, then you certainly won't keep details of the peace treaty under wraps until the Societal Order is ready to release official announcements."

Imperant just watches her with an amused grin. His dark hair and chiseled features only lend to his arrogance. He's perfectly put together and he must agree with everything Kiera says. If not, he just doesn't care enough to correct her.

"I'd say you never wanted a peace treaty or a delegation." Beckett mutters. His tone isn't bitter, it's matter-of-fact, as if he doesn't need her confirmation. Still, she can't resist providing it.

"Finally, you got something right." Kiera mockingly claps her slender hands together while taking a step closer to us. My eyes search the floor, intent on avoiding her scrutiny. I feel so small anytime she's near. Maybe it's because she always has all the control and looks down on us. Or maybe because most of the time the delegates were together in a group, so we didn't have to face her so directly. Either way, Kiera's demeanor screams that I'm insignificant. We're insignificant. And she can't wait to tell us why.

"Think about it," she sighs, as if we're the dumbest people on this planet. "If twelve teenagers can't even get along and follow simple instructions to work together, how can three separate governments lead effectively? This country needs to be united again under one leader."

"And you think you can just . . . change that?" Beckett asks flippantly. Imperant watches the conversation with mild interest.

"It's past time for a change." Kiera saunters over to Imperant's side and leans against the side of his desk. "Your way of life is antiquated and it doesn't have to be that way. Leader Imperant can make life better for everyone across the country, just like he's done here. We tried to make this a peaceful transition, but Leaders Ault and Huntsman wanted no part of that. So, they left us no choice but to take what should be ours."

"So your big plan was to use a bunch of teenagers to start a war?" Beckett snarls. "We found the stories you made up, blaming the delegates for the power grid blowing up. How would we have any idea how to even do that?"

"You see, most people are stupid enough to believe what their beloved leaders tell them." Kiera winks at us as if we've just shared a private joke. "I guarantee you, I can make up just about any story and most citizens will believe it. A few may question it, yes, but we can easily sway them when they see how much better life will be when we are in charge of all three Territories."

"There's something you need to understand." Leader Imperant speaks quietly as he folds his hands. "Everything we do is for the future of the Divided States. Look at your own Territories – they barely function. Do you like eating slop for every meal? Do you like being shut in your homes for half of each day because your leaders can't figure out how to take care of your needs? Well, Centrestates has it all. We have food, electricity, and we even allow our citizens to enjoy themselves. This is how it should be in every Territory. And unfortunately, your leaders refuse to listen to reason."

"So why bother telling us all this?" Beckett asks.

"Because I trust you'll take our secrets to the grave." My stomach drops as she tilts her head and smiles. "You know too much and a few of you are too smart. Hayes and Vanen, now that is a real shame. They were the only ones who truly deserved to be here. Unfortunately, they used their skills and the trust we afforded them against us."

"So it's all true, what they found?" I find my voice, although it's shaky. "This delegation was just an experiment and when you got what you wanted from it, you just . . . " I can't finish the thought. Trepidation flashes through me, stealing my words. Shifting on my feet, I'm suddenly unable to stand in place.

Kiera thrusts her shoulders back in a perfect portrayal of confidence. "I must admit, I didn't expect anyone to break into our network. But once Hayes and Vanen made their little discoveries, it was fascinating to watch what you did with that information." She glances at her fingernails as if she's growing bored with the conversation. "And when the time came that you all had learned too much, difficult decisions had to be made." She pauses before finishing. "Let's just say that this experiment must come to an end. The delegation is officially terminated."

She smirks, letting the words sink in. My stomach plummets. It feels like we're trapped in a very small room that's quickly closing in on us.

As if they're tag-teaming, Leader Imperant rests his elbows on the desk and steeples his hands, his dark eyes focusing intently on us. "You see, with the power grid comes . . . power. Centrestates should have been controlling everything from the start. If we had been in charge, everyone's lives would be better." He tilts his chin back, awaiting one of us to release words of defiance. Anger seethes within me but I press my lips together. *Nothing I say can change anything.*

Kiera's lips purse into a pout when no one responds. "Look how good we have it here." She sweeps a hand around the room, referring to what lies beyond these walls. "We can provide for all our citizens' needs. And we can protect them." *Protect them from what?*

Hayes' question from that first day slams into my mind. He asked why Centrestates would have security. I'm guessing there's not much of a threat from the north and south, but rather the leaders here wish to create a threat – to the east and west.

# CHAPTER 35 ~ EVERLY

## UPPER DIVISION, CENTRESTATES

"The train," I mutter. They all turn to me, confused but curious. "On the train ride here from Eastates, I overheard the transport overseers talking. They said Hayes and I weren't on the list to go back home." Beckett presses his lips together and squints his eyes. I can tell he's processing the information and he doesn't like it.

"We thought it was a mistake, but it wasn't." My eyes drop to the floor. Even though my words are directed at Kiera and Leader Imperant, I can't meet their gaze. "You never intended for us to go back home. Our families would never know what truly happened to us." Fury blooms in the pit of my stomach.

Kiera takes a step toward us and plants her hands on her hips. "That is pure speculation, and I've answered enough of your questions. Now it's time to answer one of mine." Her request catches us both off guard. Beckett and I share a nervous glance. I suck in a breath, bracing myself. *What could she possibly want to ask us?*

"Why did you refuse to wear your pin? Even after I specifically encouraged you to do so?" The question is clearly directed at Beckett because I wore my pin every chance I got, just like all the other delegates.

"I saw it as one more way for you to control us," he answers sternly, locking eyes with her.

Kiera claps her hands together, just a few times slowly. "Bravo!" She flashes him a wide smile. "I can share a little secret since I know you won't take it anywhere."

"Kiera." Leader Imperant warns, crossing his arms. "We don't have time for this."

"Sir, you'll love this," she gushes. "Remember the pins we bestowed upon each delegate on their first day here?" He only stares at her with growing impatience. It doesn't deter her from continuing. "Well, they were quite clever actually. Besides tracking the delegates' every movement, they also hold microphones. Let me tell you, it took Wynter and Lisum a lot of time to review the recordings, but the information we gleaned was worth it."

"Enough!" Leader Imperant slams a fist down on the desk so hard that the reverberations seem to bounce off the walls. "Make this mess disappear and let's move on." He turns his dark eyes on Kiera. Her previous giddiness evaporates. Fueled by pure fear, I slip a trembling finger under my collar, searching for the transmitter. *It's working, right?*

This would be a great time for the Uprising to bust in here. Hopefully they recorded enough of the conversation, but even if they didn't, I don't want to find out what Kiera's plans for us are now. Just as my finger brushes over the small device, it rolls with the movement and plummets to the floor. The whole thing takes a few seconds but feels as though it's in slow motion. There's no sense in praying that no one notices because Kiera's eyes fly open wide. Trailing its bouncy landing, she scrambles to pick it up.

Holding it in the air, she twists and turns her wrist, inspecting the transmitter from every angle. Both she and Leader Imperant stay silent. They must know what it is, or at least suspect that it's a recording device of some sort. After a brief shared glance, they turn their glares on us. Leader Imperant drops his hand behind the desk and slowly slides a drawer open. He reaches in and grasps a gun. Sweat trickles down my back as my heart races. Beckett reaches over and captures one of my clammy hands in his. He squeezes it, reminding me that we're in this together.

"What's going on?" Beckett asks, but they don't fall for it. Kiera purses her lips closed and narrows her eyes at him. Leader Imperant motions toward us both and nods his head up and down slowly. Kiera promptly approaches Beckett, patting him down. She retrieves his transmitter and holds it up like a prize. When her fingers flutter over his chest, she tilts her head with realization. Reaching under his shirt, she tears off the wires wrapped around his torso. She side-steps to me and repeats the process – feeling along my arms, waist and legs before ripping my wires away.

She marches back to Imperant's desk and slams the equipment down. He raises the gun and rams the handle down on the devices, sending broken pieces skittering across the smooth surface and over the edge to the tile floor. While he's busy destroying our only means of communication with the outside world, Kiera finds a pair of scissors and cuts the wires into several segments. I hope the Uprising got what it needed, because everything they sent us in here with is completely useless now.

Imperant raises the gun and points it toward us. "Just one thing left to do." He bends down to reach a drawer and retrieves a cylindrical tube. He screws it onto the weapon. It's a painfully slow process. While I don't know much about guns, I have a feeling that the part he's adding is only going to make what they're about to do that much easier.

A sharp crack pierces the room just before the door slams open. Beckett pushes me to the floor and huddles beside me. My hands instinctively cover my ears and I lower my head. Feet stomp into the room and a deep male voice commands, "Stop right there! Drop your weapon and raise your hands!"

Even as terror courses through me, I need to see what's unfolding. Crouched into a ball, I raise my head slightly to peek around the room. Beckett's father, Zai, is the one who spoke. He clutches the largest gun I've ever seen in his arms, and it's aimed at Leader Imperant.

My mother stands beside Zai. When our eyes meet, she mouths, "You okay?" I nod frantically. Physically I'm fine, mentally it's another story, but she doesn't need to know that now. Two others file into the room with weapons trained on Kiera and Leader Imperant. I don't recognize either one, but they're clearly on our side.

Beckett starts to stand but Zai grinds out, "Stay down until that weapon is secure." As he speaks, he doesn't take his eyes off his targets.

"I will not lower my weapon. You have broken into my capitol building in my Territory. You're terrorists!" Leader Imperant snarls. I dare glance at him. Kiera stands by his side, her nostrils flared and her chin raised defiantly.

"We're part of the Uprising," my mother says, "and we're here to discuss a more equitable Societal Order."

"This is clearly an invasion by a terrorist group. No one goes in guns blazing when they want to discuss something civilly," Imperant smirks. "You're here to eradicate the Societal Order, the very leadership organization that serves every citizen of the Divided States. I vowed to protect the citizens of Centrestates and I do not take that promise lightly."

"Protect them?" Zai laughs. "How about preventing them from spreading the truth? If someone speaks out against you, you just snatch them away from their families and drop them in another Territory." When Imperant says nothing, Zai continues. "How about injecting a compliance chip into babies' brains when they're born? Is that protecting them from having their own thoughts?"

Kiera's mouth drops open as her eyes narrow to angry slits. "How dare you! How dare you break in here and accuse Leader Imperant of such things. Every citizen owes the Societal Order leaders everything. Those chips are necessary! They virtually eliminated mental illness. A century ago people claimed weakness and inability to contribute by throwing around diagnoses like depression and anxiety. Now, with the implant, those disorders no longer exist. We are a stronger nation because of it."

Beckett rises slowly, his blue eyes cast in a darkness I don't recognize. His movement blazes with fury as he points an accusatory finger at Kiera. "No one has a right to get inside our heads! It's just one more thing you think you can control!" His tone is a low growl.

If we weren't allies, instinct would caution me to take a few steps back, inserting some distance between us, in case this is just a flare of his temper on the verge of erupting.

"Well, apparently not, since you refused to be controlled from day one," Kiera says. "So either there's a flaw in the system or you're an anomaly."

"All of you, shut your mouths!" Imperant snaps. "I don't negotiate with terrorists, so I guess we'll just stand here and point our guns at each other until my security detail arrives and blows all of your brains out."

Tension slithers through the room. The temperature seems to rise with each passing second. As sweat beads on my forehead, Leader Imperant stands at complete ease. With four guns pointed at him and his accomplice, he holds his aim on me and Beckett.

"Your security isn't coming," my mother says. "They've protected you all these years but the Uprising had some information to share with them that wasn't very flattering to you. They're reviewing it at this moment." She raises her eyebrows, awaiting a response.

"You have nothing!" Kiera snipes. "Leader Imperant has done nothing but provide for our citizens and they know that! They've lived it!"

With a quick glance around the room, Leader Imperant turns his weapon on Kiera and fires before anyone can even react. She drops to the floor instantly. A scream chases the air out of my lungs and I press a hand over my gaping mouth. Another crack pierces the air and this time Leader Imperant staggers back a step. His gun drops to the floor, bouncing on the slick surface. My mother scrambles to retrieve it as Leader Imperant looks around in shock, cradling his wounded arm. Blood seeps from a round crimson stain on his shirt, just below his bicep.

"You shot me?" he mutters in disbelief. "How dare you shoot a Societal Order leader?"

Zai shakes his head slowly. "Not only did you refuse to drop your weapon, you started firing."

"We came here to talk, but considering you just murdered your top advisor, it's obvious you would have shot one of us next," my mother adds, holstering Leader Imperant's gun.

"I eliminated the real problem here." He glances at Kiera's lifeless body. Her open eyes fix on the ceiling in a never-ending stare. "Kiera Saign was the mastermind behind this whole delegation. It spun out of control without my knowledge. Obviously, I gave her too much power and she abused it. This is my Territory and I have always done what's best for it." He straightens his back and squares his shoulders. "I'm just as dismayed as you by what she tried to do here."

"Is that so?" Zai asks, eyebrows raised in question. He doesn't wait for an answer. "Well, we'd like to see if Leaders Ault and Huntsman agree with that." Terror flashes across Leader Imperant's face but only for a second. If I had sneezed I would have missed it.

My mother gives the other two Uprising members in the room a slight nod and they rush forward. Only then do I notice the bulky black bags slung over their shoulders. They meticulously empty the contents on Imperant's desk. It's a variety of handheld devices, keyboards and monitors – nothing even comparable to the equipment back in their communications center, but an impressive stash of electronics. They mimic each other, setting up two of the same configurations on the desktop.

"What is this?" Leader Imperant demands, clutching his wound.

"I think it's time we gathered all three Social Order leaders and had a chat," my mother says.

# CHAPTER 36 ~ CARO

## UPPER DIVISION, CENTRESTATES

Leader Imperant's features twist into a scowl. Zai continues to train the gun on him while everyone just ignores the fact that there's a dead body in the room with us. Whenever my eyes drift to the floor and land on Kiera, my stomach churns with disgust. Everything she did, everything she planned . . . was it for Leader Imperant's approval? And with no hesitation, he just murdered her right in front of us. I think she was even in the middle of saying how great he is when he pulled the trigger.

Clearly this man would have no trouble exterminating my daughter and the other delegates. He executed one of his own in a ridiculous ploy to place all the blame on her. Blinking away the thoughts, I shift my focus to the Uprising members that Harley sent with us. They tap and type away on the devices set up before them. I share a glance with Zai when Imperant starts shifting on his feet. He's probably not used to waiting for direction on what's going to happen next. Not to mention that he's bleeding.

Within a few minutes, a black rectangular block emits two beeps followed by two high-pitched screeches. Unease settles across the room, weighing heavy in the air. I step forward and one of our allies holds out a palm-size square part that connects to the beeping radio. I depress the only button on it and speak.

"East Team report, this is Centre Team." I struggle to keep my voice even. Worry chases my every word, but I refuse to show weakness.

"Your East Team is not available to talk right now."

A faceless man speaks directly to us, his tone oozing power. I press a fist to my mouth and squeeze my eyes shut. *Were they captured like Orla's team was in Westates?*

Zai's hand shoots out but I won't let him snatch the radio from me. Besides, he has to stay focused on Imperant. If we're not watching that guy, who knows what he'll try to do. I depress the talk button once again.

"This is Caro Scott, a leader of the Uprising. Who am I speaking to?"

"Societal Leader Ault." As I expected. The confirmation makes my throat go dry and I gulp. This is exactly what we wanted, yet it's still intimidating.

"Well, Leader Ault, did you speak with Daxton and Welch before you decided they were . . . unavailable?" I'm pushing it, but I justify it by imagining what Zai would have said if he had the radio.

"They are in my presence, and they have provided a story about who they are and why they're here. I'd simply like you to verify its truth," he answers calmly. Of course he's calm. He's got power over us.

"I'd like to hear them confirm that they are unharmed."

"You're not exactly in a position to be making demands," he answers. "However, I'd like to resolve whatever issue you've brought to my Territory expeditiously. I will allow them no more than ten seconds to speak and then you will explain to me exactly what this is you think you're doing."

"Centre Team, this is Welch." After a short pause, he adds, "Daxton is with me. We're unharmed but closely guarded."

"Thank you." It doesn't hurt to maintain some sort of civility. "The Uprising is in Centrestates, in Leader Imperant's office. Now, if you will stand by for just a moment, we will contact Leader Huntsman so that all three Territories are represented in this conversation."

"Where is my security team?" Leader Imperant bellows. "I am injured and being held hostage! This is terrorism!"

"Your security team, as well as your citizens, are watching the information broadcast," Zai says with a smirk. "Because everything that's been said in this office since the kids were brought in here has been broadcast live to all three Territories."

His approach is blunt but powerful. Leader Imperant takes a staggering step backward, as if Zai's words physically knocked him off balance. His face pales, probably more from shock than blood loss.

"So, now that you've admitted to some misdeeds within your Territory, we have a few issues to discuss that span across the whole Divided States, and for once, its citizens will hear the truth right from the mouths of their leaders." Zai and Beckett both wear the same look of satisfaction. Everly watches with wide eyes and a trembling lower lip. The other Uprising member taps keys on a pad moments before her device emits the same pattern of beeps and screeches as the first one.

"Leader Huntsman, this is the Uprising," I say, knowing our West Team lost possession of their equipment when they were caught.

"So it is," his deep voice scratches through the slight static. "Time's not up yet, so I hope you aren't wasting my time. Do you have what I required in order to release your friends?"

"We do," I say confidently. "But first I want to speak to Orla."

"I'm afraid that isn't possible." I can hear the smile behind his words. "You see, your friends were placed in a holding cell, which is where we contain criminals until we decide what to do with them. But *Orla* wasn't very cooperative. She caused a scuffle and suffered an injury in the process." My grip loosens on the radio and Zai capitalizes on the distraction to grab it from my hand.

"What the hell did you do to Orla?" Zai's cheeks flush crimson with fury as he yells into the receiver.

"She is receiving medical treatment, which is quite generous, if you ask me, considering she stormed in here as if she had a right to shoot down anyone in her path." Even without seeing him, I can hear the smugness in Leader Huntsman's tone.

"Why the hell would we believe you?" For once, Zai voices my exact thought. *How did we think we could run this type of mission with teams this small? Maybe Zai was right all along. Maybe we should have waited until we were better prepared.* Doubt chews away at my resolve. I fight the urge to gnaw on a fingernail and ask Zai if we made a mistake. He's a leader too, but I may have discounted his opinions out of my own bias.

"What you're doing involves risks and danger," Huntsman says coolly. "Your friend understood that. Yet she ran to it. No one asked her to, nor did they make her." He pauses briefly but quickly returns to filling the momentary silence.

"I am not your enemy. As much as I don't like how you went about this, I can't imagine there was really any other choice. You're basically a group of traitors. But I'd rather stand with you than someone who can shake my hand one day and plan to slaughter my entire Territory the next. Even so, each Territory is ruled separately and there's no need to change that. If this *Uprising* group is taking over Centrestates, then Leader Ault and I will bring you up to speed on how things work."

"This is ridiculous!" Leader Imperant shouts. "You can't believe a word these people say!"

"Oh it's not their word you should be worried about, Imperant, it's yours." Leader Huntsman's words chill me to the core. "You see, they claimed that Centrestates was planning to start a war and that they were using this so-called inter-Territory delegation as a scapegoat to stir up Westates and Eastates. I didn't believe it until I heard it broadcast across the country."

"We cannot face war on our own soil," Leader Ault adds. "There have been several directives over the years that all three Territories agreed to, but that was during my father's time as leader. To this day, I disagree with some practices. I think this is the time to reevaluate our ethical standards."

"And this is exactly why the Uprising is here," I say, standing a little taller. In the midst of falling leaders and broken relationships between the Territories, the Uprising has finally reached a crossroads we've been crawling toward for years. "We prevented a civil war, and all we want is a seat at the table. We can all work together to make a safer, fairer country for all citizens."

"We can't allow this type of insurrection against the other Territories to happen again, ever," Leader Huntsman says.

"Noooooooo!" Leader Imperant shouts, maneuvering around the desk and charging at me with his arms outstretched in anticipation of wrapping his hands around my neck. I reach for his gun in my holster, but it's stuck. In the split second I tug at it, a crack rings through the air and Imperant crashes to the floor. I jump back, barely avoiding his flailing limbs as gravity pulls him down.

Catching my breath, I turn toward Zai, who still has his gun trained on Imperant. When it's obvious the man will never rise again, Zai relaxes his grip and allows the weapon to rest along his side. I nearly jump out of my skin when arms encircle me and squeeze too tightly. I gasp for air as Everly buries her face into my shoulder. Quickly recovering, I wrap my arms around her and gently rock back and forth in place. Having my daughter back is the ultimate reward for each moment of terror the past few hours have delivered.

"What happened?" Leader Huntsman demands. "We only have audio."

"Leader Imperant tried to attack us, so we stopped him," Zai says. "Permanently."

An eerie silence blankets the room in a macabre veil. Everly and Beckett are safe. The four of us still stand. But now we share the space with two dead bodies. I share a glance with Zai. This meeting with the other leaders has gone on long enough. We need to talk in private, but we also can't leave anyone who's listening just waiting, wondering what will happen next.

I rub Everly's arms and pry her off me, taking a step backward. Raising a hand in the air, I motion for her to wait. I sidestep over Leader Imperant's body and take the microphone in hand.

"This is Caro Scott from Eastates. I am a leader of the Uprising," I drag in a breath and glance at Zai, who gives me an encouraging nod. "There are a lot of things that have happened over the years . . . bad things . . . that most citizens never knew about. But the Uprising is willing to work with the existing leaders to create a better country. The difference is, more of us will have a say in how things are done. Please stay tuned. After we have a chance to discuss some preliminary decisions that need to be made, we will report back on the information broadcast across all three Territories."

Just when I think we're ready to disconnect, Leader Ault speaks. "There are some citizens who won't want to consider or accept change, but I urge you to join us in facing any challenges together. After what's happened here today, the Divided States will never be the same. There will be threats and there will be danger, but there is always a way to move forward. And that's exactly what we will do."

Leader Huntsman must feel compelled to make his voice heard too. "Citizens of Westates will await official word from me on what comes next. I don't foresee significant changes in our Territory, so until you receive an update, continue with your usual schedule and activities."

With that, the lines go silent. We all look around the room, searching each others' faces. Some of us release a sigh of relief and others crumple to the floor in exhaustion. It feels like I've lived a lifetime in just the past twenty-four hours. My body is physically, mentally and emotionally exhausted. And we've just reached the base of the mountain we have to climb.

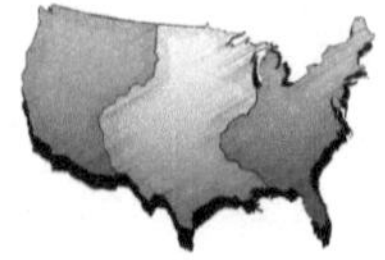

# CHAPTER 37 ~ CARO

## UPPER DIVISION, CENTRESTATES

"We need to report back home and get back on the line with Huntsman and Ault to verify their release of our teams," Zai mutters as he rubs his forehead.

"Can we send the kids back to the safe house?" I ask. Everly immediately yips a firm, "No!" but after all she's been through, she needs to rest.

"You and Everly go. Beckett and I can handle what needs to happen right now," Zai says. Suspicion clouds my thoughts. *Is he trying to send me away so he can tackle his own agenda?* He must sense the hesitation, or it's apparent from my expression. I relax my narrowed eyes and raise my eyebrows in innocent curiosity.

"I should stay and help. There's a lot to do."

Zai walks toward me and rests a palm on my shoulder. "You haven't seen your daughter in six years. You deserve a little time to catch up. Besides, what I need right now is Harley and his team. The only way we're gonna convince the people who work in this building to cooperate is to reveal who's been on our side since the beginning."

I chew on my bottom lip, considering his words as he continues. "They don't want to hear from some stranger that change is happening whether they like it or not. They need to see that people they know and trust are working with us . . . have been working with us . . . and trust us."

"You're right," I agree. "I'm just another nameless face to them."

"Glad you agree. Now take that nameless face of yours and get some rest." He smirks. "Tomorrow's gonna be another long day. We'll get started early, and I'll update you on everything we can accomplish with what's left of the night."

***

"I'm really glad we got to leave all of . . . that," Everly whispers as we make our way back to the Uprising's safe house.

"It's just for a few hours," I warn her. "I'll be back at it first thing in the morning."

"Well at least we have now," she says, pressing her clammy hand into my own. I gladly take it and flash a genuine smile. *Who would have thought after the night we had, I'd be walking out of Centrel Hall with a smile on my face?*

The streets are quiet. My guess is people are awake and buzzing with questions and speculations. If Harley's contacts got it right, they were able to send a signal through the information broadcast in all three Territories that alerted citizens to watch or listen. In that case, they're probably pacing in their homes, trying to make sense of everything they just saw or heard. Hopefully they aren't gathering to form a revolt against us. I blow out a deep breath. Whatever happens is a problem for tomorrow.

When we reach the communication center's door, it swings open. Harley greets us on the other side. "Knew yah were comin' an I got instr'utions to git yah cleaned up an settled in a bedrum."

"Thank you." It's all I can manage. My limbs feel weaker with each step and my mind swims in a sea of spiraling thoughts. Harley escorts us to a bathroom and hands us each a clean towel and set of clothing before showing us the bedroom we will share for the night. I flop onto the lumpy mattress while Everly takes her turn in the shower.

Before I know it, she's shaking me awake. On heavy legs, I stumble to the bathroom. The warm water washes away all the sweat, dust and grime from the day. When I'm dried off and dressed, I slip back into the bedroom, figuring she'll already be asleep. As soon as I crawl into bed, she rolls toward me and whispers, "Mom?"

The room is dark, but I can see every worry line creasing her forehead. Like magnets, we're drawn closer as our bodies meld into the indentation in the mattress. "Yes?"

"I know it's you, but . . . how do I know it's *really* you?" she asks as a single tear rolls down her cheek. The question stabs at my heart almost as much as her pain does. I sense she's finally allowing herself to release the emotions that have been building within her.

"Ask me anything." I smile and gently brush the hair away from her face. I'm desperate to relieve her fears.

"Why did you leave?" she asks, nearly choking on a sob.

"I didn't leave, Lyly," I whisper. "Not by choice anyway. I was told that I was going to disappear. If I cooperated, my family would be left unharmed. If I put up a fight, they would make us all disappear but we would be separated."

She sucks in a ragged breath. "And where did you go?"

"At work one day I was told to report to the infirmary. Enforcers were waiting for me. They told me what my 'crimes' were and escorted me to a train. The transport overseers turned me over to Enforcers in Centrestates and they passed me along to Westates. It was all done within a day."

"And you never tried to contact us or come home?"

I slip a lock of hair behind her ear as she swipes away her tears. "I wanted to, but there was no point in trying. If they intercepted any messages, you would all be in danger. I couldn't risk that."

Everly nods slowly, tucking her chin to her chest. She's smart and I bet the logical part of her brain understands what I'm saying. The problem is, it's probably at war with the child inside her who lived with the painful void of my absence for so many years. Too many years. When my lower lip twitches, I clamp my mouth shut. If the tears start to fall, they may never stop, and I need to be strong for her. I slowly raise her chin until our eyes lock.

"Everly, I never forgot about any of you. I made it my mission to find a way back to you. I played the Societal Order's game and used the time I had to make a plan. Not just to get my family back, but to help build a place where we could be together without having to hide because we spoke the truth."

She nods as her eyes drop. She has to know I would never leave my family. Trying to get back to them is what's kept me alive for the years I was away. They were my motivation. Squaring her shoulders, she releases a deep breath and asks another question.

"Why did they make you leave in the first place?"

"Let's just say that I figured out that the Societal Order's rules weren't in place to protect us, but were meant to control us. And once I realized just how much control they had, I wasn't willing to stay quiet about it. I thought everyone had a right to know."

"Yeah, we kind of figured that out while we were here," she says, "the delegates, I mean. Well, some of us."

"Speaking of the delegation, did you learn anything in your time here that might help us convince citizens that the Uprising is here to free them all from the Societal Order's control? Can you tell me about the past few days?" While I want to distract her from thinking about when I left Eastates, any information she may have could be useful. And I'll need it before I catch up with Zai and Harley in the morning.

"One day they let us have visitors and my visitor . . ." She pauses, chewing her bottom lip. "Well, she said she was you . . . um . . . my mother." She shudders, as if bracing for my reaction.

"I know," I say, gently rubbing her shoulder. "They did that to test you. It was just another way to observe how you'd react and what you'd tell that person, who you might have believed to be someone safe to confide in."

"Wait, how could you possibly know that?" Her wide eyes search mine for answers.

"Everly, the Uprising has contacts. Everywhere. We had planned to rescue the delegates before you were sent back home, but when I found out about the power grid and what Kiera was planning, we had to push up our plans."

"You knew the power grid was going to," she chokes on the word, "explode. And you didn't stop it?"

"All we knew was that something was going to happen on that tour, but we didn't know what or how. And we came as fast as we could. As you know, it takes time to get from Westates to Centrestates, especially when you're sneaking in."

She visibly relaxes a little, as if realization washes over her. "So you know someone close to Kiera? And that's who told you?"

"Yes, but it doesn't leave this room. We don't expose members of the Uprising. Even when they are no longer with us. It could put others in danger who may have associated with that person."

She raises her eyebrows expectantly and waits.

"It was one of Kiera's assistants. Lisum."

The name strikes Everly like a slap across the face. She wraps her arms around herself and sobs into her pillow.

"She was a good person, Everly. She helped us a lot."

"And now she's dead," she cries. "We saw her . . . Beckett and I . . . we saw her at the grid . . . after the explosion. She helped us . . . she told us about the tunnels . . . so we could get out of Centrestates."

"She was always looking out for you, for all of you, before she even met you." I shake my head slowly as tears pool in my eyes. We share in our sorrow for a few minutes. I wrap my arms around her and hold her tight as we both tremble with grief. Once our tears have run dry, we settle into an exhausted silence until Everly's breathing slows as she drifts off to sleep.

So much has happened and our minds and bodies can't take much more. This has been one of the longest days of my life, and I have a feeling tomorrow is going to be even longer.

# CHAPTER 38 ~ CARO

## UPPER DIVISION, CENTRESTATES

A sharp knock on the door jolts me awake. Panic flashes through me as my mind searches for answers. *Where am I? Who's knocking?* As I stumble to my feet, instinct draws me to the small pile of dirty clothes on the floor. My gun is tucked beneath it. I snatch it and tiptoe to the door. Not wanting to wake Everly, I twist the handle in an achingly slow motion and pull it toward me a fraction of an inch.

Beckett stands on the other side of the door, raising an arm to knock again. Swinging the door open a little wider, I peek into the hallway. He takes a step back before speaking and shifts on his feet nervously. Maybe he was hoping Everly would answer.

"Um . . . so my dad and Harley went to Centrel Hall for a meeting. They said you should join them."

"Thanks, I'll get ready and head over." I start to close the door but pull it open a little wider. "Beckett, can you do me a favor? When Everly wakes up, can you tell her where I am? I don't want her to worry."

He nods and stuffs his hands in his pockets before turning and walking back to the living room area. I slip the door closed and make sure Everly is still asleep. We must have been quiet enough, or she's that worn out, that she hasn't moved. I contemplate waking her so she can come with me. A selfish part of me wants to keep her in my sights at all times.

Taking a few steps closer to the bed, I watch her sleep. Her smooth, pale skin reminds me of a porcelain doll. Her eyes flutter but remain closed. She looks completely relaxed, and I'm certain she needs the rest. Much more than she needs to be yanked from a dream just to follow me into countless meetings.

Besides, she's in a safe house, and whenever she wakes up, Beckett will be able to tell her where I am. He could even escort her to Centrel Hall when she's ready. It might not be the best thing for her to overhear the conversations that have to take place this morning.

With my mind made up, I straighten my clothes and slip out of the room.

***

When I enter Centrel Hall, it's a completely different place than it was last night. Guards line the entrance. Each one looks more agitated and suspicious than the last. The first one I reach stops me to ask who I am and what I'm doing here.

"I'm here to speak with the leaders about the future of the Divided States," I say, raising my chin.

"And what business do you have meeting with them?"

"I happen to be one of them."

"The only leader we report to right now is the head of security forces," he sneers.

"Well, then I guess that's who I need to speak with." I'm unfazed by his supposed authority over me.

After a silent standoff, another guard approaches. They whisper to each other before a third one joins them. After about ten minutes of discussing what to do with me, one begrudgingly agrees to take me to their acting leader. "It's his problem now," he mutters before waving a hand over his shoulder for me to follow him.

People rush past us, either singly focused on wherever they're headed, or clustered in small groups that seem to be racing to their destination. They all wear the same look of determination. The guard leads me to a conference room. As we approach, the remnants of a heated exchange drift toward us.

"We need all three Territories talking right now!" Zai barks. "This situation is bigger than Centrestates!"

The guard knocks on the door, essentially extinguishing a volatile conversation. A voice calls out, encouraging us to enter. The guard motions for me to walk in first but he follows close behind.

"This person says she belongs in this meeting," he says with complete disbelief. Three men sit across the large rectangular table from Zai and Harley, who both flash a look of relief to see me. At least now they aren't outnumbered.

"Yes, she's part of the Uprising," Zai confirms. He nods to a chair beside him, and I cross the room and slip into it before anyone can question it.

"Well," the man who is clearly acting as if he's in charge starts, "to bring you up to speed, I'm Alcott Lazus, the acting leader of Centrestates. I was head of security but when Leader Imperant was assassinated, I became next in line." He's short, stocky and bald. And while I disagree with his assessment of what happened, I don't bother arguing.

"We were just discussing next steps. While I believe punishment is in order, seeing that murder is a serious offense, the Uprising seems to think its members are immune to the laws that are necessary to maintain a civil society." He folds his hands together in front of him, as if he's patiently waiting for us to prove him wrong.

The two men seated beside him wear similar smug expressions. One is older, with a neatly trimmed beard that matches his cropped salt-and-pepper hair. The third one looks younger than the other two. He narrows his eyes as he adjusts glasses that frame his narrow face. All three reek of condescension. *I've held my tongue long enough.*

"Leader Imperant was not assassinated. He murdered his assistant in front of several witnesses. During a live conversation with the other Societal Order leaders, he lunged at me with the intention to kill. Our response was purely self-defense." Although anger boils just below the surface, I manage to keep my tone even.

"Well, I guess the only thing we can agree on is that yesterday at this time, Leader Imperant was alive and you were not here. At some point you arrived and now he is dead, among others," the bald man states.

"This is useless," Zai says, pushing back in his seat and raising his hands in the air. "We need to be talking to Huntsman and Ault and agree to a plan for the country."

"I don't care about the rest of the country right now. My concern is right here." Baldy taps a stubby finger on the table for emphasis. "Whatever you're proposing could cause a wave of chaos. First our power grid blew and then our leader was murdered. Our citizens need stability and reassurance right now, not a complete change."

"Well, this is a lot bigger than just Centrestates," Zai says. "But your leader was at the heart of some pretty shady dealings. Actually, all three leaders were in agreement on some things that most citizens would be furious about if they found out." He pauses dramatically, glancing over at me and then Harley. "It would probably cause a revolt if they knew."

"You expect me to believe that?" The bald man rolls his eyes.

"We have proof," Zai says. "And it's already in the hands of our members. They will share that information across the whole country when we give the signal. And if the signal doesn't come, they'll know something is wrong. Either way, that information is going public and you can't stop it."

The older man finds his voice. "What kind of information are you talking about?"

"For starters, Centrestates' plan to destroy the power grid because they have an alternate power source. The fact that the power grid destruction was going to be blamed on the delegates, who were all supposed to be exterminated in that explosion. And that is just the beginning." Zai crosses his arms and leans back in his seat, obviously pleased with himself. It's not enough though. I can't hold back.

"Your own leader admitted they wanted to check the delegates for compliance chips," I add. "That leads to another revelation for citizens, that they all had a microchip implanted in their brain at birth. Something to control them, that they knew nothing about all this time."

"Yah underest'mate us," Harley says. "We got contacts evry'where. They got copies ah medical recurds. Hell if that ain't proof."

Baldy squeezes his eyes shut and blows out a deep breath. "Fine, we'll talk to Leaders Huntsman and Ault. But whatever you have stays quiet until we work this out!"

"That's fine with us," Zai says pleasantly. "That's all we were asking for."

***

Within half an hour, the six of us still face each other. Distrust weighs heavy in the air. The only difference is that Leaders Huntsman and Ault have joined us by phone.

One by one, we address the issues the Uprising has monitored over the years – families being punished and separated for speaking out against Societal Order practices and covert programs that were forced upon unsuspecting citizens like food additives based on citizens' gender and age. More than once, the topic swings back to the compliance chips. We find an unexpected ally in one leader.

"I admit my father was supportive of the practice," Leader Ault says. "I've never been, and we stopped it here about eight years ago. It was one of the first things I did when I came into power." Silence falls over the room. It seems the other two Territories have no issue continuing to use the chips.

"Our medical professionals advised against removing them," Leader Ault continues. "They were implanted at birth, so with any degree of growth, they would be ingrained in a very sensitive part of the body. A surgical procedure to remove the implant could cause irreversible damage. We've researched neutralizing the chips, but we felt the risk outweighed the benefit. And, as with anything produced, there is a margin for error. Some chips may be faulty or stop working over the years. We'd really have no way of confirming that."

My mind buffers with calculations. Everly was one of the last babies to get the chip. That means Easton doesn't have one. So he had more freedom in his actions. He was definitely a fussier baby.

"Okay, so Eastates already stopped using the compliance chip. So it's possible and reasonable. I'd say our first item to agree on is discontinuing it in Westates and Centrestates," Zai states.

"We don't know how that change would impact our population," Leader Huntsman says. "They've come to rely on the support that the integrated circuit provides."

The three of us look at Baldy to gauge his reaction. His eyes shift around the room before he admits that he was not aware of the practice. Memory flashes through me like a bolt of lightning. The delegate we found and brought back to Centrel Hall, he said his father was head of security. I bet this is him.

"Your son." I meet the man's stunned gaze. "He was a delegate, wasn't he?" When the man nods, I motion to Zai. "Did he tell you that we helped him escape the wreckage . . . from the power grid that your leader blew up?"

"How could you possibly know that two people helped my son?" His skepticism fades as he realizes the only way we could know is if we were there.

"This is ridiculous," Leader Huntsman hisses. "You have no power here. You're bluffing about everything."

"That's where you're wrong," Zai responds with a smile on his face. "You see, we already have what Imperant admitted to and what his assistant had in her extensive notes about the delegation. But we recently had the good fortune of connecting with a talented computer systems operator. He's actually the father of one of the delegates. And he was able to uncover some information about food additives being used in all three Territories. Maybe you know something about extra chemicals to help people stay awake or fall asleep, depending on who they are."

I can't help but smile now too. *Vanen.* The kid could barely stand on his own, but he still found a way to help us.

Tension swirls but no one speaks. Zai takes it as an opportunity to spend more ammunition. "As we see it, all three leaders have secrets. Maybe it's time to blow the lid off everything that's been kept under wraps for all these years."

"And if we disagree?" Leader Ault asks.

"Our goal is to work together for a better country for all its citizens, not just some. But that's going to take all of us, actually working together. Committing to a plan," I say. "I guess you could call it a revised Alliance Agreement, like what the delegates were supposed to be working on."

"I agree with you that there is a need for change," Leader Ault says. "I saw it with my father's laws and I've slowly tried to improve some . . . flaws in the system. But I've always been the minority. Perhaps if the Uprising has a seat at the table, we may find that our visions align more than anyone would have expected."

# Chapter 39 ~ Everly

## Upper Division, Centrestates

My senses slowly return as my eyes flutter open. My arm tingles from resting on it for too long. Releasing a yawn, I extend my arms in a deep stretch. Eyeing the surroundings, memories of last night come rushing back to me. Kiera and Leader Imperant. Shooting and death. My mother. She was there, and then she was here with me. I actually have her back and hopefully soon Easton and Dad will know too and we can all be together.

"Mom?" I call, even though she's clearly not in the room. The space is about twice the size of my bedroom back home, but other than me, all that's in it is a double bed, a nightstand and a dresser. A closet door stands open, but it's empty other than a few tan shirts and pants hanging inside.

Urgency drives me to my feet. I pull shoes on and slip through the door. Conversations drift closer as I head for the set of desks that always seem to be occupied. As I open my mouth to ask where my mother is, a familiar face draws me to the couch. Catching my movement, Beckett rises to greet me.

"Hey, sleepyhead, you're awake." My heart stutters as we draw closer together. Without warning, I crash into him and wrap my arms around him, clinging to the person who's gotten me through these past days.

"I'm so glad to see you. Where were you?" He nuzzles my hair with his nose before releasing his grip and taking a step back.

"I stayed in Centrel Hall with my dad last night. Listened to all their planning and discussions." He scratches his chin, as if he's unsure how much to say.

"How did it go? Did you get any sleep?" He leads me to the couch and we both sit, turning toward each other so our knees touch. His warmth instantly comforts me. I almost forget why I came out here in the first place.

"Let's just say there's still a lot that has to happen. I thought last night was a big step, but it seems like it was a baby step compared to what has to happen next." He scratches his chin before adding, "I got a few hours of sleep, but not as much as you." He brushes a gentle finger across my cheek, and I can't help but smile shyly, dropping my gaze to the floor.

"So what do we do?" He obviously knows more than me, and it's not like my mother bothered to let me know what's going on.

"We could stay here . . ." he glances at the people monitoring the computers and talking to nameless faces on the phone, "or we could go to Centrel Hall and find out what our parents are doing."

"Let's go," I say. "There's nothing to do here and I want some answers. Can you believe my mother just left me here this morning? I have no idea when, but she didn't bother to wake me to say where she was going or why."

"I'll help you find her." He rubs my shoulder and holds my gaze. The concern behind those blue eyes softens my anger a little. "Your mom has to be thrilled to finally have you back. I've only known her for a few years, but I know she wouldn't leave you here unless she really had to. Nothing like this has ever happened before in the Divided States, but based on how much she talked about her family, I bet she didn't want to leave without you this morning."

"Shouldn't her priority be seeing her family? Not just me but my dad and my brother? I mean, they don't even know she's alive!" I cross my arms and pout. Literally pout. I know it's childish but I don't care.

"Everything's so unstable right now, I doubt it's safe for them to come here just yet." He shakes his head slowly. "The balance of power . . . it's just . . . it could go either way." His eyes beg me to understand. "Look, I know this is all still new to you. I've been around the Uprising for as long as I can remember, and I learned that sometimes my dad was busy with stuff that I couldn't know about, but I always knew it was important. That he was doing it for us. To keep us all safe. Not just now but years down the road."

"Yeah, I guess," I agree half-heartedly. He can't understand the crushing sense of loss I felt all these years, only to have it yanked out from underneath me, giving way to shock and disbelief. And now, to know that my mother is truly still alive, it's hard to understand how it was so easy for her to leave me behind. Again.

"Come on, let's go." He stands and holds out his hand, an open invitation to join him. Even with my soured mood, I'm glad he's here. I slide my fingers across his palm and grab hold. At least we're in this together.

***

Others rush past us on the street, their faces project disoriented worry. Some eyes narrow when they spot us, obviously visitors from other Territories. If I hadn't been so angry with my mother when I first woke up, I may have thought to put on some of the tan clothes in the closet of the room we stayed in. That would have helped me blend in a little better.

The closer we get to Centrel Hall, the more bodies we see. Security officers swarm both outside and inside the building. A few stop us before we cross the threshold of the sliding glass doors.

"What do we have here? Delegates?" one sneers. His dark mustache jumps a little when he smirks.

"Yes, we're delegates," Beckett answers, taking a step closer to the man. They hold each other's gaze for a heated moment before another guard joins us, looking us up and down. Beckett motions toward Centrel Hall. "Our parents are in there. We're going to find them."

"Oh really?" the newer guard asks. "Rumor has it that the delegates caused everything that's happening now." He crosses his arms and glares at us.

"That's exactly what it is, a rumor," Beckett says coolly, motioning between us. "You seriously think we came here on some secret mission to destroy the Territory? Like we brought weapons—"

"I didn't even want to come here." I cut him off as my pent-up frustration spills out. "But no one asked me . . . they told me I was coming. There was never a choice and if I could go back in time, I'd find some way to get out of it." Each thought I share is louder than the last as my anger takes hold. Even Beckett turns to me, surprised by my harsh words and tone. When all three of them watch me as if I might explode, I add, "All I want to do right now is see my mother and go back to Eastates. Standing out here talking about it isn't helping anything."

The guards share a glance before one sighs. "Fine, I'm not sure what else to do with you anyway," he mutters. "Our orders are to maintain peace and I have a feeling the longer you're out here, the higher chance of a disruption. Follow me."

With that, he strides over to the large reception desk. We follow, waiting while he speaks to a guard behind the desk. After a brief exchange, he turns and heads for the elevators, throwing a glance over his shoulder to check that we're trailing him. The ride up is awkward and quiet, but at least it's short.

Before we reach any of the conference rooms, I spot a few familiar faces in the hallway. Rushing past the guard, I beeline directly to my mother. Surprise washes over her features but she quickly replaces it with a smile that reaches her eyes.

"Everly, I'm glad you're here."

"Really? Because I would have been here much sooner if you didn't vanish this morning."

Her smile drops and her posture stiffens. "We're on a break from our meeting right now. Why don't you and I talk privately in a room?" She doesn't even wait for me to respond. She clasps a hand around my elbow and leads me away from the others. We only take a few steps when a chunky bald man stops us.

"Miss Scott," he says. I'm unsure if he means me or her, but it becomes clear pretty quickly. "Thank you for helping my son. I appreciate your . . . compassion. You are all more than welcome to eat in our cafe downstairs. A few of us need to discuss some issues, but we'll be ready to reconvene at two o'clock." He reaches out a palm and they shake hands.

"You're welcome, and thank you. I'll see you back there in a few hours." When he turns to leave, she clamps my elbow again and continues to the closest office that's unlocked. We step inside and leave the lights off.

"Everly, you can't just barge in here disrespectfully. In case you forgot, I am still your mother and I won't be treated that way."

"I just can't believe you left me in a strange place, alone." Fury overrides any sense of being reasonable. "I woke up and had no idea where you were. I didn't know what to do."

"I had to go. You looked so peaceful that I didn't want to wake you and I knew you were in a safe place. Please understand that I'm a leader now too, not just a mother."

*What she says makes sense, but I'm not sure how to feel.* When my lower lip trembles and I wrap my arms around my stomach, she takes a step closer and wraps me in a hug. Gently rocking us both, she whispers in my ear, "I am your mother and I love you. I love your dad and Easton too. But I'm a different person now, a better person. Everything I do with the Uprising is for my family. This was my only way home. I don't care where we are, anywhere can be home as long as I have my family back. That's my ultimate goal right now. And you're part of that."

My vision blurs as tears roll down my cheeks. I drop my head, suddenly ashamed by my anger. Unjustified anger. Beckett tried to tell me, but maybe I needed to hear it for myself. She releases me and steps back, raising my chin to look her in the eyes.

"Sometimes I may have to do things you don't like, but it's not because I don't care about you. Now no more tears. We have work to do."

***

After lunch, Beckett and I are allowed to sit in on the meetings. The short bald man, who we find out is Callan's father, connects Leaders Huntsman and Ault over video. With all three Territories represented, along with the Uprising, the group discusses an outline of a plan to move forward. They actually include us in the conversation, asking for our opinions on the Alliance Agreement, which we've studied so carefully in recent days.

One of the first items agreed upon is that families that were separated by the Societal Order will be reunited. My mother and Zai insist upon this. With a few subtle reminders that the Uprising has some rather unflattering information about Leader Huntsman that could be shared across the whole country in a matter of minutes, he reluctantly becomes more agreeable during discussions.

I'm probably biased, but Leader Ault makes me proud to be from Eastates. He admits that the Divided States needs to change and that the best way forward is together.

What feels like days is actually about four hours. By the time the meeting adjourns for the day, the acting leaders have agreed to a solid plan for future discussions, and a way to move forward, at least in theory.

As we walk down the hallway, hand in hand, I can feel Beckett watching me out of the corner of his eye. Turning my head, I smirk at him. "What?"

"I just can't believe all this is happening." He runs his free hand through his hair. "I mean, three weeks ago I didn't even know you and now . . ." He gulps as he glances around us.

"And now what?" I ask.

"Now everything's changed. I don't think I can go back to Westates," he admits.

"What are you talking about? That's your home." I don't know where he's going with all of this.

"I don't think it is anymore," he stammers as his gaze drops. "All we did there was try to find my brother after he was taken. It doesn't really hold many good memories for my family."

"I'm so sorry." His admission melts my heart. I squeeze his hand and don't let go. We started as complete strangers. In the past two weeks, we faced danger and uncertainty, but at least we had each other. I should be terrified of what lies ahead. I should be heartbroken for what I've left behind. Yet every cell in my body hums with energy. Every molecule buzzes with anticipation. In spite of all that's happened beyond our control, I'm truly alive.

"Maybe we can start over right here in Centrestates. All of us, your family and mine." The words drift past my lips just barely above a whisper.

"I think that's a good idea." Crystal blue eyes sear into mine, determination passing between us. "Besides, I don't think I'm ready to say goodbye to you, Everly Scott. I think we're just getting started."

"What do you think is next for us?" My question hovers between us, but there's no fear behind it. Only anticipation.

"Anything. Everything." Those cheeks tug into the biggest smile I've ever seen on his face.

For what feels like the first time since I stepped foot in Centrestates, I have a reason to smile. I have hope. I have a future. We all do, and it's going to be bright.

# EPILOGUE ~ EVERLY

## SIX MONTHS LATER

I never would have guessed that we could challenge our government. We were expected to follow every rule to avoid being punished. But that just taught us to blindly believe anything we were told and never explore our true thoughts. Until my trip to Centrestates, I thought that was normal. Only now do I realize how stifling it was.

A board of leaders serves the United States, focused on supporting a structure that ensures history does not repeat itself. As a country, we are focused on building a responsible future. We make mindful efforts not to overburden natural resources, instead coaxing them into supporting a growing population for many years to come. Sustainable, rather than obliterating, with time.

Although the Xone walls remain, citizens are free to travel to whatever Territory they choose. My father and brother were among the first to leave Eastates and the home my mother never wants to see again. She says we have a chance for a fresh start, and she expects every one of us to take it.

I'll never forget the pure joy in Easton's eyes when he first truly understood that our mother was back in our lives. She was barely a memory to him, but now he can create new ones with her every single day. And Dad nearly crumpled to the floor when he first saw her. He knew immediately that it wasn't some cruel trick of the mind or eyes. I don't ever remember feeling such happiness. No matter where we live, what we eat or what we're doing, my family is whole again. We'll never look back on what we lost, but rather focus on the road ahead.

I promised Easton a souvenir from my trip to Centrestates and he was thrilled to get my delegate pin. Now that it's no longer being used as a tracking or listening device, it's safe for him to wear or show off to his friends. He's never owned anything so intricate, and considering why it was given to me in the first place, I don't miss having it in my possession at all.

Our family, and Beckett's, decided to settle in Centrestates. His dad, Zai, serves on the board of leaders. One of its first acts was to track and release citizens who were moved to other Territories as punishment for their "crimes." I got to be there when Beckett's brother arrived from the lower division of Centrestates. Even though I was meeting him for the first time, I felt the raw emotion and elation surrounding his family when they were reunited. He's like an older version of Beckett – tall and muscular with slightly wavy dark hair and the bluest eyes. I'm sure I'll get to know him as time goes on.

Who would have thought that we'd all choose to live here? Although it holds some memories that I'd rather forget, it's also where fate sealed my future. The delegation was a malicious experiment, a kindling destined to ignite a war. The Uprising is the only reason that didn't happen. Even though this place almost ended everything for me, it's also where I learned that my mother was still alive, and without everything that happened, I never would have met Beckett.

Before, even if we were in the same Territory, it wouldn't have been possible. The practice of day dwellers and night dwellers is being phased out. Centrestates' alternate power source is in the process of being distributed across the nation. It's more efficient than the grid was, and easier to maintain. By harnessing strengths each Territory brings to supporting an updated infrastructure, it will end up being more reliable and powerful than the grid ever was. And most importantly, it will diminish our need to allow only half the population to truly exist at one time.

The information broadcast is another priority. The board of leaders needs to communicate with everyone. They want to send the same message at the same time to each person. That means the communication system will be the same for everyone across the whole United States, with both video and sound.

Educational curriculum will include ancient history about indigenous people and how they treated the earth and its vast resources. The leaders agreed, with some added pressure from my mother, that action must be taken to heal our environment. Although not every decision is unanimous, there is always a majority, and that is what keeps us moving forward.

If there's one thing I've learned from our new leaders, it's that we all deserve more freedom to make choices. Every one of us. Not just those souls lucky enough to live in a division that doesn't enforce the rules everyone else has to follow. And while many of us have lived this way without knowing anything else, future generations can grow up in a different kind of world. A better world. An equitable world.

Josli and I actually got to make her joke come true. Before Hayes and I were announced as the chosen delegates, she said that the two of us might be picked. After she finished school, she moved to Centrestates. We're on a waiting list to move into a small apartment together.

Hayes and Vanen are still practically inseparable. They're researchers, traveling across the United States and reporting their observations and recommendations to the board of leaders. Their firsthand accounts help inform what is working in the regions and what needs further study or adjustments. Learning was never a burden for Hayes or Vanen. They truly love it, maybe even need it. And now they can make a career out of it.

While Beckett's brother has taken a leadership role alongside their father, that was not meant to be Beckett's path. He is training to become an Enforcer, not someone who wields authority over citizens to keep them compliant, but rather someone who ensures that justice is carried out in a fair manner for all.

At one time I hoped to be accepted into an occupation in nutritional research. After years of watching my little brother suffer at every mealtime, trying to force down the mush we were given as rations, I wanted to make sure no one else had to go through that. Now, it's not necessary. Using Centrestates' food growth processes, we can replicate their success in other regions.

One thing the delegation taught me is that it's important to know and question what is happening around you. That realization inspired my interest in a new career path. I got to be pretty good with taking notes on my computing device. If given the opportunity, I could spend my days weaving words and stringing sentences together. This new information broadcast will need writers and content creators to share announcements and stories. While I don't want to be in front of a camera, maybe I could be the person behind the scenes, preparing messages that will reach everyone who needs to know.

Each day I grow a little surer of who I am and what I'm destined to become. Just like our new, united country.

# Acknowledgements

Thank you for reading the Divided States series. I hope you enjoyed Everly's journey, the challenges she conquered and ultimately, her happy ending. If you have a moment, please share your thoughts with a rating or a review on Goodreads, Amazon and/or whatever retailer you may have purchased this book.

Shout out to all of the following people who helped make this book a reality.

Emily Angeline, Robin Asick, Diane Lesher and Stephanie DosSantos – thank you for beta reading the manuscript and offering your thorough feedback. I value every suggestion you provided, and you helped make the story stronger, clearer and better!

Misty Kevech and Cheryl Lindbeck – thank you for your enthusiasm and willingness to be advanced reader copy reviewers. Your input motivates me to keep spinning stories and I greatly value your ongoing support!

Jen Blackwell – as my final editor, I am always convinced that you won't find many corrections or changes for the manuscript but you always surprise me  :)  Your eagle eye has caught more typos than I care to admit! Thank you for being another set of eyes on the story and for challenging some word choices. The result was a definite improvement!

Scott, Landon and Aidan – your support means the world to me and I'm grateful to have you by my side. Thank you for sharing this journey with me.

A. E. Faulkner was born and raised in Pennsylvania. When she's not lost in a book, she loves spending time with her family, which includes three humans and five rescue cats. One of her biggest fears is the repercussions we will face when nature can no longer tolerate human destruction. As such, she never tires of reading dystopian-themed tales. To learn more about her writing, visit www.authoraefaulkner.com, email authoraefaulkner@gmail.com or connect on social media:

Facebook:@authaefaulkner
Instagram: @authoraefaulkner
TikTok: @authoraefaulkner

# ALSO BY A.E. FAULKNER

**The Nature's Fury series:**
Darkness Falls (Book 1)
Anguish Unfolds (Book 2)
Devastation Erupts (Book 3)
Allegiance Unravels (Book 4)
Hope Emerges (Book 5)
Fate Collides (Short Story)

***

The Spin (Gaia Awakens climate fiction anthology)
Culling Day (Gaia Awakens climate fiction anthology)
Hierarchy of Need (Nature Erupts climate fiction anthology)

***

**The Divided States series:**
Upheaval (Book 1)

www.ingramcontent.com/pod-product-compliance
Lightning Source LLC
Chambersburg PA
CBHW032357310726
48973CB00007B/2051